CONFESSIONS

BRANTLEY WALKER:
Off the Books

By Nicole Edwards

THE WALKERS

ALLURING INDULGENCE
Kaleb
Zane
Travis
Holidays with The Walker Brothers
Ethan
Braydon
Sawyer
Brendon

THE WALKERS OF COYOTE RIDGE
Curtis
Jared (a crossover novel)
Hard to Hold
Hard to Handle
Beau
Rex
A Coyote Ridge Christmas
Mack
Kaden & Keegan
Alibi (a crossover novel)

BRANTLEY WALKER: OFF THE BOOKS
All In
Without A Trace
Hide & Seek
Deadly Coincidence
Alibi (a crossover novel)
Secrets
Confessions

AUSTIN ARROWS
Rush
Kaufman

PIER 70
Reckless
Fearless
Speechless
Harmless
Clueless

SNIPER 1 SECURITY
Wait for Morning
Never Say Never
Tomorrow's Too Late

SOUTHERN BOY MAFIA/DEVIL'S PLAYGROUND
Beautifully Brutal
Without Regret
Beautifully Loyal
Without Restraint

STANDALONE NOVELS
Unhinged Trilogy
A Million Tiny Pieces
Inked on Paper
Bad Reputation
Bad Business
Filthy Hot Billionaire

NAUGHTY HOLIDAY EDITIONS
2015
2016
2021

Confessions

BRANTLEY WALKER: OFF THE BOOKS, 7

NICOLE EDWARDS

NICOLE EDWARDS LIMITED
A dba of SL Independent Publishing, LLC
PO Box 1086
Pflugerville, Texas 78691

CONFESSIONS
Brantley Walker: Off the Books, 7
NICOLE EDWARDS

COVER DETAILS:

Image: © smileus (64461478) | 123rf.com
Design: © Nicole Edwards Limited

INTERIOR DETAILS:

Formatting: Nicole Edwards Limited
Editing: Blue Otter Editing

AUDIO DETAILS:

Image: © smileus (64461478) | 123rf.com
Narrators: Tor Thom & Charley Ongel

IDENTIFIERS:

ISBN: (ebook) 978-1-64418-054-9 | (paperback) 978-1-64418-055-6 | (audio) 978-1-64418-058-7

BISAC: FICTION / Romance / Gay
BISAC: FICTION / Romance / General

CHAPTER ONE

Friday, March 11, 2022

Six months.

It had been damn near six months since Reese Tavoularis took a bullet to the chest.

Six months since the doctors saved his life with emergency surgery, fixing the damage done by the 9mm slug that had nicked his artery.

Six months since his family sat by his bedside, praying he would live after a minor complication had sent his ass back to the intensive care unit.

And six fucking months since he realized his dumb-ass actions had sent the man he loved running for the hills.

The worst part…

Well, that was the months following the shooting when Reese had gone AWOL. Rather than return to Coyote Ridge and make an effort to fix what he'd so clearly broken, Reese had stayed in Dallas. He'd left his team in the lurch, using his recovery as an excuse to keep his distance, hiding from the repercussions of his own fucking actions. He'd avoided anyone and everyone, with the exception of his mother, who had insisted he stay with her so she could help nurse him back to health. Oh, and Z. His brother had made it his mission in life to stick his nosy ass so far up Reese's business, it was a wonder they were still related.

Now here Reese was, pulling down the driveway of the house he'd lived in with Brantley Walker before he'd gone and fucked it all up. Everything about the place was familiar, from the old oak tree standing proud and tall in Brantley's front yard to the dirt drive that had been expanded to accommodate all the vehicles belonging to the team who used Brantley's renovated barn as their base of operations.

Everything was the same.

Part of him had expected to see an unfamiliar vehicle in the driveway. Maybe some random guy Brantley was hooking up with. Someone everyone else had hidden from Reese when he'd used lame excuses to check in via text message. God knows Reese's imagination had gotten the best of him lately, pairing Brantley up with damn near any available man Reese could think of, gay or not. He'd imagined a dozen scenarios, each one more disturbing than the one before, until he had no choice but to pack up what few belongings he'd had with him and drive the three hours back to Coyote Ridge.

But there were no foreign vehicles in the driveway. In fact, there was only one vehicle, period: Brantley's black Chevrolet Silverado parked in its usual spot. It was caked with mud and dust, as though Brantley hadn't bothered to wash it in the time Reese was gone. As though he'd been just as screwed up over this whole fucking mess as Reese was.

Relief ballooned in his chest, came out on a ragged exhale.

Doesn't mean Brantley didn't pick up some guy at the bar, bring him back here. Could be some rando is inside right this very minute, bouncing up and down on Br—

Reese shut down the idiot voice in his head before it could finish that sentence. He didn't want to think that the man he loved was getting the fuck of his life from some stranger who'd happened to catch his eye.

No, it was better for him to believe that Brantley was home alone.

He hoped so anyway, considering Reese had come to pack his things, and he damn sure didn't want to attempt this twice. Once was going to be hard enough.

If it'd been up to him, Reese would've come when Brantley was gone. He knew better than to trespass without warning the former Navy SEAL first—the last damn thing he wanted was another bullet wound—although he would've preferred the house to be empty. The sneak-in, sneak-out approach had been appealing at one point during the three-hour drive. Confronting Brantley, meeting that cold, hard stare was going to break him, there was no doubt about it, but at least he could get it over with quickly.

Now it was just a matter of making it to the door, knocking, waiting.

He sighed, realizing he was still sitting in his damn truck.

"Now or never, Tavoularis," he muttered to himself. Reese didn't know where he would go from here, but he couldn't rest his head in the same spot he had before he'd screwed up the best thing that had ever happened to him.

Putting the truck in park, he unclipped his seat belt, took a deep breath, opened the door, and stepped out. He heard an excited bark from inside the house, and his heart instantly swelled. He hadn't seen Tesha since he was shot, and it had broken his damn heart to lose her. Almost as much as it had hurt to lose Brantley.

However, he wasn't here to take her away, no matter how much he wished he could. Based on what little he'd been able to glean from Jessica James—the only person on the team willing to gossip if pushed enough—Brantley had grown quite fond of Tesha over the past six months and vice versa.

"We got company, girl?"

Reese swallowed hard when he heard Brantley's voice from inside the house, the rough baritone scraping along his spine in a sensual caress.

"Well, who is—" Brantley's big body appeared in the doorway, the screen door swinging wide as he stepped out onto the front porch, Tesha racing past him. The moment their eyes met, Brantley put his hands on his hips, his expression shutting down completely.

Oh, hell. As he drank in the sight of the big, badass Navy SEAL, he realized he'd ridiculously underestimated how fucking hard this was going to be.

Needing a minute to compose himself, Reese went to one knee to greet Tesha. She approached him as though not a single day had passed since he'd last seen her. Her training was paying off because she didn't launch herself at him like an out-of-control puppy. Instead, she trotted closer, her tongue lolling out of her mouth as she assessed him. Reese rubbed her head, then hugged her to him when she pressed her shoulder to his. He had to take a deep breath to keep the emotion at bay. He'd known seeing her would be hard, considering he would have to walk away again.

When he got himself under control, Reese stood tall, met Brantley's gaze. Had he not seen the man walk out of his own house, Reese wasn't sure he would've recognized him. Gone was the military-short buzz cut and clean-shaven jaw. In their place, Brantley's dark hair had grown out, a shaggy mess that probably hadn't seen a comb in a week. His face definitely hadn't seen a razor in a few months, maybe more.

Despite the unkempt grooming technique, he looked good. Bigger than Reese remembered. As though he'd spent a significant amount of time working out in the past six months. His charcoal-gray T-shirt hugging his broad chest, the short sleeves stretching around his bulging biceps. Brantley wore his signature black tactical pants, which fit his trim waist and thick thighs as though they'd been designed specifically for him.

"I just came to get my things," Reese said, wanting to assure Brantley he wasn't expecting anything.

Brantley held his stare for a minute, then turned and walked into the house without a word.

"Well, *that* went well," Reese muttered to himself.

He stood there for a minute, then another and another while he recalled the speech he'd prepared during his drive down. He'd come up with a few options starting with the basic groveling: *I'm sorry. I love you. Please take me back.* When he figured that wouldn't work, he'd contemplated using the straightforward angle: *Nothing happened, I was just confused. Let's let bygones be bygones.* And, of course, the pretend-not-to-give-a-fuck approach: *I'm still a member of the task force. Came back to work, that's all. So just pretend you don't see me.*

Now that he was standing here, none of those scenarios played well for him, which meant he would have to wing it.

Reese didn't know if he should just walk in without an invitation, but he also didn't feel like standing outside until Brantley decided to leave, which could've been in an hour or a few days.

Taking a deep breath, he went to the door, opened the screen, and let Tesha go inside first. He followed her, easing the door closed so it didn't slam.

The house was dark, the only light coming from the kitchen and what little of the late-afternoon sun was still filtering in through the uncovered windows. The dining room looked the same as it had the last time he'd been here. The new table and chairs they'd bought still sat stoically in the center, although they'd collected what looked to be six months' worth of dust. He'd honestly expected to find his things had been boxed up and stored in there since Brantley didn't use the room for anything else but there was nothing but the furniture.

He moved forward slowly, peered over at the couch. It was facing the television Reese had insisted they get after he'd echoed the sentiment of everyone who'd come to visit and finally convinced Brantley the space needed a couch. The living room looked as though it had sat unoccupied for quite some time, more dust coating the edges of the television and the top of the wooden cabinet it sat on.

The good news was there were no signs that anyone else was here. No one other than Brantley.

Taking the remaining steps to round the dividing wall separating the kitchen from the dining room, Reese tucked his hands in the pockets of his jeans, not sure what to expect.

Brantley was in the kitchen, a beer in one hand, the other pressed hard against the island countertop as he stared at the sliding back door. His shoulders were tense, his back muscles shifting every so often beneath the soft cotton that covered them. His chest rose and fell with every deep breath he took. He wasn't huffing and snorting like a bull, so that was something.

Neither of them said anything for several minutes, and Reese felt as though his heart was going to beat right out of his chest. It had taken him months of recovery and physical therapy just to learn how to take a deep breath again. And in one fell swoop, all that hard work seemed to dissolve. He was reduced to a panting mess, dragging ragged breaths in as deep as he could, doing his best not to draw Brantley's attention.

It didn't work.

Brantley turned, his gaze pinning him in place. His expression was arctic, the thin line of his mouth firm, the dark slashes of his eyebrows vee-d over eyes that were hard as steel.

"I'm sorry," Reese whispered, forcing the words through his dry throat.

One of Brantley's dark eyebrows rose, a mirthless smirk pulling at his mouth. "For what? For leavin' me to be with your ex-girlfriend? Or for gettin' yourself shot defending her?" He stood tall, his jaw set, his voice rising with his anger. "Or for hidin' in Dallas for the last six fuckin' months while I sat here and wondered if you'd ever fucking come back?"

There was so much emotion in his voice, so much anger and hurt, it was like a blade through Reese's chest.

Reese took one step forward, expecting Brantley to take a step back. When he didn't, Reese moved closer. Those blue-gray eyes held the same storm clouds he remembered from when they'd first met.

"I'm sorry," he said again, closing the distance but not getting too close. He damn sure wasn't prepared to take a fist to the jaw.

"So you said."

He stared at Brantley, decided he was going with the no-bullshit approach. "I'm not with Madison. Never was."

Brantley's eyes narrowed, but he didn't speak.

"That night ... I wanted to give her the closure I thought she needed." He shook his head. "That's a lie. I was seeking the closure I thought *I* needed."

Still no comment from Brantley.

"I fucked up," Reese said firmly. "I fucked everything up."

"And you think by admitting that, it'll make it all better?" Brantley's words dripped with derision and what sounded a hell of a lot like hurt.

Reese shook his head. "No. I told you. I only came to get my things."

Brantley's countenance turned skeptical. Or was that disappointment? "Movin' on to bigger and better things, are you?"

Reese's mouth fell open as he stared at the man he loved more than anything. He wasn't sure what he could possibly say to help Brantley make sense of any of this. Hell, for six months, Reese had been trying to make sense of it on his own.

No matter how hard he tried, it never fucking worked.

BRANTLEY HAD KNOWN THAT ONE DAY HE would be face-to-face with Reese again. It was inevitable since their lives had been entwined before the events that had ripped them apart.

However, had he known that day would be today, he never would've gotten out of bed.

He'd spent the past six months trying to figure out where he'd gone wrong, how he'd managed to fuck things up bad enough to send Reese running back to the arms of a woman he'd previously proposed to. A woman Reese said had turned him down because their relationship hadn't been as solid as either of them pretended. No matter how Brantley played it in his head, nothing he'd told himself made sense; there was no logical reason he could come up with. Yet, he'd lived through it. Had seen Reese laid up in the hospital bed, a bullet having gone through his fucking chest because he'd been having dinner with a gangster's sister.

That was the day Brantley had walked away, shutting himself down in the process. Since then, he'd focused solely on work and Tesha, nothing else. He'd put in time with his family just to keep them off his ass, but aside from that, he'd become a shut-in. He went for a run every day because he knew Tesha enjoyed it. He worked out in an effort to exhaust himself so he could sleep. And he dedicated the rest of his time to training Tesha because she'd become the only thing that mattered to him.

And every single minute of every single day, whether awake or asleep, he thought about this man.

"It's all where you left it," Brantley managed to say, lifting his beer bottle to his mouth and turning back to the island.

He planted his hand on the top again to keep himself upright. It took every ounce of his strength not to unleash on Reese, not to tell him how much he hated him while still fucking loving him. Never had he allowed anyone to hurt him, and the one fucking time he'd opened himself up, the man he'd thought he would spend the rest of his life with had shredded him.

As though once hadn't been enough, here Reese was, coming to get his shit. Brantley would never admit it aloud, but seeing him again ripped at his already devastated insides.

"I'll just pack it up," Reese said softly before turning away.

Brantley took a swig of his beer, set it down, unable to watch Reese walk down the hall to the bedroom they'd shared.

He waited for Reese to return. One minute turned into twenty, then into thirty. Two beers later, when he thought his heart was going to beat right out of his fucking chest, he set down the bottle and headed for the bedroom.

Brantley found Reese sitting on the edge of the bed, his hands planted firmly on his thighs, head hanging down. He looked like he was in pain, his chest rising and falling heavily.

"Problem?" he asked, the single word coming out more of an accusation than a question.

When Reese looked up at him, Brantley felt the last tethers holding his heart together snap. Reese looked as torn up as Brantley felt. His eyes were bloodshot, as though he was battling back emotion and losing. Brantley knew the feeling. He'd run the gamut these past few months. Anger, hurt, heartache. There were days when he hurt so fucking much, the emotional pain was a physical ache, shredding his insides until he could hardly breathe from it. Never had he expected to feel so much for one person, but he'd learned his lesson the hard way.

"Why don't I help you out," Brantley hissed, hating the agony flaring to life, his consistent bedfellow these past six months returning with a vengeance.

Brantley marched toward the closet. He flung the door open, yanked the string to turn on the light. It snapped in his hand thanks to the power behind the movement, but at least the damn thing came on. He found one of Reese's shirts, jerked it off the hanger, threw it out the door. He wrenched another, then another, tossing them into a pile in the bedroom. He was so furious, plastic hangers were snapping, falling to the floor at his feet. By the time he'd created a decent pile, he was breathing hard, his chest tight.

"Brantley, stop," Reese said from the doorway.

"Why? It's what you want. You're here to pack your shit and go. Good, because I don't fucking want you here anyway," he bit out through clenched teeth, jerking another shirt from the hanger.

It got caught up, infuriating him more. Before he could rip the entire rod down from the wall, a firm hand circled his arm. Reese wasn't gentle when he spun him around.

"Stop," Reese snapped, stepping up to him.

Brantley's breaths raced in and out of his lungs as he stared back at the man. His hands balled into fists, his body primed to fight.

When Reese's hands cupped his face roughly, Brantley hissed. "Aww, fuck." His chest heaved, his heart clenching like it was trapped in the vicious grip of a jagged-edged vise.

"I don't want to go," Reese whispered, leaning in, his mouth so close Brantley could feel his breath. "I never wanted to leave."

The headache that'd started earlier began to throb violently, a sensation he'd gotten too familiar with over the years since the migraines had taken over his life. They'd grown increasingly worse in both frequency and level of pain in the past few months, taking him down three to four times a week versus the one or two he'd endured before Reese went and got himself shot.

He shrugged Reese off, stumbling out of the closet and into the bedroom. He made it as far as the bed before dropping onto it, gripping his head as the pain blinded him. It was a testament to the agony he was suffering when he allowed Reese to ease him down onto the bed. A second later, the lamp on the bedside table shut off. He was aware of Reese's footsteps as he went into the bathroom. He heard the water come on, then a minute later, Reese returned.

Brantley didn't reject the pill he handed over. He didn't thank him, either.

After passing the glass back, he rolled to his side, pulled the pillow over his head to block out all noise. He doubted it would help because nothing seemed to help him these days. He figured it had a lot to do with his mood, the darkness that had consumed him. The pain he felt was a living, breathing thing inside him, created by Reese's betrayal and fueled by the love Brantley couldn't seem to let go of.

The mattress dipped behind him. A second later, he felt Reese's hip bump his ass. He couldn't muster the strength to tell him to leave, although he desperately wanted to.

However, when Reese pressed two fingers to the base of his skull and massaged lightly, Brantley instantly relaxed. The pressure alone alleviated about seventy percent of the pain, providing instant relief. He managed to slow his breathing while Reese massaged away the worst of the physical pain, all the while stirring the emotional anguish and agony into a conflagration that burned in his chest.

A few minutes later, he drifted off.

CHAPTER TWO

Saturday, March 12, 2022

REESE SHOULD'VE LEFT THE MOMENT BRANTLEY FELL asleep. Considering how well his presence had gone over with Brantley, it would've been the right thing to do. In the span of a few minutes, Reese had managed to drive Brantley to the brink of implosion, the stress likely the contributing factor for the migraine.

Just one more thing to add to Reese's list of failures.

Nevertheless, he couldn't bring himself to leave. He wasn't ready to walk away. Not yet. Not like this.

Instead of snatching up what he could and disappearing, he left everything as it was and slipped out of the room, closing the door behind him. If he were lucky, Brantley would get a good night's sleep. The headache would be gone by morning, and they could have a rational conversation. Okay, fine, maybe rational was overreaching, but perhaps they could talk it out without violence.

Just like he'd done a thousand times, Reese went to the kitchen, pulled out Tesha's food bowl. He went to the refrigerator, found the fresh food they'd started buying for her when she'd come to live with them. He measured it out, set the bowl down on the floor, and then ensured she had enough water in the other bowl. Once that was done, he went to the couch, fell down on it.

Leaning his head back, he stared up at the ceiling. As had become his nightly ritual, he focused on the steady beat of his heart, grateful the damn thing still worked. While he relaxed, he tried to process the rage he'd witnessed in Brantley.

Reese had suspected he'd hurt the man by his actions but never had he thought it would've resulted in this. He'd spent more than a year with Brantley, and the one thing he knew to be true: Brantley Walker was not a man prone to outward displays of emotion. Not unless it was passion, but that was easily resolved with sex, something they'd engaged in frequently. However, when it came to the heavy burdens of life, like Reese, Brantley shoved that shit down, boxed it up deep inside, and left it to fester.

Or at least he'd thought that was how Brantley processed things. Didn't look to be the case now, and while it devastated him to know he was the one responsible, it also gave Reese a glimmer of hope. Hope that the two of them could make their way back to one another.

He spent the rest of the night on the couch, sleeping in short bursts. He didn't take his boots off, never bothered to find a pillow or blanket. He didn't want Brantley to think he was making himself at home. He'd been a tad hurt by the fact that Tesha had opted to sleep in the hallway outside Brantley's door rather than in the living room with him, but he understood. Reese had been here one day and gone the next. She probably thought he'd abandoned her forever.

When the clock read 5:05 a.m., he sat up, dropped his feet to the floor, and listened for sounds that Brantley was stirring. He knew the man was up with the sun, regardless of the day. Didn't matter that it was Saturday; Reese expected him to come out of the room shortly.

He wasn't disappointed. Ten minutes later, Brantley emerged dressed in a pair of shorts and a T-shirt, running shoes on his feet. He was carrying Tesha's leash, and she was wagging her tail happily as she pranced along beside him, perfectly obedient. In fact, she was so content, she hardly spared Reese a glance.

Looked as though they'd kept up with her training while he was gone. Not that he was really surprised. Brantley wasn't the sort to shirk his responsibilities. When he committed to something, he followed through with it.

Reese had been like that once. Back before he'd second-guessed his life, wondered how his world had been turned upside down because his insecurities had gotten the best of him. Rather than accept the fact that his existence was better for the changes that had taken place, he'd gone and fucked it all up.

Brantley didn't say a word, didn't so much as look his way before heading for the door, Tesha at his side.

He was still sitting on the couch when Brantley returned a little over an hour later. It took effort not to ogle him, not to admire the way his chest stretched that thin T-shirt or his leg muscles flexed beneath the hem of the shorts he wore. He'd never seen a more prime specimen in his life.

"You waitin' for somethin', Tavoularis?" Brantley asked, detouring for the kitchen on Tesha's heels as she bolted for the water bowl.

Reese pushed to his feet, shoring up his nerve. "I was hopin' we could talk."

"What's the sayin'?" Brantley mused. "Wish in one hand, shit in the other, see which one fills up first."

Reese deserved that. He knew he did.

Brantley took a long pull on a water bottle he snagged from the fridge. When he lowered it, he glared at Reese. "What's there to say?"

Well, it looked as though Brantley was still capable of bottling shit up and shoving it down deep. Gone was the man who'd lost his shit last night. In his place, the same calm, reserved man Reese had fallen in love with.

"A lot," he said confidently, not wanting this conversation to have the same fate as the one they'd started last night.

Brantley tossed the empty water bottle in the recycle bin. "If that conversation starts with you apologizing and ends with me takin' you back"—he shook his head—"not gonna happen."

Reese swallowed. "It doesn't." At least not after *that* revelation.

Brantley's steel-blue eyes shot to his face. "No?"

It took every ounce of willpower he possessed, but Reese stepped forward, held Brantley's gaze, and said, "It starts with me apologizing and ends with you"—he inhaled deeply—"marrying me."

Brantley's lack of response was priceless.

Not to mention unsettling.

BRANTLEY HOPED THE SCREECHING SOUND OF EVERYTHING coming to a dramatic halt was only in his head. Surely he hadn't heard Reese correctly.

He frowned, processed the words again, but they tracked through his gray matter the same way: *It starts with me apologizing and ends with you marrying me.* Had the bullet to his chest caused memory loss?

Brantley choked on a mirthless laugh. "Marry you?"

Reese's expression didn't change. "Yes. But that's not me askin'. Not yet."

Brantley shoved his hand through his hair, desperate to find a way out of this conversation before he did something stupid like blurt out that he still loved this man, although he damn sure didn't deserve it. "What the fuck are you talkin' about, Reese?"

"I can't walk away," he said, his voice soft. "Only if you make me. I don't want to go."

"Too late for that. You walked away six fucking months ago," Brantley blasted, fury raging in his chest like a caged animal hell-bent on breaking free.

He saw Reese's jaw harden, the muscle bunching.

Brantley took a deep breath, exhaled. In, out, he willed his blood pressure to lower. He damn sure wasn't looking to incite another migraine.

"Am I wrong?" Brantley bit out, taking a bold step closer, because damn it all to hell, his fucking resistance to this man was wearing awfully thin.

"No."

If he wasn't mistaken, that was a hell of a lot of remorse in Reese's brown eyes.

"And what's your plan for convincing me?" Brantley taunted. "Because as it stands, you're the last man on earth I'd want to marry."

Of course, that was a lie. Reese was the *only* man in the world Brantley had ever *considered* marrying. And despite the months of endless heartache, the hatred that had brewed in his gut whenever he thought about what Reese had done, Brantley couldn't confidently say he wasn't willing to give this one more chance.

He was a fucking idiot; that was all there was to it. However, he wasn't an idiot who jumped at the first chance presented to him. He did have his fucking pride, thank you very much.

"Fuck this," he snapped. "Fuck you and the horse you rode in on, Tavoularis. I'm not doin' this with you. I've got shit to do."

With that, he grabbed his truck keys and walked right out the front door.

Not until he was fishtailing out of the driveway did it dawn on him that he should've kicked Reese out because it was his fucking house, damn it.

He spent the majority of the day next door at Kaden and Keegan's, helping his cousins build a tool shed. What had started as a standard ten-by-ten building had nearly doubled in size before they'd hammered in the first nail. After months of work, they'd gotten the floor built, the frame erected, and were now moving on to the roof. Brantley hadn't minded helping out because the manual labor kept his thoughts at bay, and working with his cousins always proved to be enjoyable. They were a lively bunch, despite the fact they were sleep-deprived thanks to their nine-month-old twin daughters, Payton and Paisley.

"Hey, man," Kaden called up to him. "We're gonna knock off early. We're takin' Bristol to dinner since the folks are offerin' to babysit."

Brantley swiped the back of his hand over his forehead, peered down at Kaden, and nodded. "Don't have to tell me twice."

Kaden chuckled, waited for Brantley to come down the ladder.

"We're gonna head over to Moonshiners after we grab a bite," Kaden informed him. "Ethan and Beau are gettin' a break from the kiddos, too. Thought we'd hang out for a while. Bristol said JJ and Baz are gonna meet 'em up there, too. Why don't you join us?"

"They're not plottin' anything, are they?" Brantley kept his tone teasing, though he knew it rang with skepticism.

JJ and Bristol had formed a fast friendship in recent months, ever since Bristol had dropped by to deliver cookies. Evidently, Bristol was learning her way around the kitchen, pursuing her new love, which appeared to be baking. Her efforts had resulted in an overabundance of chocolate chip cookies, so she'd swung by to pass some off, not wanting them to go to waste. They hadn't. The team had snatched those things up like they'd been starved for months.

Kaden chuckled. "Oh, I'm pretty sure somethin's brewin' between 'em, but Bristol ain't sharin'. Meet us up there. You can interrogate 'em, and then we'll both know what they're up to."

Brantley accepted the water bottle Kaden passed over, wondered if Reese was still waiting at his house, decided he didn't care. "I can do that."

He considered asking his cousin if he could borrow his shower rather than go back to his house and risk running into Reese, but he damn sure didn't want to get the third degree. It had taken weeks of deflection before they'd stopped hounding him about Reese every time he came over.

After cleaning up the mess they'd made, he hopped in his truck and drove back to his house.

When he noticed Reese's truck wasn't in the driveway, he couldn't say whether it was relief or disappointment that swamped him. Nor did he want to think about why he might give a fuck.

Several hours later, after he'd played ball with Tesha until she was panting and practically begging for a break, Brantley showered and dressed. He was on high alert, constantly thinking he heard Reese's truck pulling down the driveway, but the man never showed. His clothes were still in a pile on the floor, the rest in the closet and dresser. From what Brantley could tell, he hadn't taken anything with him when he left.

Did that mean he was coming back? Or did he just abandon ship a second time, leaving the remnants behind as a reminder?

"Fuck him," Brantley grumbled, tucking his wallet and cell phone in his pocket. He turned to Tesha. "I'll be back in a little while, girl. Behave while I'm gone."

She lifted her head from her pillow but didn't bother to get up.

He smiled. "Get some rest, girl. You deserve it."

Ten minutes later, he was pulling into Moonshiners, weaving through the rows of cars that filled the parking lot and the adjoining patch of grass used for overflow. He found a spot at the back, parked.

It wasn't until he was inside that Brantley realized he'd made one glaring mistake. Unlike he'd been trained to do, Brantley hadn't paid enough attention to his surroundings on the way inside. He should've taken the time to scan the trucks in the lot. If he had, he would've known that Reese was here, too.

His breath lodged in his throat the instant their eyes met, and he felt a chill snake down his spine. Foreboding? Elation? He wasn't sure what prompted it, but he ignored it, offering a wave to Mack, who was behind the bar tonight, keeping his patrons supplied with liquor and beer.

Pretending Reese wasn't keeping a barstool warm and boring holes into him with that intense gaze, Brantley headed away from the temptation. He found JJ and Baz at the back near the pool tables, so he ventured that way, again not thinking about his actions until it was too late.

JJ, ever the dutiful best friend, pranced toward him like a woman with a secret to share. Her eyes glittered with excitement, her mouth pulled into a wide, satisfied grin. "Did you see him? Did y'all talk?"

Pretending not to care who she was talking about, Brantley smiled. "Nice to see you, too, JJ."

She smacked his arm playfully. "Don't play dumb with me. I know you saw him."

"Then why'd you ask?" Brantley glanced at Baz. "Can you keep her under control, please?"

Sebastian Buchanan, known as Baz to his friends, barked a laugh. "Can *anyone*?"

"Touché." Brantley laughed, then ordered a beer when one of the waitresses did a drive-by.

"What brings you out tonight?" Baz asked, leaning against a wooden post, watching as JJ took a shot.

"No reason." Not wanting to be on the receiving end of the former APD detective's interrogation skills, he changed the subject. "Kaden mentioned JJ's hangin' out with Bristol. Are they up to somethin'?"

CONFESSIONS

"They're women," Baz retorted with a chuckle. "Aren't they always up to somethin'?"

Content they weren't going to question him about Reese, Brantley accepted his beer from the waitress, then settled on a stool. It went against his nature to turn his back to the door, but he forced himself to. Otherwise, it would've been too damn easy to scope the bar.

CHAPTER THREE

JESSICA JAMES DID HER BEST NOT TO question Brantley about the man sitting at the bar wearing a forlorn expression as he nursed another glass of amber liquid. Reese had arrived shortly after she had, surprising her with his appearance. She'd offered a hello, intending to saddle up beside him, see how he was doing. The grunt he'd given in response had her rethinking her plans and ultimately had her opting to give him a little breathing room.

She still wanted to go to Reese, to talk to him, to ask how he was and whether or not he was back for good, but now that Brantley was here, it felt like a betrayal, so she kept her butt planted in her seat. They'd moved away from the pool tables when Bristol and her husbands arrived, snatching an empty table when one became available. Since then, a few more had been hijacked, pulled together so the group could congregate and shout over one another to be heard.

JJ was sandwiched against the wall with Baz on one side, Bristol on the other, and a row of Brantley's cousins sitting across from her. Ethan and Beau seemed surprisingly at ease tonight, enjoying a few hours out of the house while Beau's mother babysat their two-year-old triplets. Travis and Gage had also made an appearance. From what she'd heard, their five kids were dispersed among Travis's brothers' houses, enjoying a night with their cousins. According to town gossip, they had recently started venturing out at the urging of their friends and family. Since their wife, Kylie, died last year, they'd kept to themselves, usually neck-deep in work at Alluring Indulgence Resort or holed up in the house with their rug rats.

Not for the first time, she wondered how these people did it. The Walker family was a baby-making machine, seemingly content with popping out babies one after another. Sometimes multiple at one time.

Sure, they complained like any overly tired parent did, sought a few minutes of alone time to engage in adult conversation, but to hear them talk, it was just another day. JJ had never considered herself a kid-friendly person, but then Bristol had introduced her to Payton and Paisley, and something inside her had shifted. She knew part of that was thanks to Baz and their budding relationship. She recalled how excited Baz had been about the prospect of becoming a dad, although he hadn't been in love with the woman who'd accused him of fathering her unborn child. Now that Molly Ryan was out of the picture, the baby not belonging to Baz, JJ wasn't resisting the possibility of a future with him. In fact, she welcomed it.

"Did you ever decide what to do about your house?" Bristol prompted, drawing JJ's attention.

She shook her head, glanced around, and noticed everyone else was engaged in various side conversations. "I've considered rebuilding, but…"

"Too many bad memories?" Bristol asked, her voice rich with sympathy.

JJ had told Bristol what had happened when Dante Greenwood, her ex-boyfriend, had used her to stage his own kidnapping. Although JJ hadn't been conscious for most of the event, she still recalled how she felt when she'd come to and found herself covered in blood. Not long after, her house had been blown to smithereens—thankfully without anyone inside—and all her possessions had gone up in flames. Strangely, she didn't miss any of it, but whenever she thought about pulling into that driveway again, her insides chilled.

"Well, I might have an option for you," Bristol stated.

"Yeah? You got a house for sale in Coyote Ridge?" JJ laughed. Real estate in Coyote Ridge was scarce, hence the reason she was living with Baz in an apartment in Austin rather than in the town she'd grown up in.

"Actually, I do."

JJ's gaze snapped to Bristol, her expression sobering. "What?"

A soft smile formed on Bristol's pretty face. "It's nothing fancy, mind you, but it is in Coyote Ridge."

"Tell me more."

Bristol turned more fully toward her. "It's the house I grew up in. It needs some work, but I think it could be nice with a little elbow grease. I kept it because I wasn't ready to part with it when I moved in with Kaden and Keagan." She waved a hand. "But we've built a life on the ranch, and I know I'll never go back to it. I hate that it sits there rotting away."

JJ stared, feeling a bit giddy at the idea. "Are you sure?"

Bristol nodded. "You should take a look at it when you get a chance. You can stop by and grab the keys whenever you want. See what you think."

"See what you think about what?" Baz asked, leaning over JJ's shoulder.

"Nothin'," she exclaimed quickly, smiling to distract him.

"Y'all are schemin', aren't you?" he teased.

"Always." JJ glanced back at Bristol, hoping the woman caught on that JJ wanted to keep this on the DL for now. Of course, she would bring it up to Baz when the time was right. Just not yet.

"I was askin' her if I might be able to wrangle you into helpin' with the new dollhouse for the girls," Bristol said, her eyes conspiratorially bright. "You're good with a hammer and nails, right?"

JJ laughed when Baz's eyes went saucer-wide.

"Me? Build a dollhouse?"

"Nothin' fancy. I was thinking maybe twenty-five rooms. One-twelfth scale." She pursed her lips, scrunched her nose. "Well, maybe. I've been goin' back and forth. Maybe one-sixth is better. Barbie size, you know?"

"Twenty-*huh*?" he blurted.

"Okay, fine. We could downsize a little. Would fifteen be better?"

JJ giggled as she continued to watch Baz take it all in. He looked terrified by the idea, but she knew deep down he was likely already drawing up the plans because, while she'd grown quite fond of Peyton and Paisley, she knew Baz had practically fallen in love with the little girls. He would likely take a class on how to build a Barbie dreamhouse if that would make those little girls smile.

And just knowing that made her love him all the more.

TREY WALKER WALKED INTO MOONSHINERS TO THE familiar sight of friends getting together for a night of laughter and relaxation. The scent of pretzels and beer, combined with a variety of perfume and cologne, drifted toward him, made him feel instantly at home.

Moonshiners wasn't a big place, nor was it the type of joint one would take a date to, but it was a comfortable hangout. A venue he frequented on a weekly basis these days. He tended to swing by, see who was there. Tonight, it appeared a good portion of his family had come out for a beer or two and some laughs. He noticed a handful of his cousins as well as his brother, Brantley, congregating along the far wall. They'd crowded around a handful of tables and were currently talking over one another as they told the stories of their week.

Trey intended to join them, but he headed for the bar first, sliding between a couple of old-timers and lifting a finger to get Mack's attention.

"Hey, Mack," Trey greeted. "Can I get a beer?"

"Comin' up," he said as he drew on the tap, filling a glass for another customer.

Trey waited patiently, glancing around at all the faces. Most were regulars coming in to while away an hour or two, get wrangled into a debate about sports or even the weather. He smiled, nodded in greeting as others looked his way. When he reached the far end, he did a double take at the guy perched closest to the wall, his brain not processing immediately.

"Holy fuck," he said, squeezing out from his hole and sauntering down to the opposite end where Reese was sitting on a stool, practically hidden in the corner. Trey stepped up to him, put his hand out. "Welcome back, man."

Reese looked over, his eyes heavy-lidded and bloodshot. He'd clearly been drinking, and based on the empty glass in front of him, he wasn't fucking around tonight.

"Hey," Reese slurred, offering a weak excuse for a handshake.

"How long you been back?"

"Since … uh… yesterday?" Reese grumbled in response, sounding unsure about the timeline.

"You back for good?" Trey prodded, curious as to whether Reese had talked to Brantley but managing to keep from asking.

Reese shrugged, motioned for Mack to bring him another … it looked to be whiskey and water.

"All right, then," Trey said, recognizing a brush-off when he saw one. "I guess I'll talk to ya later."

Reese nodded, his full attention on the glass in front of him.

Knowing when to leave well enough alone, Trey stepped away, but not before getting his beer from Mack. He headed for his cousins but drew up short when he heard his name. He stopped, turned, saw Magnus Storme strolling into the place. He looked like a man on a mission, and damn it all to hell, Trey couldn't help wondering if he was the intended target.

"Don't worry. I'm not stalkin' you. Yet," Magnus said with a beaming grin. It was the same grin Magnus used when he seduced Trey during their secret late-night encounters at Trey's house. "JJ texted me. Said to come by if I was free."

Trey wasn't sure what to say.

Magnus stepped in close. Close enough Trey could see the green and brown flecks in his hazel eyes, smell the rich but subtle fragrance of his cologne. "So am I free, Trey?"

They'd spent the past year engaged in this little dance. The one where Magnus would approach him in public, taunt him, tempt him. And then, late at night when there were no prying eyes, Magnus would come back to Trey's place, and they would fuck until they could hardly move. Trey would fall asleep, exhausted from the best sex of his fucking life, and he would wake in the morning to an empty bed.

For the most part, that was working well for them. Trey battled the daily urge to fall in love with this man, forced himself to stick to his guns and keep this thing between them simple and uncomplicated. It wasn't easy, but Trey was managing. Or, rather, that was the lie he told himself.

"Go on," Trey rumbled.

"You sure?" Magnus's eyes gleamed with mischief. "I happen to know of a supply closet that's got just enough room..." He winked.

Trey was all too familiar with that supply closet. They'd used it half a dozen times already when Trey's willpower gave out before they could sneak out. Just thinking about it made his dick thicken behind the zipper of his damn jeans.

Trey responded by grunting and moving past Magnus. As it was, they'd already caught JJ's attention, and the last damn thing he needed was her hounding him about the nature of their relationship.

A soft laugh sounded behind him, but Trey pretended not to notice.

As the clock ticked on, the night transitioning to early morning, Brantley watched as Reese teetered on the barstool. More than once already, he'd nearly tumbled onto the floor.

While a few others had commented, finding Reese's intoxicated state amusing, Brantley found no humor in the situation. He also couldn't find it in himself to get Reese out of here, to save him from becoming the laughingstock of the night. The guy needed to sleep it off somewhere, but Brantley'd be damned if he was going to come to the man's rescue.

"I take it you two haven't made up?" Travis's gravelly drawl sounded from his right.

He spared his cousin a glance. "No."

"You happen to know where he's stayin'?"

Brantley shook his head, shifted his attention back to Reese. "Motel, maybe?"

He damn sure wasn't going to tell Travis that Reese had stayed at his house last night. Had Brantley been in his right fucking mind, he never would've allowed it to happen.

"Well…" Travis pushed to his feet. "We're gonna call it a night. I'll let him sleep it off on my couch."

Brantley kept his eyes on Reese because he didn't trust that Travis wouldn't read him like a fucking book if he looked him in the eye. His cousin would know that Brantley wasn't about to leave Reese on his own in this state. He much preferred Travis be the white knight and cart Reese off before Brantley was forced to do so.

Clearly seeing right through him despite no eye contact, Travis let out a gruff chuckle. "I'll catch up with y'all later."

Those who'd stuck around to waste the entire night offered up a round of goodbyes to Travis and Gage.

Brantley watched as the two men approached Reese, saw Reese offer a drunken smile. He briefly wondered if he would've gotten the same smile if he'd been the one to go over there. Doubtful.

"I think we're gonna call it a night, too," JJ said. "It's thinned out really well."

Yeah, for the most part, those with kids had already headed home. They might've gotten a few hours with adults, but come morning, they'd be right back to entertaining the little ones.

"You'll holler if somethin' comes up?" JJ asked, patting Brantley on the shoulder.

He knew she was referring to a case. Since they hadn't worked one in nearly two weeks, they'd been focusing their efforts on doing a deep dive on the social media kidnappings they'd stumbled on a while back. Unfortunately, they weren't making much headway, despite the fact the number of missing kids associated with these types of groups was on the rise.

Brantley pushed his beer away, got to his feet. He'd been nursing the damn thing for two hours now, so it was safe to say he was not headed for a buzz anytime soon. Figured it made more sense to head home.

He said good night to Trey, who was chatting it up with Rafe Sharpe. Brantley figured Rafe was hanging out until Bailey Weber got off work. He didn't know what, if anything, was going on between the two of them, but he knew Rafe often drove Bailey home when her shift was over.

With Reese no longer at the bar, Brantley made his way over, closed his tab, and added a healthy tip before heading for the door.

When he stepped outside, he stood on the old wooden porch and stared out at the nearly empty parking lot. He didn't see Travis's SUV or Gage's truck, so he assumed they'd already left in whichever they'd come in. He also didn't see Reese's truck, and he assumed the other had driven it back to their house so Reese would have it in the morning.

Not that Brantley gave a damn where Reese was or what he was doing or even what his transportation options were come daylight. He didn't fucking care. He couldn't.

He made that his mantra for the next ten minutes. It was the only thing that kept him from detouring to Travis's house on his way home.

CHAPTER FOUR

MAGNUS LEFT MOONSHINERS FOUR MINUTES AFTER TREY. He knew because he timed it.

In his defense, waiting was damn hard. Almost as hard as his dick had been all night watching Trey as he interacted with his friends and family. No man had ever captivated Magnus the way Trey did. Every single thing about him was sexy. The way he moved, the way he talked. And especially the hair. For whatever reason, Trey was letting his hair grow out. That or he simply didn't have time to go to the barber to get it cut, because it had surpassed his collar and was well on its way to being considered long. He'd always been attractive, but this change made him hot. The kind of hot that had Magnus wondering if the guy had a Harley parked out in the lot instead of his truck. Between the shoulder-length hair and the goatee/mustache thing he had going on … yeah, Magnus sported a hard-on just looking at the guy.

And damned if it hadn't been difficult to play his part as the dutiful secret lover and wait until no one suspected he could've been traipsing after Trey.

Now, as he pulled up to Trey's house, parking behind Trey's truck, he was ready to strip off his damn clothes and stroll in naked just to save time.

He didn't, of course. But he wanted to.

As was usually the case, the front door was unlocked, so Magnus let himself inside. All the lights were off, except for the one in the guest bedroom where Trey slept. Magnus had attempted to ask him why he didn't sleep in the master bedroom where he kept his clothes, but he'd been shut down too many times for him to repeat the question. He figured Trey had his reasons, and since Magnus was supposed to be a booty call and nothing more, he'd decided not to pester him.

He had just walked past the hall bathroom when he heard footsteps behind him. The next thing Magnus knew, he was pinned to the wall, his face pressed against the Sheetrock and Trey's big body crushing him.

Teeth bit into his neck, and he moaned, tilting his head, welcoming the erotic pain that accompanied it.

He sometimes had a difficult time believing they'd been doing this for the better part of a year now. Each encounter was hotter than the last, and no matter how many times they fucked, no matter how many different positions they tried or toys they used, Magnus never got enough. He wanted Trey with every breath he took, and his craving for the man intensified day after day.

Magnus reached back, gripped Trey's thigh, and squeezed.

"I hope you're not in the mood for gentle," Trey rumbled against his skin.

He chuckled. "Have you ever been gentle with me, Trey?"

"Not on purpose."

Trey sucked the skin on his neck hard, dragging a ragged moan from Magnus's throat. Trey reached for the hem of Magnus's T-shirt, jerked it up, then yanked it over his head. He tossed it to the floor, and then Magnus was pressed to the wall once again. The heat of Trey's body was a welcome relief, but it disappeared instantly when Trey gripped his arm, spun him around, and slammed him into the wall. A second later, those smooth, warm lips were molded to his mouth, and Trey's tongue was thrusting inside.

Magnus moaned, running his hands over Trey's arms, up to his shoulders, down his back. He touched him everywhere, knowing that was how Trey liked it. He'd never known anyone as responsive to touch as Trey, and yeah, that was another fucking turn-on.

While Magnus explored the impressive planes of Trey's upper body, Trey worked free the button on Magnus's jeans. The zipper was jerked down, then his jeans shoved down to his thighs. He had just enough time to suck in a breath before Trey was on his knees.

Thank fuck for the wall at his back. Magnus leaned into it, using it for support when Trey's seductive mouth wrapped around the throbbing head of his cock. He wasn't sure why Trey was so worked up, but Magnus didn't care. He loved Trey like this. Hell, he loved Trey any way he could get him. Not that he could tell the man that. Revealing that he'd fallen in love with him an eternity ago would've sent Trey into a panic and ruined the best fucking thing Magnus had going for him.

"Oh, fuck," Magnus hissed, gripping Trey's hair in his fist, urging him to slow down. "Keep it up, I'll come."

That seemed to spur Trey, because he took him to the root, swallowed, his throat muscles caressing the sensitive head and nearly sending him right into that glorious freefall. Trey drew on his cock, releasing him before taking him down his throat again. Hard hands gripped his ass, tugging his cheeks apart. Trey's skilled fingers dipped along the crack of his ass, teasing as they brushed sensitive skin.

Magnus pumped his hips, eager to get more everywhere, but he knew he wasn't the one in control, regardless of what their positions looked like. Trey was always the aggressor, and Magnus was helpless to resist. Another fucking turn-on.

He focused on breathing, fighting off the urge to come down Trey's throat. He moaned and groaned, repeating Trey's name over and over. It was all he could do to keep from exploding.

Finally, Trey released his cock and got to his feet. Magnus barely managed to get his jeans up high enough not to hinder his movements before Trey was dragging him down the hall, into the bedroom.

"Strip," Trey demanded, stepping back and doing the same.

Magnus wasted no time, kicking off his boots, shucking his jeans and underwear. He didn't dare sit down, not sure what Trey had in store for him. Whatever it was, Magnus knew he would love the hell out of it. Instead, he looked his fill, admiring every lean inch of Trey as he stripped down to nothing, his beautiful cock bobbing proudly out from his body, eager for attention.

"Turn around," Trey demanded before Magnus could offer up his oral services.

He slowly turned away from Trey.

"Put your hands on the bed."

He did.

"Spread your legs."

Magnus shifted his feet apart, bent at the waist, and assumed the position.

And while it should've seemed obvious, he knew that he would never be able to predict Trey's next move because Trey Walker was not a predictable man. He was quite possibly the most incredible, the most attentive lover Magnus had ever had.

He listened for clues: the telltale click of the lube that Trey used, the slick, messy glide of a lubricated hand on a cock. He heard none of those things, but he remained just like that, bent over, spread-eagle, his cock throbbing and his asshole clenching in anticipation.

Something hard pressed against his anus. It wasn't a finger or a cock, but he couldn't quite place it. Because he trusted Trey with his life, he didn't ask questions, didn't panic.

Trey's hand moved to Magnus's hip, held him as something pressed more firmly against his hole. It wasn't big enough to be Trey's cock, but it was too big for anything else.

"Fuck me," Trey rasped. "I like watching your asshole stretch wide."

A chill ran over his skin, covering his entire body in goose bumps. Anticipation built, made his cock swell and throb. Whatever Trey used was being pushed into his ass slow and deep. A dildo? A plug? A vibrator? Magnus didn't know.

Trey tormented him, sliding it in, pulling it out. Again and again, while Magnus's ass gripped the intrusion.

A soft hum sounded a second before Magnus realized there was a vibration deep inside him.

"Oh, fucking hell," he shouted when the fucking vibration grazed his prostate. His cock jerked, and he damn near came.

"Yeah? You like that?"

"Fuck … Trey … oh, fuck, yes."

Trey fucked him with it, his hand tightening on Magnus's hip as though he was holding himself back. Magnus clenched his teeth, his muscles coiling tighter with every pass of that damn thing over his prostate. He wasn't going to last. He wasn't. It was too much. Too good.

"Trey … oh, God. I'm—"

Suddenly the vibrator disappeared, and a second later, Trey was ramming his dick inside him. Magnus gripped the comforter, locked his elbows, and took every punishing thrust of Trey's hips as he fucked him. Hard.

It was so fucking good.

He let Trey use him for long minutes, accepting the deep thrusts that rocked his entire body. He held himself still, urging Trey to rail him harder, give him more. It would never be enough, he knew, but it would be enough for now.

Trey gripped Magnus's hips hard, jerking him back every time he impaled him. The brutal intensity had his cock leaking. If he could just touch his cock, stroke it once, he would come. That was all he needed to go over.

"I'm gonna come in your ass; then you're gonna come in my mouth," Trey growled.

Magnus moaned in response. He was game for whatever Trey wanted. The man had never left him wanting before, and he didn't suspect he would start now.

"Oh … fuck … Magnus…" Trey drove into him, his words punctuating every aggressive drive of his hips. "So … fucking … tight."

When Trey came, it was with a hard grunt and a violent shudder. Magnus resisted stroking his cock, waiting until Trey dropped down to his knees, then urged him to turn around.

Two strokes of Trey's wicked mouth was all it took to shatter his mind and body at the same time.

AFTER THAT INSANELY HOT ENCOUNTER, TREY COAXED Magnus into the shower. He took his time washing them both, enjoying the way Magnus's eyes rolled back in his head as Trey touched him, relishing the soft, satisfied moans that rattled in his chest.

He was no longer capable of pretending he didn't want Magnus. It took effort to keep up the facade in public, but when they were alone, he'd stopped trying. He knew that if Magnus would just look hard enough, he would see every emotion written on Trey's face. He wished he could've kept the man at arm's length, wished he could've kept it at the level where pleasure was the only thing he sought. He'd long surpassed that point, even if he would continue to outwardly deny it.

As he rinsed Magnus with the sprayer, he trailed his fingertips over his velvet smooth skin, admiring the thick slabs of muscle. Magnus had bulked up some recently, and he suspected Brantley had convinced Magnus to take up lifting weights the way he did. He knew Brantley and Magnus had spent more time together since Reese left, knew they'd established a friendship while Magnus taught Brantley the necessary steps to train Tesha.

Admittedly, Trey was jealous of that friendship, but not because he worried. No, he merely wished he had that sort of easy interaction with Magnus outside of the bedroom.

Trey hooked the sprayer back to the wall then turned off the water. As he turned to get towels, Magnus grabbed him.

"Trey?"

He met those beautiful hazel eyes. "Hmm?"

Magnus was staring deep into his soul, and Trey wondered what was going through his head. Unfortunately, he wouldn't know because Magnus's "Never mind" ended the moment.

Trey pressed a kiss to his lips, pulled back. "Come on. Let's sleep."

When Trey drifted off, he knew he would sleep soundly for the few hours Magnus would remain in his arms. The man would slip out before dawn, leaving Trey wishing for another moment like they'd shared in the hotel in Dallas the night Magnus had surprised him with a visit. Those moments didn't happen, though, and Trey constantly reminded himself that this was what he'd asked for. This was what he continued to push for.

And until he decided to move forward, this was what he would get.

CHAPTER FIVE

Sunday, March 13, 2022

REESE BRUSHED THE TICKLE AWAY FROM HIS nose as he came awake slowly. He didn't open his eyes right away because something felt off.

He wasn't at his mother's, he knew that much. And he wasn't at Brantley's because he would've known since that was the only place that felt like home.

Another tickle had him rubbing his face as he peeked open an eye only to flinch back into the cushion behind his head.

Three small faces stared down at him, all of them smiling, their eyes glittering with amusement.

Kate, Kade, and Avery, three of Travis and Gage's five kids, were hovering over him.

"I told you it'd work," Kate said proudly, waving a small feather in victory.

Yep, they were responsible for the tickle. Being that they were Travis's offspring, it was a wonder Reese didn't have shaving cream—or worse—smeared over his face at his own doing. He figured that was a prank they'd learn soon enough.

"It's about time," Avery said gleefully. "The daddies said you might sleep all day." She dragged out the *all day* part as though that was inconceivable.

"The daddies?" he said, rolling his head on his neck to work out the kinks.

Kate smiled. "Yep. We've got two dads."

Reese shifted his gaze to the left then to the right, trying to see if those two dads happened to be somewhere close. Maybe they could call back the rug rats who were all but sitting on top of him.

"Daddy-O said you're gonna have a headache," Kade relayed with a smile. "Do you have a headache? Huh? Do ya?"

If he didn't, he certainly would now.

"I'm good," he told them as he attempted to sit up.

They each took one step back, which didn't allow much movement, but Reese managed to prop himself up on an elbow. And sure enough, as soon as his head went vertical, pain throbbed behind his eyes, and there was a ringing in his ears.

It all came back to him. Downing whiskey and water at Moonshiners while the people he'd once considered friends had laughed and joked without including him. Well, to be fair, a couple of them had tried, but by then, Reese had been committed to drinking himself under the table, so he'd brushed them off. He'd indulged in his very own pity party while he fought the urge to declare his love for Brantley right there for the whole world—or the small town of Coyote Ridge, anyway—to hear.

He hadn't, had he?

"Let's give him some space," Gage called out when he walked into the room.

He held out a cup of coffee, and Reese nearly wept at his feet.

"Figured you'd need this. Water and aspirin are in the kitchen," he said before turning to the munchkins, still holding vigil around him. "Go on, let's get dressed. We're goin' to Nana and Pops's house today."

"Yay!" they squealed, dancing around, oblivious to the machete slicing through Reese's brain.

Reese sipped coffee, praying the caffeine would help cease the throbbing in his head.

He remained where he was, listening as little feet pounded the floor over his head. Every so often, there would be a squeal or a shout, along with a steady stream of chatter. He worked himself to a full sitting position, stretching his legs out in front of him. He still had on his boots, and if he wasn't mistaken, that was his wallet imprinted on his ass. Luckily he didn't seem to have his keys on him.

"Daddy! Kade stole my Barbie!" Avery shouted. "Give it back!"

Reese took a deep breath, prayed his stomach wasn't going to join in the riot now pounding intently in his head.

Fifteen minutes later, after Gage had taken the three bigger kids with him, Reese managed to get vertical. He stood and stretched, wondering if he'd have permanent kinks in his neck from all the couch sleeping he'd done as of late. His legs weren't completely steady, but they kept him upright as he made a quick trip to the bathroom.

He took a piss, washed his hands, splashed cold water on his face. He looked around for toothpaste, wishing to get the fuzziness off his tongue. Not finding any, he decided more coffee would have to do the trick.

He was coming out of the bathroom as Travis stepped out of his office.

Travis's gaze narrowed on him. "You look like shit."

"Yeah. Thanks for that."

"Gage get you coffee?"

Reese nodded, then followed Travis into the kitchen, grabbing the empty cup on his way.

"Ibuprofen?" Travis offered.

"Please," he said gruffly.

He thanked Travis when he passed over the bottle.

"Tell me I didn't do somethin' stupid last night."

"You mean besides get shit-faced and wallow in it all night?"

"Yeah. Besides that."

"Nope. You even managed to stay on the stool although half the bar was takin' bets as to when you'd fall on your head."

Fuckin' fantastic. Now he was the laughingstock of the town. Just what he needed for his already bruised and battered ego.

Reese downed the pills when Travis passed a glass of water.

"Sit," Travis said, using the tone Reese suspected he used on his kids when they were in trouble.

Reese sat.

Travis topped off Reese's coffee, then poured himself a cup and joined him at the small table in the middle of the kitchen.

"You back for good?"

Reese studied his mug, his hands, anything to keep from looking up at Travis. "I don't know."

"You apologize to him yet?"

Reese's gaze snapped up at that. "To who?"

Travis gave him a look that said he was quite possibly the biggest idiot on the face of the planet to ask that.

"Yeah," he admitted with defeat. "I tried. He's not havin' it."

"Can you blame him?"

"No."

Travis sipped from his cup, his steely gaze pinned on Reese, making him feel like a bug under a microscope. He did his best not to fidget even as his discomfort level rose.

Finally, Travis leaned toward him, his expression stern when he said, "You fucked that boy up but good, Reese."

"I know."

"But he loves you. That much is obvious."

Was it? Reese wasn't so sure.

"If he didn't, Brantley would've fucked every willin' man in three counties by now. He's no saint."

Reese stared back at Travis, not sure what to say. He wasn't in denial. He took full responsibility for everything that'd happened, and he wanted to make it right with Brantley. Hell, that was the only thing he wanted; he just didn't know how to do it.

"I can't blame him if he tells me to get lost," Reese grumbled.

"Oh, for fuck's sake. Stop feelin' sorry for yourself and man up." Travis's voice lowered another octave when he said, "Take it from a man who lost one of the loves of his life, Reese. This life is too goddamn short. Don't throw yourself a fuckin' pity party. You should be over there grovelin' at his fuckin' feet if that's what it takes."

"What if it doesn't help?"

"Who fuckin' cares?" Travis blasted. "Goddamn, Reese. Do you love him?"

Reese took a deep breath and said the most honest thing he'd ever admitted aloud: "With everything I am."

"Then tell him that. And don't waste a fuckin' second. I'm serious. One day they're here; the next they could be gone." There were tears glistening in Travis's eyes. "Don't waste time with what-ifs."

Reese swallowed hard.

Travis's tone smoothed out, his frustration dialing down a notch. "Tell him, Reese. And make him believe it."

With that advice penetrating his pounding skull as thoroughly as the headache, Reese got in his truck and headed for Brantley's.

Brantley woke up like he did every day. He made his way to the bathroom, took care of business, then pulled on shorts, T-shirt, and shoes, and headed out with Tesha for their morning run.

His pace was for shit today, and he knew it had to do with the fact he'd tossed and turned for most of the night. Evidently, it wasn't enough for him to know Reese was in Coyote Ridge. He wanted the blasted man under the same roof even if he wasn't ready to forgive him yet.

He managed six miles before giving up the ghost and heading back to the house. He was unhooking Tesha's harness when he heard tires on gravel, then turned to see Reese's truck pulling down the drive.

"You think we should go easy on him, girl?" he asked the dog.

She didn't answer. Then again, she never gave him advice, but he appreciated the fact she listened to his endless bullshit anyway.

He didn't wait for Reese, rather going inside and grabbing a water bottle from the fridge. He added more water to Tesha's bowl after she gulped down most of it before flopping in a heap on the floor. He was putting the water pitcher back in the fridge when the screen door opened. Footsteps sounded.

Brantley tipped his bottle to his lips, turned to see Reese stepping into the kitchen.

"Ouch," Brantley said aloud. "You look like hell."

"So I've heard."

Brantley didn't feel sorry for Reese. Or rather, he didn't *want* to feel sorry for the man, but Reese didn't make it easy. Considering all the times Reese had taken care of him when he'd suffered a migraine, it wasn't easy to pretend he didn't care. Even if the devil sitting on his shoulder told him now would be the perfect time to turn on some music and blast it through the house.

"You need somethin' for it?" Brantley asked.

"Took somethin' already. I wouldn't say no to coffee, though."

Brantley pointed the bottle toward the coffee maker. "Have at it."

Reese watched him for a moment, then headed for the cabinet, pulling out the coffee and starting a pot.

Brantley stepped back out of the way, tossed his empty bottle in the recycle bin, then leaned against the island and crossed his arms over his chest. When Reese turned around, Brantley asked, "You back to pack your shit?"

Reese's expression softened. "If that's what you want me to do."

Brantley frowned. "It ain't about what I want," he said hotly. "It's *never* been about what I want, obviously."

"That's not true," Reese countered.

"No?" Brantley felt his ire rising, the pain he'd suffered these past six months returning with a vengeance. "If I recall, I'm the one who was makin' an effort. And you were the one runnin' toward the ex-girlfriend."

Reese's mouth opened, closed. It was apparent he wanted to say something, but he held it in.

And then there they were, staring at one another while the coffee maker hissed and gurgled. Brantley's breaths had grown labored; his heart was pounding as he fought the urge to punch something.

Reese spoke first. "I know it means nothin', but I am sorry. If I could take it all back, I would."

Of course he would. Hindsight was always twenty-twenty.

Brantley held Reese's gaze, not even sure what he wanted from the man.

"Can we start over?" Reese asked.

Brantley's eyebrows shot to his hairline. "Start over? As in what? You want me to court you again? To have you turn tail and hide when someone looks at you funny?"

"It's not like that anymore," Reese declared.

"Oh, fuck that shit," Brantley grunted, dropping his arms and turning away from him. "What the fuck does that even mean? You've missed me so much that you're suddenly willin' to go on a date? Out in public? You won't freak the fuck out like you did before?"

Brantley recalled all the times he'd sucked it up, making excuses for why Reese wasn't willing to date him like a normal couple. He'd forgiven him too easily, passed it off as confusion because Reese had never been with a man before Brantley.

No fucking thank you. He was not putting himself through that again. Although he'd abided by the military's *don't ask, don't tell* policy even after it was repealed, he'd kept his sexual orientation on the DL, hidden from his teammates because it made things simpler for him. However, Brantley had never been in the closet. He had a family who had always supported him, raised him to be who he wanted to be, so he'd never felt the need to hide. Then Reese had walked into his life, and he'd regressed, doing what was necessary to ensure Reese felt comfortable around him.

And Reese had the audacity to want more *now*.

Brantley shook off thoughts of a future with the man who'd shattered him and scrubbed a hand over his face. "I don't have time for this right now. I've got to take Tesha to Magnus's. She's scheduled for training today."

"I'll take her."

Brantley stared at him, considered telling him to fuck off. It would be just his luck that Reese would take Tesha and bolt, leaving him high and dry once again, only this time without the dog he'd come to love like she was his own damn child.

He took a deep breath, reined in the thought. Reese wouldn't do that. He was a lot of things, but vindictive wasn't one of them.

"Fine," he said, figuring he could use a few hours to process everything that had happened since Reese walked through his door the other night. At the very least, he needed time to gather his thoughts so he could decide whether or not he was ready to kick Reese to the curb once and for all. Plus, he had seen how happy Tesha was now that Reese was back. He refused to see her love for Reese as a betrayal, although it would've been easy to.

Reese's eyebrows popped up. "Really?"

"Yeah. Just so you know, we've long since gotten out of the basics."

"I'll let Magnus catch me up," he said softly. "When I get back, we'll finish this discussion."

Brantley narrowed his eyes, unwilling to concede just yet. "Maybe."

"Better than no," Reese muttered, looking over at Tesha. "You wanna go for a ride, girl?"

Her ears perked up, and she trotted over, staring up at Reese as though sniffing out the command in his question.

"Truck," Brantley commanded.

Tesha's entire body wagged because she knew exactly what that meant.

Five minutes later, after Reese left with Tesha, Brantley headed for the bathroom. He needed a shower.

He made it as far as the mirror over the sink, leaning in and taking a good long look at himself. He ran a hand over the scraggly beard he hadn't bothered to cut, then over the mop of hair that he'd refused to do anything with mainly because his brothers and sisters had started giving him shit about it. Didn't seem to matter that Trey was growing his hair out long and looked as much like a homeless person as Brantley; they all seemed to gang up on him for some reason. Then again, Trey had gone through these phases before while Brantley'd always been within strict military regulations.

The next thing he knew, he was pulling the clippers out of the drawer.

It took twenty minutes to buzz the hair off his head and shave his face. By the time he was finished, he almost recognized the man staring back at him. It was the first time in months he'd given a shit about anything at all.

"Goddamn, Reese," he grumbled, marching over to the shower and turning the water on.

When it was hot, he stepped beneath the spray. It felt weird for the water to pelt his scalp, but he ignored it. He washed up, rinsed off, and was about to turn off the water when he paused. He took hold of his semi-hard cock, stroked it once, twice … by the third time, he was fully hard, his eyes closing as he thought about Reese walking up to his porch the other day.

Despite his anger at the situation, there'd been that familiar zing that always came from looking at Reese. Something about the man spoke to Brantley on a primal level. From the very first day he met the man, he'd been attracted to him. Even through their painfully slow courtship, he'd been aroused by the mere thought of him.

And now Reese was back, spouting off shit like apologies and starting over. Oh, and marriage. Yeah, he hadn't forgotten that tidbit Reese had laid on him the other day.

How the fuck was Brantley supposed to keep his distance? Hell, he'd fantasized about this exact thing a time or two in the past six months. Granted, those fantasies were generally obliterated by the self-loathing that would smash those thoughts into smithereens. But still.

Brantley leaned against the tiled wall, tightened his fist on his rigid cock. He closed his eyes, jerking himself, imagining it was Reese's hand on him. Or better yet, his fucking mouth. Brantley knew his anger was no match for those fantasies. There was no doubt in his mind that he would give in if Reese were to seduce him. Hell, it had been six fucking months since he'd gotten laid. While he'd attempted to talk himself into finding some stranger to tap for one night, Brantley hadn't been able to do it.

He was panting, his fist jerking roughly, the wet sound of his cock tunneling through his fist rivaling the soft groans that started down deep. In his mind's eye, he saw Reese going to his knees before him, opening that wicked fucking mouth…

"Fuck," he growled, squeezing his cock as it spurted.

His knees went weak, and he used the wall to hold himself up while he fought to catch his breath.

"Goddamn you, Reese," he bellowed. "Why the fuck do you make it so goddamn hard?"

This time he wasn't referring to his dick.

CHAPTER SIX

TREY WAS SITTING AT THE BREAKFAST BAR in his mother's kitchen when he heard Brantley's voice, followed by shouts from their nieces, Meghan and Ashley. He glanced at his mother, who gave him that look that said she had no idea another one of her sons was stopping by for a visit.

Considering Brantley hadn't ventured much farther than his own house for the past six months, Trey had to wonder whether something was wrong. Two outings in just a few hours? Had Reese's reappearance triggered that?

Brantley stepped into the kitchen, and Trey did a double-take similar to the one last night when he'd spotted Reese crammed in the corner of the bar.

Gone was Brantley's shaggy mop of hair, the hard line of his jaw now visible without the scraggly shit growing on his chin.

"You look..." Trey tried to come up with a way to describe it and blurted out, "Less like a caveman."

"You're one to talk," Brantley retorted. "Your hair's longer than Mom's."

Trey chuckled. "It's a fashion statement."

Brantley waited until their mother turned away and flipped Trey the bird.

"Mama, did you see that?" Trey said, adding a petulant whine for good measure. "Brantley's bein' mean to me."

"Probably serves you right," their father's voice boomed as he joined them in the kitchen. "Just payin' you back for all the times you roughed him up when you were boys."

Brantley smirked, clearly pleased that their father was on his side.

"You boys want somethin' to drink?" Iris offered.

"Nah. Too early for beer," Trey grumbled good-naturedly.

"But it's never too early for coffee," Brantley noted. "You have any made, Ma?"

"I'll make some fresh," she said sweetly, turning toward the coffeepot.

"So, what's got you all showered and cleaned up this mornin'?" Frank asked Brantley.

Brantley's eyes narrowed even as he said, "It was time."

"Any chance it has somethin' to do with——"

"Shut the hell up, Trey," Brantley bit out, cutting him off.

He would've found significant pleasure in giving Brantley shit about Reese, but he noticed the gleam in his eyes and decided to back off. He'd seen how hard it'd been on Brantley after their split. The least he could do was hold off until he figured out whether or not the two of them were going to patch things up.

It was then Trey realized Brantley had come solo. He looked down to confirm, then back up to his brother. "Where's Tesha?"

There was a rough exhale, and then Brantley looked away. "Reese took her for her session with Magnus."

Did that mean Reese had spent the night? Were they back together?

He kept those questions to himself, let out a short whistle instead. "Well, I'll be damned. I shoulda known there was only one reason you'd get all prettied up."

"Shut it," Brantley snapped.

"Boys, behave," Iris chastised.

Brantley's phone rang, and Trey took a reprieve from harassing him, turning back to his mother and father. He was about to strike up a conversation when Brantley's curt tone had him pausing.

"You get lost or what? I thought you——"

When Brantley's words abruptly cut off, Trey looked up. Brantley's body language did not inspire confidence. His eyes were squinted like he was concentrating, his hand was inadvertently rubbing the back of his neck, and he'd already started to pace. Something was definitely wrong.

"All right. Yeah. Lemme see what I can find out. You stay there, see what information you can get from the officers on scene."

Trey's back straightened as he turned to face his brother. "What's goin' on?"

Brantley simply stared at him for a long moment.

"What?" Trey felt the hair on the back of his neck stand on end. "What's wrong?"

"It's Magnus."

A cold chill slithered down Trey's spine as he slowly stood up, eyes pinned on his brother, waiting for more information.

"When did you last see him?" Brantley asked.

Frowning, Trey tried to figure out what that had to do with anything.

"Trey? I need to know. Did he leave the bar with you last night?"

"Why?"

"Don't play dumb with me, Trey. Did you or did you not see Magnus after you left Moonshiners?"

"Yeah," he lamented. "Why's that matter?"

Brantley's exhale sounded a hell of a lot like relief.

"What the fuck is goin' on?" Trey demanded.

"Mouth, boy," Frank scolded.

Trey ignored him.

Brantley continued with, "What time did he leave your place?"

Trey shook his head. "I am *not* answerin' any more of your fuckin' questions till you tell me what the hell's goin' on."

Brantley stared him down, his lips pursing as he breathed through his nose.

Trey stood his ground. No fucking way was he going into detail until someone told him something.

"Goddammit, Brantley, what the—"

"The police just picked up Magnus."

Trey's entire body stilled, and his responding, "What?" came out a little higher-pitched than he would've liked.

"Tesha's trainer?" Frank asked, moving closer, coffee cup in hand.

"Yeah."

"Start from the beginning," Iris insisted, stepping around the island, her soft tone morphing into the one Trey was all too familiar with. Iris Walker might seem passive in spirit, but the woman had raised seven children, so beneath that sweet exterior was the heart of a lion.

"What happened to Magnus?" Frank asked.

Great. And now Trey's parents were going to find out that Trey had been mixing it up with a twenty-six-year-old for the last fucking year. And he'd thought his day couldn't get any better.

Brantley exhaled, his full attention on Trey. "Right now, Reese knows very little. Aside from the fact they're cartin' Magnus down to Round Rock PD for questioning."

Questioning.

Trey continued to breathe, pretending he wasn't a little freaked at the knowledge. What business did the police have with Magnus? And what the hell were they questioning him for? More importantly, why did Trey feel the need to defend the man?

"Do they think he did something?" Iris asked.

"He's currently their main suspect in the disappearance of Ava March."

"And she is?" Frank prompted.

"We don't have that information," Brantley stated. Looking at Trey once more, he added, "Unless you do."

Trey immediately looked at the floor, recalling the one and only time he'd been introduced to the woman.

He'd gone to Magnus's house on New Year's. Not one of his finer moments, no, but he'd gone in an attempt to show Magnus he was capable of making the first move when it was warranted. What he found when he arrived had weighed heavily on his mind since then.

He pulled the door to Camp K-9's small office open slowly, trying to avoid making the bell overhead ring and announce his presence, then came to an abrupt halt at the scene before him.

There was Magnus, his arms around a woman, her head resting on his shoulder. She appeared to be distraught. Crying. But the way Magnus was holding her ... it was...

Trey didn't know how to describe it, but it reminded him of the fact that Magnus was openly bisexual, that he enjoyed both men and women and made no apologies for it.

Magnus must've heard him because he turned his head, peering over and meeting Trey's gaze briefly. He didn't release the woman, waiting for her to calm down.

Trey had plenty of time to leave, to walk right back out the door and into the night. It would've been easy to get in his truck, go home, pretend this never happened. He could avoid Magnus, use this as an excuse to put an end to their intimate encounters. But something kept him there, had him watching the way Magnus's hand cradled the back of the woman's head, his fingers tucked into her sleek golden-blond hair in a gesture that spoke of intimacy that went far beyond friendship. Who was she? Why was she here?

He met Magnus's gaze, tried to read him, to gauge what was going on here, but he couldn't. Their eyes locked and held for long moments, but neither of them spoke. It was in those few brief seconds that an image flashed in Trey's mind, vivid and clear. Magnus with this woman, the two of them naked, Magnus pushing inside her, slow, deep strokes as they panted and moaned. Trey felt his body heat, the mental image making his cock thicken in his jeans.

Christ. Was he turned on by the thought of Magnus with a woman?

"I'm sorry," the woman mumbled softly, stepping back. "I shouldn't be here, I know."

Magnus released her, his hands sliding to her arms, going downward until he was holding her hands. "Don't ever be sorry. I'm always here if you need me."

She sobbed softly, then pulled away, wiping her eyes with the heels of her palms.

Trey cleared his throat, trying to announce his presence without scaring her. It didn't stop her from jerking around, her eyes slamming into him.

It was then Trey noticed she had a swollen lip and what looked to be a black eye forming. If it hadn't been for those marks, she would've been possibly the most beautiful woman he'd ever seen. Her delicate features were smooth, rounded, her eyes a brilliant blue. She looked young. Early- or maybe mid-twenties. Young and innocently beautiful.

He instantly shot a look to Magnus.

"Ava, this is Trey Walker. Trey, Ava March. She's ... a friend."

"Are you all right?" Trey asked on instinct, pained by the sight of her face. It was clear someone had hit her, and they hadn't pulled the punch, either.

Ava sniffed, her voice soft, sweet when she said, "Yes. I'm sorry for comin' here."

"No, you're not," Magnus countered, taking her arm and pulling her back to him. "I think you should stay here tonight. You can sleep in my bed. I'll bunk out here."

Ava was shaking her head. "I can't do that."

"You can and you will." Magnus met Trey's gaze, something that looked a lot like a dare flashing in his eyes.

What? Did Magnus think Trey was going to get upset? He had no claim to the man. If he wanted to have this woman ... this stunningly beautiful, this much-closer-to-Magnus's-age-than-Trey *woman to sleep in his bed, who was he to stand in his way?*

Ava pulled back again, wiping her eyes and steeling her spine as she glanced over at Trey momentarily, then turned her attention back to Magnus. "I appreciate it."

Magnus nodded. "Go on in the house, get settled. I'll check on you in a little while."

"It's nice to meet you," Ava said as she stepped toward the door.

Trey moved out of the way, forced a smile. "Likewise."

He shook off the memory, his full attention turning back to Brantley.

"You said he's in police custody," Iris said, her voice soft and even. "Did they arrest him?"

"According to Reese, they haven't yet. They've produced a warrant to search his house, and they intend to question him about her disappearance."

"So they don't have any proof that he's responsible for the girl's disappearance?" Frank inquired.

Brantley shrugged.

Trey waited, knowing his brother would repeat his question from earlier.

"How long did Magnus stay at your house last night?"

Trey felt all eyes on him, hated that they were. While everyone assumed he was some sort of man-slut, it had never been the case. Yet, the one time he was openly questioned, his answer would give substance to the rumor.

Figured.

"This'll help us, Trey," Brantley stated firmly. "How long was he there?"

Trey stared at his brother, exhaled, and resigned himself to sharing more than he cared to. If it would help Magnus, it wasn't like he had a choice.

"Until at least three," he said, glancing down at the floor. "We fell asleep around that time. When I woke up at six, he was gone."

Brantley nodded. "All right. Well, that narrows it down some."

"What time did the girl go missing?" Frank asked, obviously curious.

"I don't know. Reese didn't have any answers."

"What now?" Trey prompted.

"You have to figure this out," Iris said smoothly. "Find this woman they're worried about."

"Yes, Ma, we do. We need to figure out who saw him next. I figure someone at the dog place did. Question is, when?" Brantley's gaze shifted back to Trey. "I need to head over to HQ."

"You gonna call in the team?" Trey asked.

"I'll wait to hear back from Reese."

"No!" Trey demanded. "Call 'em in now."

Brantley's blue-gray eyes locked on Trey's, held firmly for a few painfully long seconds before he nodded, his tone less aggressive when he said, "Okay. I'll call 'em."

Trey nodded though he wasn't sure why he did.

THIS WAS ONE HELL OF A WAY to be pulled back into the fold, Reese thought as he made his way to Magnus's front door, Tesha walking alongside him.

He knew the trainer wasn't home because Reese had witnessed him being escorted to the back of a squad car when he arrived. He'd had just enough time to get the gist from a cocky officer who'd seemed thrilled with the idea of taking a suspect in for questioning.

Reese had absorbed the few details the officer offered, heeded Magnus's plea to find Ava, then told Magnus he'd take care of things. As the car was driving away, Reese called Brantley, filling him on the little he'd learned in the span of a twenty-word conversation. Magnus wasn't being arrested, but he was being taken in for questioning, and the police had produced a warrant to search the house.

Now, after receiving a text from Brantley to let him know he was calling in some of the Off the Books Task Force to, at minimum, assist with the case of the missing Ava March, Reese had every intention of inserting himself into this investigation, finding out what angle the cops were playing and how Magnus fit into it.

"You can't be in here," someone called out when Reese stepped into the house, Tesha beside him. He closed the door, letting the officer know he had no intention of leaving.

"Actually, I can," he countered, heading toward the man glaring a hole through his face. "Reese Tavoularis. Off the Books Task Force." When the man's jaw set, Reese held up his credentials from Sniper 1 Security, let the guy scan it briefly before tucking it back into his pocket.

"What the hell's Sniper 1 Security?" the guy asked, his mouth a hard line.

"Private security firm. We're looking into the case. And you are?"

"In charge," the man said, a tic in his jaw.

Based on the glint in his narrowed eyes, this guy was short on pleasantries and obviously not impressed to see Reese. Not that Reese cared. Nor was he going to let that distract him from his objective: finding out what they had on Magnus.

"And you are?" Reese prompted.

"Detective Ron Weatherby."

"What's goin' on here?" Reese asked, glancing around at the men and women who were currently going room by room. "What exactly are you lookin' for?"

The detective didn't answer, so Reese gave him his full attention, held the guy's hard stare.

"Look, I know you don't like others in your sandbox, Detective, but we'll either work together or my boss'll make one call to the governor and officially take over the case. Up to you."

Sure, it was an empty threat, but Reese knew if push came to shove, Brantley would call in a favor to the man they used to work for. Governor Greenwood owed the task force more than a few favors after all they'd done for him since the task force had been disbanded and forced into the private sector.

"Well, I'll trump your *governor* with one Texas senator," Weatherby said with a smarmy grin. "Missin' woman's his wife."

"That right? Why're you questioning Magnus?"

The detective exhaled roughly. "We believe he's responsible for the disappearance of our missing person."

"How'd you come to this conclusion?"

"An anonymous tip," Detective Weatherby said snidely.

"A tip?" Reese cast a sideways glance at an officer carrying a laptop. He nodded. "Does the warrant cover his electronics?"

The detective didn't look pleased by the question. "No." He peered over at the officer. "Leave the computer."

"Yes, sir," the man said, setting the laptop on the fireplace mantel.

Worried this detective was overstepping his boundaries, Reese continued with the questions. "When was she reported missing?"

"This morning. Her husband called it in when she didn't come home last night."

"What time?"

"Shortly after six."

It was eleven forty. "Isn't it standard for the MP to be gone for forty-eight hours?"

"It's been escalated," Weatherby snapped.

Which meant someone was making a stink. More than likely due to the senator's political clout.

Not that Reese didn't think they should be spurred into action as soon as a person was suspected to be missing, but something sounded off. Not to mention, Reese knew Magnus, knew the man would not be responsible for anyone's disappearance.

"And you've been workin' the case since she was reported missing?" Reese asked.

"I … uh…" Weatherby looked sheepish. "The officer who answered the call wrote the report, yes. I was assigned when the tip came in."

"So one call to report and another with a tip?"

Weatherby's eyes narrowed. "That's right. It's cut and dried if you ask me."

"Why's that?"

"First off, she's been havin' an affair with this guy," he rattled, his tone insisting Reese was an idiot. "Husband said she's been trying to end it, wanted to make the marriage work."

"He said that when he reported her missing?"

The detective looked sheepish again. "The anonymous caller informed us."

"An anonymous caller who seems to know that little detail that wasn't supplied by the husband?" Reese frowned. "And you didn't think to get their name?"

"Ah-non-ymous," Weatherby repeated slowly. "What part don't you get?"

"Sounds to me like it's got some merit." Reese watched as an officer pulled the cushions off the couch, tossed them haphazardly on the floor. "I know for a fact you can't use an anonymous tip as the basis for a warrant."

Another sheepish look passed over the man's face.

"Mind if I see the warrant?" Reese asked, holding the detective's stare.

Weatherby pulled open his suit jacket, snagged a folded sheet of paper from the inside pocket, slapped it in Reese's direction.

He unfolded it, skimmed the page. "You talk to the husband?"

"Yes. I called him directly, asked him to come down to the station when he has time so we can get more information."

"And you said he's a senator?"

"That's right."

That certainly explained the precedence and expediency.

"And you think she came here?" Reese peered around again, looking for any signs a woman had been in the space.

"Not confirmed at this time. But I think Magnus Storme played a part in her disappearance."

"You *think*? That good of a tip, huh?" Reese glanced toward the kitchen when he heard someone rummaging through pots and pans.

"It holds water."

"An anonymous tip holds water?"

Weatherby stared at him, which told Reese everything he needed to know.

It wasn't that he was knocking the detective or his methods. Reese understood the need to work every lead, regardless of how credible. What he didn't understand was taking someone into custody before there was any proof of involvement. No way did they have credible proof in that short of a time. The only reason they'd gotten a warrant had been the fact the man had influence as a government official.

"What's her relationship to Magnus?" Reese prompted.

"They've been having an affair."

"For how long?"

"A few months."

"This you also learned from the anonymous tip?"

Weatherby didn't respond, but his eyes narrowed again.

Now Reese would admit, he didn't know everything going on with his friends since he'd been in Dallas for months. He didn't have the first clue what the team had been up to recently, much less Tesha's trainer. However, except for the day he'd met the man, right here at the camp, Reese had never seen Magnus with a woman. Not that it wasn't possible that Magnus was seeing one. He was admittedly bisexual.

"Was it serious?" he asked the detective.

"Unconfirmed."

Based on the answers he was getting, Reese knew better than to ask for personal information. Obviously, Detective Weatherby didn't have much of anything to go on aside from a questionable phone tip and a preconceived determination of guilt. More than likely, JJ would uncover more before the Round Rock Police did, so he would have to wait. Until then, he was more interested in confirming when this woman was with Magnus.

"What exactly did you base your warrant on?"

The detective gave him a look that said he was irritated by the interrogation.

Oh fucking well.

"Her Lyft account shows her coming and going from this residence numerous times over the past year."

"You just said they've only been involved for a few months."

"Best guess, she was a client," the detective mused. The detective's use of words like *guess* and *think* told Reese they had nothing.

"She has a dog?"

Weatherby's jaw ticked. "Unconfirmed."

"So you don't know that she was a client." When the detective didn't respond, Reese said, "I take it she still lives with the husband since he reported her missing? They're not separated?"

"Happily married," Weatherby noted with a smirk.

"You just said the wife's been havin' an affair. Which is it?"

The detective's phone rang. With relief smoothing out his features, Weatherby excused himself, leaving Reese with unanswered questions and a shit ton of doubt.

He took the opportunity to wander through the house. Although he'd been to the dog day camp numerous times, he'd never had reason to come into Magnus's personal domain.

The house was a single-story brick ranch with a detached two-car garage. It had been updated at some point since it was built, which he would guesstimate to be sometime in the fifties based on the architecture. The front door opened directly into the living room, which looked to be in the vicinity of twelve by thirteen with hardwood floors and a fresh coat of gray paint. The room consisted of a single floor-to-ceiling window on the front of the house and two narrow windows on the other exterior wall, a dark gray microfiber couch situated between them. No frills in the space, not much color, either. Across from the couch was a wood-burning fireplace with a gray marble-tiled hearth and a thick-beamed mantel.

At the end of the living room were two doorways, one turning left and leading down a hallway, the other wider and opening into a small kitchen and eating area. The breakfast nook was on the right side of the long, narrow space, the kitchen on the left, a door leading outside directly ahead at the back of the house.

Reese moved to the left, surveyed the space. The same hardwood from the living room swept through here, too, and the L-shaped countertops looked to be gray-veined white marble, likely installed in the past few years. Appliances were all black and also new, Reese noted when he opened the refrigerator, which was tucked into a space to the left of the back door. Inside were a couple of Chinese takeout containers, a half-gallon of milk, a six-pack of Sam Adams with one missing, a small tub of butter, a jar of mayo, a sealed tub of lunch meat, a package of mild cheddar cheese slices, and what, at a quick glance, looked to be thirty-plus bottles of water. The guy drank a lot of water.

Reese closed the door, opened the freezer. Far less in there, only a box of waffles, a bag of steamable broccoli, and a stack of ice trays.

To the left of the refrigerator were the dishwasher and the sink with a single window over them. On the short end of the inverted-L counter was the range with microwave above; dark gray cabinets finished it off. The only appliance on the counter was a small toaster oven. The symbol for heat was lit red, so he opened it, saw there were two of those frozen waffles—no longer frozen—inside.

"Makin' breakfast, Magnus?" he mumbled to himself as he continued through the doorway into the hall, then to the right.

Three doors. One on the left, one on the right, and one at the end. Two bedrooms, one bath, he guessed.

He checked out the smaller bedroom first, which appeared to be Magnus's game room. There was a computer setup, complete with a gamer chair, desk, and some sophisticated steering wheel contraption, probably used for racing games. One large floor-to-ceiling window overlooked the front porch and the yard. Finishing it off was a tiny closet that held a couple of coats and what looked to be extra blankets.

As with what he'd seen so far, there wasn't much clutter and no dirty dishes or stray cans or bottles.

The other bedroom was the master, and if Reese wasn't mistaken, it had been renovated at some point. Two baths, he amended when he noticed the attached bathroom. He stuck his head in, saw that it was large, with a walk-thru shower, double sinks, and a jacuzzi tub. He ventured in, checked the doors, and found the closet. It was a decent size, holding primarily jeans and T-shirts, several pairs of boots—work, hiking, and casual—as well as flannel and denim button-downs. Looked mostly like work clothes, nothing fancy.

Back in the bedroom, Reese glanced around. Something felt off about the space, like the angle of the wall wasn't natural. He studied it, glanced up at the ceiling. It took a moment, but he realized it had likely been expanded, along with the master bathroom, to incorporate what was originally a third bedroom. Had to take the space from somewhere, right?

A grouping of photos tucked into the sides of the dresser mirror drew Reese's attention. He headed over, leaned in to get a better look.

He recognized Magnus instantly. A much younger version—ten, maybe eleven years old—with what Reese assumed to be his parents and a younger girl. Sister, probably.

Reese skimmed the other pictures. All of them were of the same people, just in varying poses and situations. One was of Magnus and the same older man from the other photos standing in front of a sign that read: Storme Kennels.

Family business? Had he renamed it? Or was there another?

Reese checked out the next picture, pulling it from its perch to get a better look.

It was the house he was standing in, only a significant portion of it was burned. He thought back to the layout, to what angle the picture was taken from.

Moving to the window, he pulled the blinds back, saw the new windows.

The burned house in the picture was this one. The portion that had been destroyed had been rebuilt. Had Magnus's parents done that? How did he end up with the house? Where were the parents now?

Not that any of those questions would help to solve the disappearance of a young woman, but as far as Reese was concerned, they were important. He needed to know more about Magnus Storme before he could figure out what part he played in all of this. If any.

CHAPTER SEVEN

JJ PULLED AWAY FROM THE BIG, WARM body she'd been curled up to, smacking the nightstand in search of her ringing cell phone.

She recognized the ringtone, which was the only reason she answered with a gruff, "Hello?"

"Hey. Did I wake you?"

If he'd meant to hide his condescension, Brantley had just failed epically.

"It's Saturday," she said, resuming her position, her head resting on Baz's shoulder. "I'm allowed to sleep in."

"Well, you better get up and get some coffee in you."

"We have a case?"

"Technically, no. We do, however, have someone to find."

"I don't get dressed for just anyone, B," she teased. "What's goin' on?"

"The police took Magnus down to Round Rock PD for questioning in a missing person's case."

"Who's the missing person?" she dared to ask.

"JJ," he said slowly, succinctly. "I'd greatly appreciate it if you'd get your ass out of bed and get over to HQ. Bring your boy toy along with you."

The call disconnected.

JJ pulled it away from her ear, stared at the screen that showed the call had ended.

"He hung up on you?" Baz asked, pressing his lips to her forehead.

"The shithead," she muttered, then relayed the ridiculously little information she had regarding the not-really-a-case that was getting her out of her comfortable bed on a Saturday morning. "He called you my boy toy."

"Mmm," he mumbled, rolling toward her, his hand sliding over her naked hip. "You can play with me anytime you want."

JJ moaned softly, wishing she could sink into his embrace for a few hours, let his skilled hands bring her awake the way she was growing to enjoy. Unfortunately, she could still hear Brantley's stern tone in her ear, knew there was no time for canoodling—as Brantley liked to refer to it—this morning. They had work.

"Careful, Detective. I'll tell Brantley you're the reason we're late."

Baz chuckled softly, releasing her before sitting up and dropping his feet to the floor. "If you get ready quick, I'll run you through Dazzle on the way in."

JJ didn't need to be told twice. She lived for her morning coffee.

Just shy of an hour later, Baz was pulling the truck down Brantley's drive. No sooner did JJ see the other Chevy truck parked behind Brantley's than her hand shot out and smacked Baz's forearm.

"Do you see that?" she whispered, shaking his arm to signify the importance.

"Reese's truck?" Baz cut his gaze to her. "Yeah. I see it."

"Holy shit. He's here."

"Doesn't mean he's here for Brantley. Just means he's *here*."

"Don't poop on my parade, Detective."

When he laughed and shook his head, JJ couldn't help but smile. She still couldn't believe how well things were going between the two of them. Ever since Baz learned that Molly Ryan had lied to him about the baby she was carrying being his, they'd been back together. Or, she figured, *really* together. She couldn't say that they'd been much of a real couple back in the beginning, since before JJ was attacked and before Baz had met Molly. But that wasn't the case now. JJ was giving this relationship everything she had because she'd found real happiness for the first time in her life.

"Do not give him a rash of shit," Baz warned, meeting her at the front of his truck as they walked toward the barn behind the house.

"You're just tryin' to take *all* the fun outta my day, aren't you?" she groused.

"I'm sure you'll get over it." Baz took her hand, lifted it to his lips, and kissed the backs of her knuckles.

JJ let him, walking steadily at his side. "I'm more curious to know what happened between them. How long's he stayin'? Did they work things out last night?"

Baz punched in the code to unlock the barn doors and gave her a sideways glance. "Behave yourself."

She pouted, ensuring he saw it, before stepping into the barn ahead of him, her gaze swinging around to find Reese. He was nowhere in sight, but he was suddenly the last thing on her mind when her eyes came to an abrupt stop on Brantley. He looked like the man she knew, the clean-cut Navy SEAL who'd been her best friend since they were kids. No longer did he look like he'd be searching for his next meal in a dumpster behind a building.

She whistled. "Lookin' good, military man."

Brantley flipped her off.

JJ smiled, holding his gaze. She managed to refrain from giving him shit, but only because she knew he would be legit pissed off, and she didn't want to start a fight while they were working.

However, she did silently appreciate the fact that her best friend had cleaned himself up because the man he loved had returned. And if anyone wanted to dispute that theory, they were welcome to, but they would be wrong.

She knew Brantley, and this was his way of making an effort.

WHEN JJ STROLLED INTO THE BARN, TREY managed to keep from barking orders at her. Barely.

He'd been not so patiently waiting for her to arrive so she could start doing a deep dive into what was going on with Magnus. They'd attempted to get Luca Switzer's help, but the OTB Task Force's other hacker extraordinaire was out of town for the weekend, which meant they'd had to wait.

Trey looked at his brother, willed Brantley to get on with it. For the past hour, they'd been sitting in the tricked-out barn they used as their base of operations waiting for the rest of the team to get there. Brantley hadn't called everyone in, but he had reached out to the heavy hitters. Evan Vaughn and Slade Elliott, two of their more recent hires, had been more than willing to pop over to help out. The rest of the team was enjoying their day off. For now, Brantley had assured him. If and when the case called for it, he would reach out and get all hands on deck.

Only because he was playing down his feelings for Magnus did Trey resist the urge to smack his brother. He wanted every damn person he knew to help out, to figure this shit out. The thought of Magnus sitting in an interrogation room pissed him off to no end, but he wasn't ready to out his relationship with Magnus just yet, if at all.

"JJ, I need to know everything you can find about Ava March," Brantley finally said when Reese returned from the kitchen, carrying a single cup of coffee and looking as though he wasn't sure he belonged.

"On it," she said, grabbing the iPad docked on one of the desks.

"Could you run through the gist of it for me?" Evan requested.

"Sure." Brantley's gaze skimmed each person as he spoke. "Reese took Tesha for her training session this morning. When he arrived, Magnus was being escorted down to RRPD for questioning. Evidently, he's got a relationship with Ava March, who was reported missing this morning."

JJ's head never lifted from what she was doing, but she asked, "Does that mean Reese spent the night last night?"

Brantley continued as though she hadn't said a word, looking at Reese, "You wanna tell them what you learned?"

Reese stepped forward, glanced around, still looking out of place. "I spoke to the detective—"

"Mind if I ask who?" Evan prompted.

"Ron Weatherby."

"You know him?" Brantley asked.

"Yeah."

"He solid?" Trey questioned before he could think better of it.

"A little quick to make assumptions, but he's thorough."

Reese continued. "He was serving a warrant to search the house. Honestly, he was not a fount of information."

"Did you see the warrant?" Evan asked.

Reese nodded. "Search only for the property. Not a seizure warrant.

"Meaning?" Trey asked, feeling like an idiot.

"Means they didn't have permission to seize any of his property," Evan explained.

"Correct," Reese agreed. "It didn't extend to electronics, so I'm not sure what they were hoping to find."

"A body, maybe," Slade noted.

"Ava March," JJ interrupted, reading from her iPad, "twenty-three-year-old white female. Reported missing six a.m., today, by her…" JJ's gaze lifted, her eyes widened. "She's married to Harrison Rivers?"

"Who's Harrison Rivers?" Slade asked, clearly sensing her disbelief.

"A senator," Reese supplied.

"*Junior* senator," JJ noted.

Trey didn't ask what that meant because he didn't give a fuck. He wondered what the hell Magnus had gotten himself involved in. He recalled the way Ava had looked the night he'd met her and prayed like hell her politician husband hadn't done that damage to her face.

"Go on," Brantley urged.

JJ looked at Trey then back to Brantley. "Her husband claims she went out with friends last night and didn't come home. According to notes entered this morning, she was last seen with Magnus Storme, a man she was attempting to break off a long-running affair with."

"Where'd they get that information?" Trey asked.

JJ's eyes skimmed the screen as her fingers continued to type, but Reese spoke up with, "An anonymous tip. Based on the information the caller offered, they're focusing their efforts on Magnus."

"Did the anonymous tipper happen to state what time they saw her with Magnus?" Trey asked, feeling defensive. "Because I got to Moonshiners at eight thirty last night, and he was there by himself."

"Question is what he did *after* he left," Slade remarked.

Trey knew exactly what Magnus had done last night after they'd left. He'd had his ass stuffed with a vibrator first, then with Trey's cock.

Not that he intended to share that information with the team.

"It does not clarify in the case notes," JJ confirmed. "I'll see if I can figure out where the anonymous call originated from. It'll take some time, though."

"Do that. Anything'll help," Brantley stated.

Then Evan asked the very question Trey was thinking. "Is this our case now?"

Brantley nodded. "Since Magnus is a friend of ours, we owe it to him to find out what happened."

"I hate to be the one to ask this," Baz said, glancing between Trey and Brantley, "but are we certain he *didn't* do this? I mean, I know y'all consider him a friend, but how well do you really know him?"

"We're certain," Brantley and Trey said at the same time.

Although Trey did not want to go into detail with his teammates, he would bet his life that Magnus did not have anything to do with Ava's disappearance. Based on what Trey had witnessed between the two of them on New Year's, Magnus cared for her. If he were a betting man, he would put his money on the husband. The night he'd met Ava, she'd been sporting a bloody lip, and he had a damn good guess who was responsible for it.

"Good enough for me," Baz said as he headed to his computer. "I'll start prepping the board."

"I'm gonna call Round Rock PD, talk to some buddies of mine, see what they can give me," Evan said, pulling his phone out of his pocket.

"You might talk to Weatherby," Reese said. "See if you can smooth the waters with him. I don't think he was all that impressed with my questions."

Evan smirked. "I'll do that."

"While you do, I'm gonna head down there, see if I can spring Magnus," Brantley stated. "Trey, you're with me. Everyone else, let me know as soon as you find out more."

"You should warn him Brantley's comin', too," JJ told Evan, chuckling. "Maybe send donuts to let him know you care."

Trey grabbed his cell phone, tucked it in his pocket, and followed Brantley. He caught up to him in the driveway, where Brantley was standing beside his truck, phone to his ear.

"I understand that. I'm not askin' permission." Brantley rolled his eyes, nodded for Trey to get in the truck.

While Trey walked around to the passenger side, Brantley climbed into the driver's seat.

"I understand that," Brantley repeated slowly. "And I'm not steppin' on your toes. I will if I have to." Brantley paused, then exhaled. "We're on our way now. But just know this, if you're not chargin' him—" Another pause, followed by a gruffly rumbled, "We'll be there in ten."

Brantley disconnected the call, started the engine.

Trey didn't know what to say, so he kept his mouth shut. Not that it helped, because a minute into the drive, Brantley began his interrogation.

"Trust me when I tell you, I don't wanna know the details of your personal life, but you can understand why I have to in this case."

He understood, all right. He didn't like it, but he got it.

"When you left the bar last night, you went straight home, right?"

"Yes."

"Did Magnus ride with you? Or did he follow you from the bar?"

"Followed."

"How long'd it take him to get there?"

"He literally followed me," Trey said through gritted teeth. "He was parked in my driveway before I had a chance to start flippin' on lights."

"Okay, so you had eyes on him from roughly twenty thirty until oh three hundred."

"Yes." Trey didn't bother to mention he had more than eyes on the man. Definitely didn't need to share *that* much information with his brother.

"Have you talked to him since?"

Trey cleared his throat, kept his eyes forward. "No."

Brantley remained quiet for a moment.

"What is it?" Trey asked, knowing Brantley had something on his mind.

His brother cut his gaze over briefly. "Tell me this. Is it serious between you two?"

"Define serious," he retorted.

"Trey," Brantley drawled. "I'd like to know what I'm dealin' with."

Trey huffed, stared out the window, and opted to tell the truth. "It's serious."

"Meaning?"

Jesus fucking Christ. Trey exhaled heavily. "Meaning I'd lay down my life for his, Brantley. Even if I haven't admitted it to him yet."

"All right. Now we've gotta figure out why someone believes he's responsible and who else has had eyes on him since. Not sure you're enough of an alibi as he'll need."

Alibi.

Jesus.

What the fuck had Magnus gotten himself involved in?

"I'M GOING TO ASK YOU AGAIN, WHERE were you last night, Mr. Storme?"

Mr. Storme. Every time the officer said it, Magnus fought the urge to smile. He was not Mr. Storme. That title belonged to his father, God rest his soul.

He stared back at the detective who had not so kindly placed him in this small room with the single table, ass-numbing chair, and the two-way mirror. Magnus wasn't exactly sure why this guy thought he would be intimidated by this room or by him, but clearly, Detective Arthur Rosenthal believed that his beady-eyed stare was doing something to help things along when, in reality, it only pissed Magnus off, made him want to continue to be petulant and ornery.

"Mr. Storme," the detective repeated. "I can do this all day long."

Could he? Could he really?

Magnus offered a purposely vague answer because he was too frustrated to sit there any longer. "I went to a bar with some friends. Now can you tell me what the fuck is going on? Where's Ava?"

Magnus had been read his rights but informed he was not actually under arrest, yet they hadn't bothered to tell him why he was there, only that they had some questions for him related to a case they were working on. A case involving Ava March, who was deemed a missing person as of this morning.

"Who were these friends?" Detective Rosenthal asked.

"Why do you care?"

"Mr. Storme, you're not doing anything to help your case."

"*My* case?" Magnus cocked his head to the side. "I wasn't even aware I *had* a case. Maybe if I knew what *case* I might be helping, perhaps I'd answer your questions."

Sure, he was being a dick, but who could blame him? They'd dragged his ass out of his house while he'd been waiting for his toaster waffles to heat up, and he was starving. What did they call that? Hangry? Yeah. That's what he was. Hangry.

And scared, but not for himself. He was terrified that something had happened to Ava, and the police wanted to sit on their asses rather than get out there and look for her.

"I'll need the names of the friends you were with so I can verify your alibi."

Ah, Jesus.

Magnus sat up straight. "Alibi? Why do I need an alibi?"

Please, please, please God, don't let Ava be dead.

Before the detective could answer, the door to the small room opened enough for Magnus to see a woman standing in the hallway. She leaned in to say something to Detective Rosenthal. Magnus probably would've been paying attention to those words if not for the man he saw standing behind her.

A hot rage filled his blood and had him standing tall. "What the fuck is he doin' here?"

The woman, eyes wide, immediately stepped out of the room and shut the door.

"Sit down, Mr. Storme."

Magnus glared down at the detective sitting across from him. "Am I under arrest?"

"We've already informed you, not at this time."

"Then I'm free to go?"

He could see the indecision on the man's face and knew what the answer was, so he started for the door. In the hall, he looked left then right, attempting to find—

"Hey, you okay?"

His attention shot over to the scattering of desks and the familiar, concerned voice. It only took a second to find Trey weaving his way through the clutter on his way over, and when he did, something shifted inside Magnus's chest. He couldn't quite pinpoint what it was, but it felt a hell of a lot like relief. As though he wasn't alone in this. Whatever the fuck *this* was.

"Where'd he go?" Magnus asked, stepping closer. "The guy who was in the hall. Which way did he go?"

Trey was staring at him, clearly unsure whether to answer. "Do you know him?"

"Where'd he go, Trey?"

Trey stepped closer, put his hand on Magnus's arm, and steered him toward the exit door. "We need to talk."

"You ready?"

Magnus jerked his attention behind him, and there stood Brantley, watching him closely.

What the fuck was going on here?

"Come on," Trey said, nudging Magnus toward the door. "Let's go talk."

"I don't want to fucking talk," he snapped, a red-hot rage boiling in his veins. It had started to bubble when the cops dragged him here, got hotter when he realized no one wanted to tell him a damn thing, and then seeing Harrison Rivers … it'd turned into lava, and Magnus was seconds away from detonating. Why the fuck wasn't anyone telling him what the hell was going on? And what the hell was Ava's bastard of a husband doing here?

"What the fuck?" he bit out, jerking his arm out of Trey's grip.

Magnus wasn't an idiot. He knew everything centered around Ava and whatever relationship they believed he had with her. And that could mean only one thing: something had happened to Ava, but they weren't admitting it.

He spun around, stared directly into Trey's eyes. "Where is she, Trey? Where's Ava?"

An answer didn't come, but Magnus saw something shutter in Trey's gaze.

"Please, God, tell me she's all right," Magnus insisted, keeping his voice low.

"We'll talk in a minute," Trey growled softly, once again guiding him outside.

Magnus gave in, headed out the door, down the ramp, and to the parking lot. He even continued toward Brantley's truck when he realized that was where they were headed. But when they reached it, Magnus refused to get in.

He faced off with Trey. "Tell me what the fuck is goin' on."

Trey's eyes locked on his face, narrowing as he spoke. "Ava's missing. And someone called in a tip claimin' you're responsible for her disappearance."

Magnus swallowed the desert that had formed in his throat. "Missing?"

"According to her husband, yes," Trey stated, that steel-blue gaze piercing him.

Magnus felt the cold chill sweep down his spine at the news.

Missing.

Christ.

The hair on the back of his neck prickled, and Magnus glanced over, saw Ava's husband walking out of the police station all cocky and proud, as though he was the king of the fucking world.

Before he knew what he was doing, Magnus was marching toward him. He could see the evil in that bastard's eyes, knew what he'd done.

"Where is she?" Magnus demanded, storming up to Harrison Rivers, grabbing him by the shirt, and jerking him like a rag doll. "Where the fuck is she?"

"Get off me." Harrison shoved him back, but Magnus held tight, ignoring the burly bastards in suits who were quickly moving in his direction. He figured the private security, or whatever the fuck they were, would be drawing on him any second.

"What did you do to her?" Magnus demanded to know.

"Magnus!"

The sharp bark of his name barely registered, and he ignored Brantley, his rage having found a target.

"Did you kill her?" he growled.

Harrison's expression gave nothing away, but he held up a hand to hold back his dogs coming to his rescue.

Magnus could see it in the man's eyes. There was evil in there, pure evil.

"Ah, fuck," he groaned, pain consuming him at the thought of this bastard having killed her. The sorrow that filled him at that revelation nearly took him out at the knees, but he forced it back, allowing the rage to take over.

When Harrison tried to shove his hands off, Magnus let go, but he redirected them around the man's skinny neck, gripping tightly, choking. He wanted to see the bastard's eyes bulge out of his head, see the fear that came with knowing he was going to die. It would be so fucking easy to squeeze the life out of him right here and now. The man deserved it. Hell, he deserved a death worse than that.

"Magnus, let him go," Trey demanded from behind him.

He didn't, continuing to squeeze as he held Harrison's gaze. "You will go down for this, you bastard. I swear to you."

The evil Magnus had seen before glinted in Harrison's eyes then. "Not if you go down first," he choked out.

Hard hands gripped his arm, pulling him back. Forced to release Harrison, he stumbled away, never taking his eyes off the man.

"Get in the goddamn truck," Brantley barked, shoving him so he stumbled again, this time farther away from Harrison. "Before they do fucking arrest you."

"Come on." Trey's tone was calmer, smoother. "Let's grab some coffee and talk."

"I don't fucking want coffee. And I damn sure don't want to talk. I want to know where Ava is."

"And that's the question we have to find the answer to," Trey explained. "To do that, we need to know everything you know."

Magnus sighed, resigning himself to talking as fear consumed him once more.

After all, Trey was right. They had to get answers to find Ava.

He prayed to God she was still alive.

Because if she weren't, Magnus would be back here soon enough. However, the next time they'd be questioning him about murder, because he was going to kill that son of a bitch.

CHAPTER EIGHT

BRANTLEY HAD NO FUCKING CLUE WHAT SET Magnus off, but for a minute there, he'd thought the usually laid-back dog trainer was going to kill the other man. There were only a few times in his life when Brantley had seen that sort of rage on a man's face, and it always reflected a deep-seated hatred. Whatever the situation was between Magnus and Ava's husband, it was based on a dislike of astronomical proportions.

He waited until they'd made it to the main road, then glanced in the rearview, caught sight of Magnus. Before he could ask a question, though, Magnus spoke up.

"They wouldn't tell me anything," Magnus explained, his tone one of a defeated man. "Just that Ava's missing but nothing else."

"Right now, that's all we know," Brantley assured him. "When's the last time you saw her?"

Magnus blew out a breath. "Shit. I don't know. It's been a few weeks."

"Not last night?" Trey asked, turning to look back at him.

Brantley caught Magnus's frown in the rearview. "No. You both know where I was last night."

He remembered seeing Magnus at Moonshiners, but he'd been so preoccupied watching Reese that he hadn't paid attention to what time he'd arrived. Nor had he kept up with the man throughout the evening.

"Who is she to you?" he asked Magnus.

"My sister's best friend."

There was something in Magnus's tone that had Brantley refraining from asking the natural question of where Magnus's sister was. Unfortunately, it didn't appear Trey heard it.

"Maybe she's seen her recently," Trey stated. "Where's your sister?"

"Dead."

Silence choked the cab of the truck. Brantley focused on the road, tried to order his thoughts, mentally outlining all the details he'd obtained by talking to the police chief a short time ago. Not that they had much, aside from the fact Ava March was missing. According to her husband, she'd gone out with friends and never come home. He got worried because he feared Magnus had done something to her.

"I'm sorry," Trey said, breaking the tension in the air.

"Don't be. You didn't know."

Brantley cast a sideways glance at Trey. The question was: should he have known? Considering these two had been hooking up for … well, Brantley didn't know exactly how long they'd been hiding whatever this was, but he knew it'd been a while. Sure, Trey had copped to the fact he cared about Magnus; however, based on their reactions to one another, Brantley had already suspected it was more than just a routine booty call. Seemed logical that they would've gotten down to the personal details by now, but evidently not too personal.

"The person who made the anonymous tip—"

"If there was a tip," Magnus ground out, "anonymous or otherwise, it came from Harrison or one of those assholes on his staff."

"Maybe," Brantley acknowledged. "Regardless, the caller claims you've been stalking her. Said you've been having a long-running affair with her. When she refused to leave her husband, you made threats." Brantley peered in the rearview mirror again, kept going before Magnus could interject. "And yes, *we* know that's a load of bullshit, but the police don't."

Brantley felt more than saw the shift in Trey.

"Like I said, I haven't seen Ava in weeks," Magnus explained. "The last time was when she dropped by Camp K-9 to chat. I was filling in for Gia, my head trainer, because she was sick. Didn't get a chance to spend much time with her."

"Do you talk on the phone?"

"Every now and again, I'll shoot her a text to check in. She'll usually get back to me right away, sometimes not until the next day."

If there was a text thread, there was proof of a relationship between Ava and Magnus. Maybe just friendship, but it was a relationship, nonetheless.

"You two close?" Trey asked, his eyes now on the road in front of them.

"We used to be, I guess. Growing up, she lived next door, was best friends with my sister. Her mother and mine were good friends. After my mother and sister died, Renee was too devastated to live there anymore. Packed up and moved with Ava."

Jesus, the guy lost his mother *and* his sister? Fuck.

When Trey didn't speak up, Brantley did. "Where does Ava live now?"

"Austin. We lost touch for a little while after she left. Came back to visit right after she graduated from high school. We've kept in touch ever since."

Trey cleared his throat. "Do you have a … relationship with Ava?"

Brantley didn't look over at his brother, although he wanted to. Why didn't Trey know these little details about the man he so clearly cared about?

He couldn't help but think about Reese, about all the things he'd learned about him since the day they'd met.

A memory surfaced of the trip they'd taken for a stakeout. He recalled being shocked to the roots of his hair when Reese admitted he'd been engaged at one point. Okay, so maybe he wasn't the best person to pass judgment. Up until that point, he'd thought he knew all of Reese's deep, dark secrets. Maybe not the nitty-gritty details, but he'd thought he knew the high-level stuff. He'd been so very wrong.

Clearly offended, Magnus didn't respond.

"You seem convinced her husband had somethin' to do with her disappearance," Brantley said to redirect.

"Harrison Rivers is a monster," Magnus stated, his voice low, dangerous.

"Has he hurt her before?"

The sigh that came back told Brantley far more than Magnus probably thought it did. The problem was he needed to know everything.

And if they had any chance of finding Ava March, he needed to know it now.

TREY FELT LIKE AN ASS. HE COULD practically feel Magnus's concern, yet he'd spouted off stupid fucking questions in the hopes of helping things along.

Okay, maybe that was a lie.

Maybe he was asking stupid fucking questions because he wanted to know the stupid fucking answers. Oh, and he had more. Lots more. Like: Was Magnus involved with Ava March? Were they sleeping together? Was she someone Trey had to worry about? What had happened to Magnus's mother and sister?

The bigger question, the one he should've been asking himself: Why the fuck should he fucking worry in the first fucking place?

Yeah. Those were the kinds of stupid fucking answers he was looking for.

Trey took a deep breath, vowed to mentally erase the F-word from his vocabulary for the next hour at least. It was getting out of hand, even in his head.

And yes, he knew he had no business sticking his nose in Magnus's life. He was the one who'd said no strings and had managed to keep Magnus at arm's length for the past year. Magnus had held up his end of the bargain. Just because they would be in close quarters for this case didn't mean Trey had any business making it personal.

"You still wanna grab coffee?" Brantley asked when they entered the Coyote Ridge town limits.

"Yeah," Trey muttered.

"The diner?"

"Sure." Anywhere was fine with him just as long as there were other people around. Just as long as he could keep himself in check and remember that this was about a missing woman and not about his own fucked-up personal life.

He wished he could say he hadn't felt anything when he saw Magnus, but that would've been a lie, too. In fact, he'd felt something from the moment he'd learned Magnus was in police custody. What spurred that defensive feeling, the need to protect Magnus, he didn't know and wouldn't think too long or too hard on it, but that didn't mean it wasn't there.

When Brantley pulled into the diner and found a spot, Trey was the first out of the truck. He didn't look back as he headed into the restaurant, told the hostess they needed a table for three. Thank God she had one, because he would've lost his shit if she'd told him they only had booths left. He was not going to sit that close to Magnus. He didn't trust himself right now.

Once seated, it only took a minute to place an order for coffee, everyone waving off the idea of lunch. Trey wasn't hungry, but even if he was, he wasn't sure his stomach was in any condition to eat right now.

Brantley looked up from texting on his phone. "Reese kept an eye on the police while they did their search."

Magnus nodded, his expression blank. "I don't know what they were lookin' for, but it won't matter. Ava hasn't been in the house since New Year's."

Trey thought back to the night he'd stumbled upon Magnus with Ava. He'd suspected something was going on between them. Their interactions had been innocent enough—Magnus consoling her, offering her a place to stay—but he'd sensed something deeper.

He then recalled what had transpired once Ava had gone to Magnus's house, leaving him and Magnus alone together. As was usually the case when they were in close proximity to one another, things had gotten out of hand. Magnus had ended up on his knees with Trey's cock in his mouth. The look on the man's face that night had been so full of passion and pleasure. It was difficult to see him like this, to know he was hurting.

When the coffee arrived, Trey focused on adding Splenda—three packets, one at a time, when he only needed two—and doing his best not to watch Magnus.

Brantley kicked things off. "Although I can't speak for the Round Rock Police Department, who's lookin' at you for this, my goal is to find Ava. I've called in a few others, and we'll do whatever it takes to find her, independent of whatever the police are doing. That means we'll need as much information as you can give us, so we know where to start lookin'."

Magnus nodded, stared at Brantley as though waiting for the first question.

"Ava was reported missing this morning," Brantley continued. "We can only assume yesterday's the last time Harrison saw her."

Magnus took a deep breath. "I wouldn't know. Like I said, I haven't seen her in a few weeks. And I haven't heard from her in several days."

"Did she hang out with anyone specific?" Brantley prompted. "If she did go out with friends, do you know who?"

Trey glanced at Magnus, who was shaking his head. "I don't know any of them well. I've only met one or two of them. But it doesn't matter. Ava doesn't hang out with her friends. Harrison doesn't let her out of the house unless he's with her. He keeps her on a tight leash."

"You said she came to see you? If that's the case, how'd she get away from him?"

"I figure she snuck out. I know on New Year's she ran away."

Trey knew she'd had a valid reason based on how her face had looked that night.

"Speaking of the husband," Brantley prompted, "what's your beef with him?"

Magnus's gaze shifted to Trey, those hazel eyes burning with what appeared to be banked fury, then back to Brantley. "If Ava's missin', he's the reason."

"Why do you say that?"

"Because she's been tryin' to get away from him for years."

Brantley's tone was empathetic, not accusatory, when he said, "Has she been having an affair?"

"No. Doesn't stop him from accusing her, though."

"Does he hit her?" Brantley asked.

Trey listened intently, wanting an official confirmation that her husband's fist had been what damaged her beautiful face that night.

"Hits her, beats her, talks down to her. He's a bastard."

"Why's she still with him if it's a volatile situation?" Brantley asked.

Magnus sighed. "Her mother. She's not … well. Harrison holds that over Ava."

"Not well? In what way?" Trey asked because, based on Magnus's tone, he seriously doubted she had a cold.

Magnus tapped his temple. "She was diagnosed with bipolar depression years ago. Every few months, she'll be put in a mental health facility under suicide watch."

"Ava's close to her mother?" Brantley inquired.

"Her mother lives with her. Ava takes care of her physically, Harrison financially." Magnus's brow lowered. "Which is why I don't buy that she was out with friends. That's not something he lets her do."

"When you say physically," Brantley prompted. "Is there something that keeps her from takin' care of herself?"

"The drugs." Magnus exhaled roughly. "Harrison keeps her doped up. Says it's the only way to protect her from herself."

Trey already didn't like the fucker, now he downright detested him.

"Okay. Say she snuck out, as you said. Is there anywhere she might go?" Brantley asked. "Somewhere she usually goes to get a break from it all?"

"My house," Magnus admitted, glancing between them. "It's her safe haven. She used to show up to talk. Sometimes, she'd stay the night."

Trey knew the unsettled feeling wasn't normal. Odd thing was, it wasn't jealousy. Well, maybe it was. A little. However, it was something else, something … he didn't know how to classify it.

"Anywhere else?" Trey asked in an effort to ensure he didn't ask another stupid question, like *where does she sleep when she's there?* Or worse: *where do you sleep?*

"Friends? Co-workers?" Brantley prompted.

Magnus took a sip of his coffee. "I wish I knew."

"You're not close?" Brantley asked.

"Not really, no. We were before Harrison put a leash on her." Magnus exhaled and leaned back in his chair. "I've known Ava all her life. She was my little sister's best friend. They were close, always at our house. Ava would spend the night with Tabby, hang out, watch movies. Seemed she was always around."

"Before they moved?"

Magnus was quiet for a moment, his eyes taking on that faraway look as though he was attempting to search the past. He finally shrugged, said, "Before my sister died."

Neither Trey nor Brantley spoke, but all eyes remained on Magnus as they waited.

"As much as I want to remain hopeful, I fear finding Ava alive is slim to none." Magnus's tone was rough. "I've feared Harrison was going to do something to her for a long time."

"Why would he call it in if he did something to her?" Trey asked.

"To insert himself into the investigation, take the heat off him. He knows I'd realize she was gone sooner or later, and I'd start lookin'." Magnus cleared his throat, looked away. "By bringing it to light, he's puttin' the spotlight on me."

"I've asked JJ to do a deep dive on this guy," Brantley said, meeting Trey's gaze. "To get me everything there is to know about Harrison Rivers."

Trey had figured as much. Considering the scene earlier, there were a lot of unanswered questions when it came to whatever the issue was between Harrison and Magnus. It was apparent Magnus was protective of Ava. As for his reasons, Trey didn't know. Was it a brotherly connection? Or was there more to it? More that Magnus didn't want them to know?

Brantley's phone buzzed. He glanced at it, then at Trey. "That's Evan. He's gonna pick me up. We'll head over to talk to Harrison ourselves, get a read on the guy."

Trey was tempted to offer to go with Evan and let Brantley go with Magnus, but he refrained. He wasn't a coward. He could survive a couple of hours with Magnus without doing something stupid.

At least he hoped he could.

CHAPTER NINE

As soon as Brantley left, Magnus felt the tension ratchet up a few notches. And it wasn't the good kind of tension, the type that came with sexual chemistry between two people. Although that was still there—despite the circumstances—still going strong even if Trey was fighting it, obviously none too happy to be out in public with him.

"Mind if I ask how they dragged you into this?" Magnus prompted when it was clear Trey was looking for a way out of the building and not necessarily through the door. He imagined a Trey-sized hole in the wall when the man went right through it.

Trey's dark eyebrows lowered, those steel-blue eyes searching Magnus's face. "They didn't drag me."

"You look like you'd rather be anywhere but here."

"There's a girl missin'," Trey bit out, his voice pitched low.

"I'm aware," he snapped back, pissed that Trey would even *think* Magnus wasn't thinking about that every second. "So why didn't you go with Brantley? That's what y'all do, right? Solve missing person cases?"

Trey didn't answer, merely held his gaze.

"Look," Magnus finally said on a sigh. "This thing between us … I'm aware it's superficial. You don't have to worry about me expectin' anything from you."

Still no response from Trey.

Magnus decided to let Trey off the hook. "I'll just see if I can find someone to call for a Lyft so you can get back to it."

"Where's your phone?"

"They didn't let me get it," he admitted, remembering how the cops had dragged him out of the house, patient only long enough for him to pull on a T-shirt and shoes. "I need to get home, anyway. My day help's probably wonderin' what the hell's goin' on."

"I'll drive you," Trey stated, pulling out his wallet and tossing a twenty on the table.

"Not necessary." The last thing Magnus wanted to do was put Trey in a situation that made him uncomfortable. As it was, their interactions were kept mostly to the privacy of Trey's house. They didn't interact in the light of day. In passing, maybe, but not in close quarters, and while Magnus would welcome more time with Trey, he damn sure wouldn't make the suggestion.

"I said I'll drive you."

Magnus heard the frustration in Trey's tone, peered up when Trey stood. He considered arguing again, but he honestly didn't want to cause another scene. One was his quota for the day, and he'd met that back at the police station.

Plus, he had to begin his own search for Ava, and he needed things from his house to do it.

Without a word, he followed Trey out to Brantley's truck, climbed into the passenger seat. Neither of them said a word as Trey pulled out of the parking lot, headed toward the highway. Magnus tried to relax, but there was too much anxiety coursing through his veins. His thoughts drifted to New Year's after Trey had left and Magnus had gone to check on Ava.

"Hey. You doin' okay?"

Ava's big blue eyes peered up at him. "Where's Trey?"

"He left?"

Her smile was sweet and maybe a little sad. "Is he the one?"

"The one what?" he asked, sitting on the edge of the sofa where she'd curled up with a throw blanket.

"The guy you're in love with?"

Magnus nodded, unable to lie to Ava. While he didn't see her nearly as much as he'd like to, Ava had become important to him over the years. He wasn't sure whether it was the physical attraction he had to her or some warped hero complex that drove him, but he found he liked when she came to him. He just wished she would stay longer and her visits didn't coincide with a beating from her bastard husband.

"How does that work?" she prompted, shifting so she fully faced him. "I thought you said you couldn't be with only a guy or a girl. That you wanted both."

Magnus leaned back against the cushion, repositioned her legs so that they were across his thighs. "I do."

"But you love him?"

He nodded, not sure he wanted to say the words aloud.

"Does that mean you'd give up the need for someone else?"

Magnus shrugged. He wasn't sure what it meant. Trey Walker had torn through his little world like a tornado, disrupting everything, making him consider things he'd never thought he would. Namely, an exclusive relationship with a man.

"Is he bisexual?" Ava asked.

"Not that I know of."

"So he's never been with a woman?"

"No."

"Hmm."

Magnus looked over at her. "What does that mean?"

She giggled, then winced when it pulled at her swollen lip. "I just figured if you ended up with a guy, it'd be one who also wanted a woman. Then y'all could do that sharing thing."

Magnus's eyebrows rose. "What sharing thing's that?"

She smiled again but not as wide. "You're not gonna get me to say it out loud, Magnus Storme."

God, he loved how innocent she was. But it was her curiosity that intrigued him most. He suspected that if Ava weren't married, he would've made a move on her long ago. Problem was, he figured, like Trey, she would have the power to change his life, shift his priorities. He wasn't sure he could handle two of them, but he couldn't deny he'd like the opportunity to find out.

Magnus remained silent for the twenty-minute drive from Coyote Ridge to Camp K-9. When they finally reached the sign that guided people to the camp, he felt some of his tension ease. When the house came into view, he noticed the police cars were gone and another level of tension faded away. Once they pulled up to the house, Magnus motioned for Trey to park between the house and the Camp K-9 building.

He opened the door, stuck one foot out. "Thanks for the ride. I'll … uh … I guess I'll see you around."

Without waiting for a response, he shut the door and headed for the camp building. He first had to check on the dogs currently in residence. Six were boarded overnight, plus twelve more were scheduled for day camp. At this point in his day, he would've already assisted in cleaning things up, getting breakfast and lunch delivered, the morning playtime underway, administering meds if needed. If all were well, the dogs would be tucked in for an afternoon nap by now. Thanks to the police, his entire routine was wrecked.

"Hey, Gia, how's it goin'?" he asked his trainer when he stepped into the building to find her looking at the computer.

Her eyes were filled with concern when she looked up at him. "Are you okay?"

"No," he said truthfully. "But right now, it doesn't matter. Everything good—"

The door opened, and Trey walked in, all big and brooding and distracting. Gia glanced over at him, her eyes wide. Magnus could tell she had no idea what to say, although she was usually adept at greeting strangers.

When her gaze swung back to him, Magnus forced a smile. "This is Trey Walker. He works for the OTB Task Force. Trey, this is Gia Billingsworth. She's one of my staff trainers and fills in on overnights when we have dogs staying with us."

Trey gave a chin nod and a clipped, "Hey," in greeting.

Gia smiled, but it didn't quite reach her eyes. "You're with a task force? Doing what?"

"Ava's missing," Magnus informed her. "That's why the police were here this mornin'. Harrison told them I had somethin' to do with it."

That seemed to snap Gia out of her stupor. Her eyebrows lowered, and her brown eyes sparked with banked fury. "He's an asshole."

"You know him?" Trey asked.

"Everyone knows him," she answered, then looked back at Magnus. "All that glitz you see on TV … his smug smile … it's all horseshit." Her attention swung back to Magnus. "She's missing?"

"Yes," he said somberly. "The police, as well as Trey's team, are currently looking into it. Which is what I intend to do as soon as I can check on a few things."

Gia shook her head. "You don't worry about a thing here. We've got it covered. I've already called Randy in to help out. And I'll stay as long as I'm needed."

He knew better than to argue. Gia was fierce when she set her mind to something. And since finding Ava was more important to him than anything else, he wanted to give the search his full attention so he would take all the help he could get.

"I'm gonna run in the house and change," he told them, motioning toward the door.

He wasn't sure why Trey was there, what he needed, or how long he intended to stick around. Nor did he care to ask. The man was making things awkward because he clearly didn't want to be here, yet he refused to leave.

Magnus didn't wait to see if Trey would follow when he headed for the house. He didn't care whether he did or not.

Sparing a glance at the waffles still inside the toaster, he headed down the hall to his bedroom. He grabbed his phone from where it was charging, tapped the screen. No messages and no calls. He swallowed the disappointment, set the phone down, and headed for the bathroom. After giving his reflection a quick once-over while he washed his hands, he decided on a quick shower but opted to forgo shaving. He was in and out in two minutes, then dressed and pulling on his boots when he heard the back screen door slam shut. He wandered back down the hall, grabbing his cell phone from the charger on the way.

Stepping into the kitchen, he dialed Ava's number, although he knew it would go unanswered. When he got her voicemail after several rings, he opted to text.

"Her phone's still on," he said, glancing over at Trey. "You think JJ could see if she can locate it?"

"It's worth a shot. What's the number?"

Magnus knew it wouldn't be that easy, but it was something. He rattled off the number, praying Ava was hiding out, refusing to go home. He knew that wouldn't be the case because she would've come to his house if she didn't go home. Ava knew he would keep her safe, protect her from Harrison at all costs. She damn sure wouldn't have to go it alone.

He began typing a text to Ava, wanting to send it just in case.

"She's been tellin' me she's gonna leave," he told Trey, not looking at him. "Ava. For years she's claimed she would leave that house to get away from Harrison. She ends up goin' back to take care of her mother every time."

"Why not take her mother with her?"

"She can't afford it." Magnus had offered to help, but Ava had refused. She was too proud to accept handouts, or so she'd told him.

"You said Harrison abuses her. How long's this been goin' on?"

Magnus hit send on the text and turned his attention to Trey. "He … uh…" Unable to force the words past the bile rising in his throat, he peered over at the coffeepot, opted to make some.

"Magnus. Talk to me. It's the only way we're gonna find her."

He nodded, understanding, but still couldn't get the words out.

"Magnus." Trey's voice was lower this time, and he'd moved closer. "Talk to me."

Slowly turning, he leaned against the kitchen counter, crossed his arms over his chest. "Yeah, he beats her," he said, his voice rough with the anger that began flooding his system. "Started up shortly after they were married."

"He's the one who gave her the split lip?"

Magnus remembered the night Trey had shown up shortly after Ava had. She'd been so upset because Harrison had threatened to kill her. "He's the one," he confirmed.

Trey's eyes flashed with something that looked a lot like the anger Magnus felt. While he appreciated the guy's fury on Ava's behalf, Magnus knew there was one emotion the man couldn't take on: guilt. Magnus couldn't shake the guilt that consumed him knowing if he'd only done something sooner, perhaps Ava would be safe and not—

He cut off the thought. He couldn't think along those lines. She wasn't dead. She couldn't be.

"She used to deny it," he told Trey. "I knew she was lyin'. I finally got her to admit it, but now she tells me it's no big deal. Probably because I told her I'd kill him if I ever saw him." He sighed. "I've offered to let her and her mother stay here, but she refuses."

"Does her mother know..." Trey swallowed. "Is she aware he hits her?"

"Doubtful. If she's noticed, I'm sure Harrison's made up excuses. According to Ava, Renee's not well, and I don't think Harrison helps matters. He's a dick."

"Do you believe Ava's a threat to herself?"

"No."

"What about her mother? If her daughter's missing, could that send her into a spiral?"

"That's a good question." Magnus turned to grab two mugs from the cabinet. "According to Ava, no. If you ask Harrison, he'll say yes. Honestly, I haven't seen Renee in years. Not since they moved from next door."

"I take it your father doesn't talk to her anymore, either?"

Magnus met Trey's gaze, felt the overwhelming sadness when he said, "My parents are dead, Trey. I lost them all in the house fire."

FOR FUCK'S SAKE. HE'D DONE IT AGAIN.

"Shit, man. I'm sorry," Trey blurted as it sank in.

He could see the pain in Magnus's eyes, knew he still felt the loss, and Trey felt like such a jackass for not knowing something so important. He'd fucked this guy senseless at least a hundred times over the past year, and he didn't know the first thing about him. What did that say about him?

Deciding he wouldn't think on that now, he asked, "When did it happen? The fire?"

"Thirteen years ago."

Fucking hell.

Trey thought about his sisters, his parents, his brothers. He couldn't imagine losing any of them, much less more than one at a time.

"I was stayin' with a friend," Magnus said, as though he sensed Trey's next question. "I wasn't here that night. Shit, I was only thirteen and never here unless I was working the kennels."

Magnus nodded toward a hallway off the kitchen.

Trey glanced back, not sure what he was referring to.

"Fire started in my parents' bedroom. They say it was from a propane heater. Caught the curtains on fire. Spread from there." Magnus swallowed, inhaled deeply as though to hold back the emotion. "Carbon monoxide put them to sleep; fire killed them all."

Trey shook his head when Magnus offered him coffee. There was a knot in his throat, one he didn't think he could choke down. He could practically feel Magnus's pain, even all these years later. Trey wondered if that sort of devastating loss ever got any easier.

"I should've been here," Magnus said softly.

Trey didn't know what to say to that. He could understand Magnus's grief because he would've felt the same if he were in his position. Even knowing there wouldn't have been anything Magnus could've done. He would've probably died along with them, and Trey would honestly say he was glad that hadn't happened.

Magnus stood tall as though he refused to let the grief weigh him down. "Anyway. My mother's relationship with Renee had started going downhill before that. Renee never was very stable, but my mother knew how to handle her. I think Renee started dating some jackass, though, which came between them. My mother didn't like him." He waved a hand. "It's true what they say about abusers. They isolate their victim, shut them off from the world. He did it to Renee from the beginning." His gaze swung to the window overlooking the backyard.

Trey wondered if that was how Ava had ended up in a similar situation. Had she not seen the warning signs because she'd seen it so much it had become familiar? Or maybe Harrison had come along and treated her like a princess, promised to solve all her problems before revealing he was actually a monster in disguise.

"After they moved," Magnus continued, "Ava stopped by once or twice, but then I didn't see her for several years. Not until she graduated from high school. I think it was hard for her. When my sister died, she was so distraught. Eleven years old and lost the family who'd been there for her when her mother wasn't."

"You stayed," Trey said. "In this house?"

"Yeah." Magnus looked at him. "I had nowhere else to go. No other family. Not that we kept in touch with, anyway. We had a kennel helper who'd become good friends with my parents. He lived on the property and took legal responsibility for me after. He made sure I went to school and kept my nose clean. Told me no one would hassle us about the situation as long as I stayed off the radar. House was paid for, insured. Edgar helped me with all that. I kept up the kennels, had income from that. I expanded it when I graduated. Finally got around to renovating the house a couple of years ago."

"What happened to Edgar?"

Magnus's Adam's apple bobbed, and Trey realized more bad news was coming.

"He was killed by a drunk driver. He'd gone to San Antonio to visit his daughter. Head-on collision ended his life."

Fuck.

Nothing about Magnus had given him the impression he'd had such a traumatic childhood. He was quick to smile, always laughing. It was one of the things Trey loved—

He swallowed, cut off that thought immediately.

It didn't stop him from wanting to know more about Magnus. Truth was, he found he wanted to know everything, but they needed to focus on Ava. Finding her was critical, considering they didn't know exactly how long she'd been missing.

"Does Ava have any friends she keeps in touch with? Anyone else she might turn to?"

"There's only one girl I know she still keeps in touch with from high school. Her name's Jane Ross."

"You know how to get in touch with her?"

He shook his head. "I know she works at the Round Rock Outlets, but I don't know what store."

"I'll get JJ to look into that, and we'll head up there," Trey suggested. "See if she's workin'. Maybe she'll know somethin'."

Magnus nodded, some of those clouds clearing from his eyes.

Trey shot a quick text to Baz, giving him the friend's name and asking for employment data, then he shot a text to Brantley, letting him know where they were headed.

When Magnus dumped his coffee into the sink, Trey headed for the back door.

He decided to focus on the task at hand, filing away the details he'd learned about Magnus for later. He didn't want to like the guy, didn't want to get close to him, but he'd surpassed that a long damn time ago. It was pure stubbornness that had kept him from pursuing something more. Then again, that was Trey's nature, wasn't it? He was always looking for someone to fix. It had been the case with his ex-husband, Paul.

Paul had been down from Dallas, visiting his mother in the hospital when they first met. Paul had gotten a room in the hotel Trey worked at as a third-shift security guard. Paul had been outside smoking a cigarette when Trey came by on his rounds. That night, he'd learned that Paul's mother had fallen, broken her hip, and was recovering from the surgery.

Paul had been shaken, worried he would lose his mother, and felt guilty for living so far away. For the first few nights, Trey had been there, helping him through it, listening, consoling, ensuring Paul knew he wasn't alone. The next thing he knew, they were having dinner, and Trey was staying with Paul in his hotel room; then Paul stayed with Trey on occasion after his mother was released, and he decided to move to Austin to be closer to her.

It had been a whirlwind; everything happened so fast. Marriage hadn't been an option at the time, not for them, but as soon as it was, they'd jumped at the opportunity. Only for things to fall apart two short years later.

Trey knew better than to think he was a white knight. He'd never actually saved anyone despite his misguided desire to do so. In fact, he'd go so far as to say he probably made most situations worse.

Until now.

With his resources, he could find Ava March. That much he could help with.

As for saving Magnus ... sounded like the only person he needed to be saved from was Trey.

CHAPTER TEN

———————————

At Brantley's request, JJ was digging up information on Harrison Rivers. When she'd first dived in, she'd thought it would be easy. And it had been. Maybe a little *too* easy, actually.

Everything she uncovered told her that Harrison David Rivers, married to Ava March Rivers, was a stand-up guy. Well, as stand up as a forty-two-year-old man married to a twenty-three-year-old woman could be, she figured.

Not that JJ put too much emphasis on age.

Okay, fine. That was a lie. She'd been hung up on age her entire life, which was the reason she'd pushed Baz away in the beginning. Not until recently did she learn he was, in fact, younger than she was, but she had suspected it. At least she wasn't old enough to be his mom.

"Is that why you beat on her?" JJ mused to herself. "Because she's young and vulnerable, and you're a big bully?"

From all accounts, Harrison Rivers was an upstanding citizen. He'd been a resident of Texas for the past nine years, having moved from Colorado. There were a couple of speeding tickets on his record but nothing else. His credit score was just short of excellent, mostly affected because they carried a little more debt than they should. Then there was his family. He came from a long line of politicians, so it made sense that he'd followed the same career path. Both his father and grandfather had been senators, so he had an in with Washington.

Problem was, there was so much she *wasn't* finding about Harrison Rivers. She should've found a wealth of detail about his childhood—where he'd gone to school, where he'd grown up—but it appeared a good portion of that had disappeared from public record. Based on her search, he'd never been married, never so much as dated anyone. His social media footprint was glaringly sparse before five years ago.

"Was that by design?" she muttered, staring at her computer screen. "Were there other abused women before Ava?'"

JJ knew there were signs, but she found nothing in his past signifying he'd ever hurt anyone. And yes, maybe she was being deceitful in her pursuit of dirt, but she knew abusers tended to leave a bloody trail behind them. Former co-workers, neighbors, school friends. She couldn't imagine Ava was the first person he'd laid hands on.

"I got an update from Trey," Baz called out from downstairs. "He's goin' to see if they can find Ava's best friend from high school. Her name's Jane Ross. He wants employment history."

"I'm still diggin' into the husband. Could you do that?" JJ hollered back.

"Yeah, sure."

JJ stayed completely focused on her research. She could not afford to be distracted by Baz. She found it too easy to let herself be seduced by him, even when he wasn't making any effort to do so. It was safe to say she was smitten, and in times like this, it didn't help matters. Just thinking about the man had her blood running hot. If they hadn't had an active case, there was no doubt in her mind she would've found a way to be alone so they could scratch that itch one more time.

"Not an option," she whispered. "Not yet."

However, tonight, when they reached a stopping point, she would be getting that man naked—and keeping him that way if she was lucky.

Half an hour later, JJ was frustrated with her inability to find that string that would lead to who Harrison Rivers had been before someone had glossed over his past and given him this squeaky-clean identity. She'd searched all the databases, tried variations of his name, looked for relatives but came up empty at every turn. She was just about to get up and seek input from Baz when she heard footsteps coming up the stairs.

JJ turned in time to see him ambling toward her, his gaze moving over her slowly. She could practically feel the heat coming off of him, and damn if that wasn't a heady sensation.

"Don't worry," he said with a grin, "I'm not here to seduce you."

"Aw, shucks," she teased, spinning in her chair to face him. "If not that, then why're you gracin' me with your presence, Detective?"

"Can't I come see you without having a reason?" He smirked, leaning closer until his lips met hers.

Unable to resist, JJ cupped his face, let herself fall into the kiss. His lips were firm and warm and oh so skilled.

"I was thinkin' about you earlier," she whispered when he pulled back.

"Is that so?"

"I was thinkin' about you naked."

His smile widened as he stood tall. "Tell me more."

"I'll just have to show you. Tonight," she added quickly when he leaned in.

"Is that a promise?"

"Oh, yeah."

"I'm gonna hold you to it."

JJ knew he would.

It was weird, this light feeling she had. JJ couldn't remember a time when she'd felt quite like this. Having something to look forward to. Someone, actually.

Her cell phone rang, and she snatched it up, hoping it was someone who would keep her mind off of the detective who held her heart in the palm of his hand even if he didn't realize just how hard she'd fallen for him. She might've been plagued with this fluttery feeling nearly every minute of every day, but she was trying to play it cool to a degree. Letting him know how hot she thought he was seemed to be an innocent way to keep the embers burning.

"You got an update for us?" Brantley asked.

Knowing she was on speaker, JJ explained what she had so far. "It's like the guy didn't exist before he married Ava," she said after she'd explained the searches that continued to come up empty.

"Clearly, he did," Brantley grumbled, "which means you've gotta keep lookin'."

"Trust me, I am. Where're y'all headed?"

"Over to the grocery store she worked at her senior year, see if they can tell us anything about who she is. According to Harrison, that's where they met."

JJ snorted. "Harrison Rivers did his own grocery shopping? Doubtful."

Brantley continued as though she hadn't spoken. "If we're lucky, someone who knew Ava might still work there."

"Was he not helpful?"

"He certainly pretended to be," Brantley said, disappointment in his tone. "He talked us in circles, probably figured we didn't notice."

"He's a politician. That's his job." JJ sighed. "What about Ava's mother? You talk to her?"

"Negative," Brantley replied. "She's so zoned out, I doubt she even realizes her daughter's missin'."

JJ hated to think about what that meant. The fact Ava's mother had tried to take her own life more than once told her something was very, very wrong with her situation.

"You think the husband's hidin' somethin'?"

"I think he's deflectin' for sure," he replied. "Kept comin' back around to Ava and Magnus havin' a relationship."

"Jealousy?"

"Without a doubt."

"But you don't think that's true?"

"No. I talked to Magnus this mornin'," Brantley explained. "I think he cares about her, but I don't think they're involved romantically."

JJ remembered the article she'd read about the house fire that had killed Magnus's family after Reese told her to look into it. His sister would've been the same age as Ava at the time, and the two girls had probably spent a lot of time together. She could see how Magnus would care about her.

"And he's worried about her," Brantley continued. "I think he's convinced the husband did something to her."

"You mean like...?" She couldn't get the word out.

"Yeah. Which is why you've got to keep lookin'."

"I know," JJ said. "I'll find it. I just need time."

"We don't have time, JJ," Evan said, his tone hard. "She's been missing too long as it is."

Her first instinct was to argue, to tell him that wasn't her fault, but Evan already knew that. She'd come to understand him over the past couple of months working with him, had picked up on the fact he took every case personally, and while it sounded like he was taking it out on her, she knew he wasn't. He simply wanted to find Ava the same way the rest of them did.

"I'll let you know when I have somethin'," she told them before disconnecting the call and shifting her chair to the other desk that held her special computer.

There was always another way to dig. But for this, she needed one that could effectively hide what she was digging for.

Stretching her fingers, JJ smiled. And did what she did best.

"I DON'T MEAN TO PRY, BUT IS it safe to assume Reese is back with us?"

Brantley glanced over at Evan, behind the wheel, while Brantley rode shotgun. He fucking hated the passenger seat, but unlike the rest of the team, Brantley'd yet to force Evan to trade places so he could drive. Despite the fact he desperately wanted to.

"I don't know," he said truthfully. He'd yet to get that far in a conversation with Reese, but he had a feeling they would be tackling it in the very near future.

"I was glad to see he looks like his old self again," Evan noted, focusing on the road.

Brantley would admit, at least to himself, that Reese did look good. Healthy and strong. He'd gotten tidbits of information from Z and RT over the months Reese had been in Dallas. Reese's brother and brother-in-law had been worried at one point, mentioned that Reese had lost some weight. At six foot five, Reese had weighed somewhere in the low two hundreds before the bullet ripped through him. Even then, he'd been a little on the slim side, although he was solid muscle. If Brantley had to guess, he'd added more muscle during his recovery.

He looked good. So good, Brantley was having a damn hard time focusing on what he should've been, which was finding Ava March so he and Reese could finish the conversation that had included *marriage* as one of the topics. Although he'd put up a good front, letting his anger come between them, Brantley couldn't deny he was already considering seducing the man just to ease some of the tension that had started to coil inside him the instant Reese showed up on his doorstep. No doubt about it, the desire to abstain had faded, and his libido was kicking into high gear. Only he knew once he gave in, that would be it for his resistance.

Thankfully, they were pulling into the grocery store Ava had previously worked at, forcing his thoughts off Reese and back to where they belonged.

"Let's do this," he said as Evan pulled his SUV into a spot that opened up near the door.

They headed into the store, past the rows of checkout lines, most of them ten people deep due to it being Sunday. They located one of the wandering employees, asked for the manager, and were told they could find him in the back of the store.

With directions—not very clear, but still directions—on where to go, Brantley led the way.

"This must be him," Brantley said under his breath when a man wearing the same shirt as the other employees, but just a little more put together than the rest, came toward them. His hair was cut, styled, and combed, his wire-rimmed glasses were straight on his nose, and he looked like he might've shaved within the past hour or so, which was the *little more put-together* part. Plus, he carried himself well and looked as though he might have at least a few concerns going on in his head.

As Brantley approached him, he caught the man's attention. "Are you the manager?"

His expression shifted to pleasant, his eyebrows lifting above those wire rims. "I am, yes. Joseph Sutherland. How can I help you?"

Evidently, he hadn't gotten a heads-up from the other helpful employee that they were coming to find him.

"We'd like to talk to you about Ava March."

"Ava?" His expression morphed to confusion. "I'm sorry, she no longer works here."

"We're aware of that. Right now, she's missing, and we're trying to find her. We're hopin' you might be able to give us something to go on."

"Are you with the police?"

"Private security firm," Brantley told him, pulling out his credentials and flashing them. "Can you tell us about her?"

He glanced between Evan and Brantley.

"It's not a difficult question," Brantley said when the man didn't respond.

"I'm sorry." He shook his head as though to clear it. "I'm trying to process the missing part. She's such a nice girl, one of those you could depend on. Never late, never missed a scheduled shift. She would come in when we needed someone to fill in."

Sounded like a model employee.

"What did she do here?"

"She was a customer service assistant."

Because retailers tended to have creative names for the same job, Brantley decided to ask, "And that means…?"

"She would bag customers' groceries and assist them to their vehicles if they needed help. She worked her way up to cashier. Did that for a few months."

"When did she last work here?"

"Oh, goodness. It's been several years. I'd have to look at her file to be certain. I know it was during the school year. She would work after school and on weekends."

"Why'd she leave?"

Joseph looked concerned, once again, his gaze bouncing between them. "We had to terminate her employment."

"You fired her?" Evan didn't sound impressed. "Thought she was a hard worker."

"She was," Joseph confirmed with a vigorous nod. "Definitely was. But her boyfriend … he was always coming up here, following her around, interrupting her while she worked. It got to be a problem, and I warned her several times. Finally, I had to let her go."

It certainly tracked, Brantley knew, based on what they'd learned so far. A lot of things were because of the husband—too many, in fact.

"What exactly did he do to interfere with her duties?" Evan probed.

Joseph appeared to relax a little. "He claimed to be checking on her, making sure she made it to work. But often, we would see him in the parking lot, waiting for her if she assisted someone with their groceries. He would approach her then, talk to her." He looked down briefly. "At first, I thought he was maybe her brother or something. A relative."

"Why's that?"

"He just … uh … seemed a little too old for her."

Brantley was definitely in agreement.

"The nature of their communication?" Evan asked. "Could you tell if there were issues?"

"It didn't seem they were unfriendly if that's what you're asking. I asked Ava a couple of times if there was anything she needed. She would assure me she'd take care of it. If she spoke to him at all, you wouldn't know it. He was up here at least once during every one of her shifts."

"Is there anyone here she might've confided in?" Evan asked. "A co-worker?"

"Not Ava, no. She kept her head down at all times. She would speak if spoken to and was always polite, especially to customers, but she didn't seem to have many friends."

"Thank you for your time." Evan produced a business card. "If you think of anything else, don't hesitate to call."

They left Joseph nodding in the aisle and headed back to the SUV.

"I'm not liking Harrison Rivers all that much," Evan said, spinning his keys on his finger. "Assuming he'd been pursuing her at the time, she could've been underage."

Yeah, Brantley'd picked up on that, too. Based on the facts JJ had supplied, they'd married when Ava was eighteen, which meant the courtship likely started before then.

"Where to next, boss?"

"Back to HQ. We'll see if JJ's learned anything that'll help."

"Baz texted," Evan noted. "Said Trey and Magnus were going to talk to the best friend. They found out she works at Spencer's in the outlet mall."

"What the hell is a Spencer's?" Brantley asked, glancing over at Evan.

He got a shrug in response. "Got me."

"Well, if we're lucky, Ava's hidin' somewhere, and the best friend's keepin' her secret." Brantley didn't think that would be the case, but he was aiming for optimism here.

When they returned to HQ thirty minutes later, he had only one thing on his mind. They weren't professional thoughts plaguing him, either. He knew it was in his best interest to shove them down, but the moment Reese stepped out onto the front porch, he knew he had to face them head on. If he didn't, there was a good chance this heat would blaze into an inferno, and Brantley would snap at a less convenient time.

"I'm gonna head in the house for a few minutes," Brantley told Evan as he parked. "I'll catch up to you in a bit."

"I'll see what JJ's got," the other man said, sauntering off toward the barn.

Brantley closed his door and walked toward the porch, meeting Reese's gaze as he did.

"You wanna sandwich or somethin'?" Reese offered, motioning toward the house behind him. "I'm tryin' to find a way to be useful."

"Is that a euphemism?"

A myriad of expressions flitted across Reese's face. Surprise, confusion, followed by feigned innocence, belied by the spark in his brown eyes. "Why would you say that?"

He stared at Reese, letting him see just how tightly he was wound. "Just checking."

Perhaps Brantley could forgive him for just a little while.

Reese must've read his mind because he grinned, and that dimple in his cheek flashed, making Brantley's entire body go hot. Christ, it had been so long since he'd seen this man's smile. At the same time, it felt like only yesterday.

Now, as he followed Reese up the steps and through the front door, the only thing he could think about was having his wicked way with him. It wasn't appropriate considering the circumstances, not to mention the status of their relationship. However, Brantley had never been able to resist Reese before, and it looked as though some things never changed.

"If you haven't had lunch," Reese began, closing the door, "I'll make— *Oomph.*"

Before Reese could get out his lunch offer, Brantley had him up against the wall, crushing him to the wall while he plundered his mouth with his tongue.

Aww, Jesus. He was so fucked. If he'd thought giving in would be beneficial in any way, he was damn wrong. There would be no turning back, and while he wasn't ready to move forward, he couldn't seem to help himself.

Every fucking time… Every kiss, every touch was like the first time. It lit Brantley up from the inside out. And he fucking loved that Reese instantly gave in, softening beneath his weight, hands roaming, tongue seeking and searching.

"Fucking hell," Brantley groaned, overwhelmed by Reese's touch, his taste. It had been an eternity since he'd last felt him, and he hadn't realized how much he missed this.

"Brantley," Reese groaned, his hand palming the back of his head. "You sure you wanna do this?"

No, he wasn't, but he couldn't seem to stop himself.

"Unless you're tellin' me no," he answered, nipping Reese's bottom lip.

"Fuck," Reese hissed, jerking Brantley, their mouths crashing together once again.

And just like that, six months' worth of pent-up passion blazed in the swirl of their tongues and the insistent press of their hands.

Not knowing how much time they had before JJ came looking for them—it was inevitable that she would—Brantley began fumbling with Reese's jeans. Before he could release the button, Reese was swatting his hand away, reaching for Brantley's jeans instead.

A soft growl escaped him as he watched Reese slide down to his knees.

This was so fucking wrong. He was giving Reese the wrong impression, but Lord help him, he couldn't resist.

"You look good down there, you know that?" he said, sliding his hand in Reese's hair, holding firmly.

Staring up at him, Reese licked the swollen head of his cock. Brantley's eyes glazed as the wicked heat blazed through every nerve ending, his mouth going slack as euphoria consumed him. It had been too fucking long since he'd had a mouth—*this* mouth—on his cock, and he wasn't sure how the hell he'd survived it.

"Fuck, yes," Brantley moaned, dropping his head back against the wall, savoring every second as Reese focused his full attention on licking, sucking, stroking. It was sheer perfection, the way he worshipped him. Brantley remembered every single pull of those delicious lips as he sucked him to completion, yet none of those times had felt remotely as good as this.

"Reese … oh, fuck…" Brantley's fingers tightened in his hair, pulled as he pumped his hips.

The instant Reese surrendered control, letting Brantley use his mouth how he needed, he knew he was doomed. Although he wanted nothing more than to pretend this thing between them was over, he knew better. It was far from over.

"I'm gonna come," Brantley warned.

Reese squeezed the backs of his thighs, silently urging him to let go.

When he did, it was with a grunt and Reese's name on his lips.

Twenty minutes later, after Brantley managed to regain some semblance of control, they took a plate of sandwiches to the barn. If he'd thought for one minute that no one would realize what they'd been doing, he was sorely mistaken. There was no sneaking around and getting away with anything here. The only good thing was no one dared to say anything, knowing it would embarrass Reese, which, in turn, would piss Brantley off.

"What do we have?" Brantley asked when he walked upstairs to JJ's lair.

She was sitting at her corner desk, neck craned, a Blow Pop stick wiggling against her lip as she stared at her computer screen.

"This bastard thought he'd be sneaky," she said, words obscured by the candy until she popped the sucker out of her mouth. "But I found him."

"Was there ever any doubt?" he joked, sliding one of the sandwiches onto the desk.

JJ spared the paper plate a glance before turning back to the computer. "He was born Franklin Joseph Harris. Figure that's how they came up with the name Harrison. He was adopted by the Rivers family when he was three."

"Not related?"

JJ's smile was smug. "Oh, he's related, all right. His mother's one of the maids who worked for his father."

Brantley grunted.

"Looks as though his father's wife took him in, somehow glossed over his past, and treated him like their own son."

"What happened to the birth mother?"

"Deported," JJ said with a snarl. "From what I can find, Harrison lived in Colorado until roughly nine years ago when he relocated to Texas. According to his public announcements, he wanted to make a play for a senate seat in Texas, so that's why he came. Moved through the state from Dallas to Houston, then back up here a few months before he married Ava."

"Months?"

"Some men move fast," she said snidely.

"Criminal record?"

"Public record, no. But I found some stuff, and let me tell you, this guy's bad news. Cited several times for drunk and disorderly from the time he was eighteen. Arrested for inappropriate actions with a minor, then—"

"Details on that," Brantley interrupted.

JJ tapped the keyboard, pulled up a document. "He was twenty-two; the girl he was with was sixteen. Charges were eventually dropped, and not long after, he applied for a marriage license."

"Same girl?"

"Yep. The license was never filed, and everything was swept neatly away, kept out of the public eye."

"Can you find out why?" Brantley feared the worst, but he hoped it was simply a matter of the girl—or her parents—coming to her senses. Or better yet, maybe his family intervened and forced him to toe the line for the sake of their political affiliations.

"Did y'all learn anything with Ava's former employer?" JJ asked, fingers flying over the keys.

"Model employee. Fired because he stalked and harassed her at work."

JJ's gaze flew up to him. "Seriously?"

Brantley nodded. "I'm thinkin' Magnus might be on to somethin' here. I want to keep lookin' into him. Find everything you can. See if there's anything else they've buried."

"Probably a lot," JJ said softly.

Unfortunately, Brantley thought. Guys like Harrison Rivers preyed on innocents and managed to get away with it because they were slippery and had people who could clean up their messes.

If he was responsible for Ava's disappearance, he wasn't going to slip through this time. Not if Brantley had anything to say about it.

CHAPTER ELEVEN

MAGNUS WALKED INTO SPENCER'S, PAST THE ROWS of T-shirts depicting bands and pop fiction, beyond shelves of lava lamps and a variety of specialty lamps. The place was dark, with spotlights highlighting the variety of novelty items they sold. At the moment, there were only a couple of teenagers picking through items on a shelf, snickering to themselves.

He made his way to the center of the small store where an employee was standing at a register, folding a stack of shirts on the cluttered counter.

"Can I help you?" the young woman asked, setting her folded shirt aside and giving them her full attention.

Magnus noticed her nose and lip rings glittering from the spotlights above.

"Are you Jane Ross?" Trey asked, holding up his credentials.

Magnus decided he'd let Trey lead the charge because this was Trey's job and the man probably knew the right questions to ask to get the information they needed. That and he looked damn good with the sidearm holstered to his side. There was something distinctly sexy about an armed and dangerous man.

"I am," the woman confirmed.

Magnus figured she couldn't have been more than twenty-one, maybe twenty-two years old. Her blond hair, streaked with purple, pink, and blue, was cut short and at an extreme angle that, along with a fringe of bangs, framed her small face. Her eyelids were coated in dark shadow and lined with a thick black liner, making the light blue irises pop against her pale skin. No more than five feet tall, maybe a hundred pounds, Jane Ross looked like a strong breeze could take her down.

"Trey Walker. I'm with the OTB Task Force. We're here about Ava March."

Magnus was watching Jane closely, so he caught the flash of concern in her eyes, understood exactly what she was feeling. Those who knew Ava understood the danger she was in because of her bastard of a husband.

"This is Magnus Storme," Trey introduced.

"You're the guy Ava talks about," Jane noted.

Magnus nodded.

"Have you heard from her lately?" Trey asked.

"In the past few days, specifically," Magnus added.

Jane was shaking her head, glancing between them. "I haven't talked to her since right before New Year's. We were supposed to go out that night. New Year's Eve. She was gonna meet me at my house so we could go to a couple of clubs. She never showed."

Magnus knew that was because Harrison had beat her up, and Ava had come running to him to get away for a little while.

"And you haven't talked to her since?" Trey asked.

Magnus listened as their questions and answers volleyed back and forth.

"I've tried. I called, texted, even went by her house. She didn't answer. I assume she wasn't there."

"You went to her house?"

"Tried. It's like a fortress, though."

"Was Harrison there?"

Jane shrugged. "No one answered the door."

"Any cars there?"

"They only have one car. Harrison's. It wasn't in the driveway, but he sometimes parks in the garage, so I don't know for sure. He has a driver, but that car wasn't there either." She pulled out her phone. "The last time I texted her was last Saturday, just to check in. She responded the next day." She tapped the phone screen. "Said she would catch up later, but that she was out and about, and then going to see a guy."

"A guy?" Magnus asked, taking the phone when Jane passed it over.

"Yeah. You know her, right?" Jane asked him.

"I do, yes."

"Then you know that's not like her," Jane told him as he read the text. "And that doesn't *sound* like her."

The text definitely did not sound like Ava at all. For one, there weren't any emojis in the message, and Ava was almost obsessive about them, to the point there were times Magnus couldn't decipher what she was trying to tell him.

When Trey held out his hand, Magnus passed over the phone, watched while he read it, and handed it back to Jane.

"I don't know who texted me that, but it wasn't Ava," Jane concluded. "I wish I could help you. I've texted her since, but she hasn't responded. Do you think she's all right?"

Her eyes held more concern when she peered over at him. As much as Magnus wanted to tell the truth, that he believed Harrison had hurt her, he couldn't do it. Not only because he didn't want this nice girl to spend the rest of her workday in tears, but also because he was still holding out hope that Ava was all right, that she was taking care of herself.

"We're gonna find her," Trey answered for him. "If there's anything you can think of that might help us do that…"

Jane considered for a moment. "I know she wanted to leave Harrison last year. She told me she couldn't stand being there anymore, but she said her mom disapproved. Said Ava owed it to her husband to work things out." Jane shook her head. "Renee's messed up, you know. Half the time, I don't think she knows what day it is."

Magnus was still thinking about that when he and Trey walked out of the store, through the parking lot. It was crammed with weekend shoppers, all out to enjoy the early spring day while spending a little bit of money.

"How well do you know her husband?" Trey asked as he climbed inside Trey's truck.

"Not really at all," Magnus admitted. "I didn't meet him until after Ava married him. She introduced us, but there was no budding friendship. Until today, I hadn't seen him since he told Ava she couldn't talk to me anymore. So I only know what Ava's told me. Which wasn't much, and none of it was good."

He could feel Trey's eyes on him, knew he should keep talking but didn't know what else to say. Instead, he pulled out his phone and brought up his text thread with Ava. He skimmed the past messages back and forth to see if someone else had been responding in her place. She hadn't responded back as much as she normally did, but that was the only oddity he noticed.

Trey finally broke the silence. "I need to head back to HQ to check in with the team. You wanna head over there with me? Or you want me to drop you at home?"

Magnus shrugged. He honestly didn't know. Right now, his mind was on Ava, on where she might be.

"To HQ it is," Trey finally said.

"I … uh… Actually, I need to get back to the house. Need to check on the dogs." It wasn't a complete lie. He did need to check in, make sure Gia didn't need anything. Although he trusted her to handle the business, he hated leaving it all on her.

Trey studied him momentarily as though he wanted to argue. It wasn't surprising when he didn't.

REESE WAS STUDYING THE BOARD, REVIEWING THE timeline they'd drawn up depicting where Ava March had last been seen. Based on the text they'd just gotten from Trey, the friend they'd met with hadn't heard from her since last Saturday. Although Trey's message had mentioned they didn't believe Ava had been the one to text the friend back, they were using that as a last-confirmed.

He had updated the details and started the timeline because he was making every effort to stay focused on the case and remember that was the only reason he was here.

Of course, his thoughts were scattered, more so since that intense encounter he and Brantley had shared in the house a short time ago. When they'd succumbed to the passion that seemed to burn out of control the longer they were around one another. He had to keep reminding himself that just because they'd indulged, given in to their desires, it didn't mean things would work out with him and Brantley. Ever since then, Brantley had been keeping him at a distance, back to business.

Reese refused to be hurt by it all because it was his own fault. The instant Brantley kissed him, he'd known that it was a reaction to the situation.

Didn't mean he couldn't use it as a building block for their future. Reese had every intention of using that to his advantage if it meant getting to spend even a little more time with Brantley. He'd missed the man fiercely; only his own insecurities had kept him from coming back. Now that he was here, he didn't want to leave.

Brantley's cell phone rang, pulling Reese from his thoughts.

"It's Trey," he announced, then answered the call on speaker. "You find anything out?"

Reese went back to staring at the board, shook his head. That was Brantley for you. Couldn't even say hello. Good to see some things hadn't changed.

"Jane didn't know where she is. Said Ava was supposed to go out with her on New Year's but didn't show. Hasn't seen her in the past three months."

"And she hasn't heard from her?"

"Just the text I messaged Baz about," Trey answered, "but Magnus and Jane don't think it was from her."

Reese glanced at Brantley, spoke up when he didn't. "Why doesn't he think it was her?"

"The tone of the text," Magnus said, the call obviously on speaker on the other end, too. "It wasn't Ava. No emojis or acronyms. If I had to guess, someone else answered to throw Jane off."

"Would that someone be Harrison Rivers?" Brantley asked.

"Could've been anyone," Magnus noted before Trey added, "Jane did say she went by Ava's house on New Year's Day, but no one answered the door. She said they only have one car. It wasn't there, either, but Harrison could've parked in the garage."

"We need to track that car," Brantley stated, his gaze swinging to JJ, who was sitting at one of the desks near the electronic board that was slowly gaining information, but nothing that would help them find Ava.

"Maybe he has a toll tag," Reese added.

"I'm on it," JJ called out.

"I'm gonna drop Magnus at his place," Trey said, "then head in."

"Take us off speaker," Brantley commanded, his tone still all business.

Reese heard the click, then Trey's voice came in clearer.

"I want you to stay with Magnus," Brantley told him. "Don't leave his side. If Harrison's tryin' to pin this on him, I want eyes on him at all time."

"Are you sure about that?" Trey asked.

Reese hid a smile. He could hear it in Trey's voice, knew the man wasn't keen on the idea. It probably had something to do with the fact he liked Magnus. Before everything went FUBAR, Reese knew Trey and Magnus had been spending time together. He hoped that was still working out for them because he'd always liked Magnus.

"Yes. Stay with him," Brantley repeated. "We'll check in later, let you know when we have something."

Reese grinned when Brantley disconnected the call. "He's gonna hate you. You know that, right?"

"Why?"

Feigned innocence. That was what he saw on Brantley's face.

"I owe him," Brantley said by way of explanation. "Consider it payback."

"For what?"

"Growing up, he was the very annoying older brother." Brantley's grin was wicked. "I've got a long, long list."

Reese felt more of the tension ease from his chest. He wouldn't go so far as to say things were back to the way they had been between him and Brantley, but they were certainly better than he'd expected them to be.

Not that he was getting his hopes up. He knew better when it came to Brantley. Just because Brantley had initiated their tryst earlier didn't mean a damn thing. Brantley had been up-front with Reese from the beginning. The man had never seen sex as anything more than a means to an end. As far as he knew, Brantley could still be planning to kick his ass to the curb once this was done.

Of course, Reese intended to fight him tooth and nail. Yes, he'd fucked up, but he was a very determined man, and the last thing he wanted was to let Brantley go. Not without a fight.

CHAPTER TWELVE

———————

BABYSITTING.

Brantley wanted him to fucking babysit Magnus.

Why him?

Trey could not believe his brother was forcing him to do this. If he had to guess, the asshole was paying him back for something. Or a lot of things.

Trey rolled his eyes. In his defense, he'd been the oldest boy and the middle child. With three older sisters and three younger brothers, he'd had a specific role. Giving them all shit had come with the territory.

Not that being with Magnus was a hardship by any means. Oh, no. Trey couldn't get that lucky. His problem was that he *wanted* to spend time with Magnus, and after having been so adamant about that whole no-strings thing he'd been harping on since they met, it made him ... well, it made him needy.

He didn't want to be fucking needy.

"You okay?"

Jerking himself out of his thoughts, Trey forced a smile, offered a nod in Magnus's direction. "Good."

"Your brother wants you to babysit me, huh?"

Trey blew out a breath.

"You should turn down the volume on your phone," Magnus said with a mirthless laugh. "I heard every word."

What was he supposed to say to that?

"It's fine," Magnus continued. "I've got a bunk room in the office. I'll sleep out there. You can take my bed in the house."

Fucking hell. They were already talking about sleeping, and it was just now dinnertime. More importantly, Magnus was inviting him to sleep in his bed.

Shit.

"Why don't we swing through so you can check on the dogs," Trey told Magnus so he could forget about beds and Magnus, which was only snowballing to include Magnus naked in that bed.

Fuck.

"After," Trey continued, "we'll go by some of the places Ava frequents."

"We can skip the camp," Magnus said, not looking at him. "Gia's got it covered."

"But you said—"

"I was tryin' not to make it uncomfortable for you."

Trey could've said a few things. He could've lied and said he wasn't uncomfortable. He could've told Magnus his feelings weren't important, so it didn't matter. Or he could've told him that he was enjoying the time he got to spend with him, even if it wasn't ideal.

Trey said none of those things.

"Name a place Ava likes to go. A store, a favorite coffee shop."

"Truth is, I don't know what Ava does anymore. After getting fired from the grocery store, she started looking for another job. Based on what she told me, Harrison sabotaged her at every turn."

"He didn't want her to work?"

"A politician's wife doesn't work," Magnus said in a tone that mimicked a female voice. Ava's maybe? "That's what she told me he said. I know she wanted to get out of the house, but he rarely let her. All I know is she would complain that he was there everywhere she turned."

"That tracks. That's what the grocery store manager said."

"But he would never come to my place," Magnus explained, "although I figure he knew when she was there."

It was an opening, Trey knew. "You said the last time she came by was New Year's. You sure about that?"

Magnus was quiet for a moment as though he was thinking.

Because he didn't have a destination, Trey decided to head to a fast-food restaurant so they could grab a bite. He was starving since he'd skipped lunch, and he was starting to feel light-headed, which was a sign his body needed food.

"No, I haven't seen her since," Magnus finally said.

"What?"

"That was the last time Ava came by. The night you met her. She stayed the night, slept in my bed while I occupied the bunk room. I didn't get a chance to talk to her the next morning, though, because I woke up late. She was gone by the time I was finished with the morning chores."

"If she doesn't have a car, how does she get where she needs to go?"

"Rideshare. Lyft, Uber."

Right.

"So your relationship with her is purely platonic?" Trey heard himself say.

Magnus chuckled. "Up to this point, yeah."

"What's funny?"

"I'm just curious whether you're askin' because it'll help us find her or because you have a personal agenda."

"Taco Cabana or Whataburger?" Trey asked, deflecting.

"What?"

"Dinner. What're you hungry for?"

"Taco Cabana's fine."

"Perfect." Trey continued when the light turned green, pulled into the parking lot.

He managed to avoid more conversation until after they'd gone inside the restaurant, placed their order at the counter. He paid because it seemed the right thing to do. Not because he was trying to be gentlemanly. Hell no. He was merely trying to be nice after all Magnus had been through already.

After self-serving the drinks, Trey found a high-top table near the windows, sat, and waited for Magnus to join him. He did a couple of minutes later, carrying a basket of chips and a bowl of salsa.

Trey meant to ask about Ava, to keep their interactions solely focused on the case, so he was only a bit mortified by what came out of his mouth next.

"When's the last time you were with a woman?"

Magnus's gaze shot to his, and Trey saw a glitter of amusement there.

Damn it.

"Is that case-related, too?" Magnus's teasing tone did little to loosen the knot forming in Trey's stomach.

He took a drink of his tea, looked outside.

"You do the math," Magnus said, his voice low. "I haven't been with anyone but you since ... since the first time we were together. I haven't had a lot of time for dating. I spend every waking moment at the camp. I've dedicated the last couple of years to growin' the business and to ... you."

Trey couldn't help it, he looked over at Magnus.

"If you're askin' about before then..." Magnus smiled. "I honestly don't know. I don't dwell much on the past."

That shouldn't have made him feel better, but it did.

"You want the God's honest truth, Trey?"

Trey swallowed, nodded.

Magnus leaned toward him, met his stare. "I'm attracted to Ava. I've never touched her, but I've wanted to."

Trey felt a knot forming in his stomach.

"But she's not the only one I think about when I fantasize about her."

Trey's heart galloped, and he found he couldn't look away.

"I think about the three of us," Magnus whispered. "I think about how hot it would be if the three of us were together."

Trey's cock swelled as the image formed in his head. He'd never been with a woman before, never had much attraction to any. He wouldn't deny there'd been something mesmerizing about Ava, but he figured that had been based purely on his concern for her when he'd met her.

"Does that repulse you?" Magnus asked.

The image faded from his mind, and Trey focused on Magnus, then blurted the truth. "No."

He saw the shock that flashed in Magnus's gaze. Luckily, one of the servers came by, delivered their food, then moved on to clear off an empty table nearby. It was enough of a distraction for the subject to die off, leaving them in silence to eat. Trey didn't hesitate, scarfing down his meal as much to sate his hunger as to keep from going down this path with Magnus.

"Ava likes bookstores," Magnus said when they were both nearly finished.

"Are you talkin' Barnes and Noble? Half Price Books?"

Magnus shook his head. "The independent ones. There's one in downtown Round Rock she likes."

"We're not too far from there." He glanced at his watch. "It's Sunday, so they'll probably close early, but we'll swing by. Maybe we'll get lucky. Anywhere else?"

"No. She usually came to the camp and helped out with the dogs," Magnus said, tone solemn now. "I told her I'd hire her whenever she was ready, but she thought I was joking. I wasn't."

Once again, Trey could see the concern on Magnus's face, knew he was worried. He had every right to be based on the information they had. It didn't sound to him like Ava was one to go off on her own or to hide out from her friends, and no one knew where she was.

It wasn't looking good, and the grim outlook was starting to weigh on him.

MAGNUS DIDN'T BOMBARD TREY WITH QUESTIONS DURING the drive to the bookstore. Instead, he spent the time thinking about where Ava might go, all the while, in the back of his mind, that niggling feeling was still there, the one that told him Ava was dead, that Harrison had killed her.

He was doing his best not to succumb to the negative thoughts, telling himself Ava needed him to be optimistic because she could still be alive. Unfortunately, that was easier said than done.

However, Magnus didn't speak the words aloud. Not to Trey before or after they'd gone to the small mom-and-pop bookstore only to learn that, yes, the owners knew Ava well but hadn't seen her in a few months.

"Tell me about Ava," Trey prompted when they were heading back to Camp K-9.

"What do you wanna know?"

"Anything. You said she was best friends with your sister. What did they do when they were kids?"

Magnus couldn't help but smile at the memories of his sister. "What didn't they do is probably the better question," he said with a chuckle. "Tabby was always into gymnastics, doing flips and cartwheels all over the house, the yard. My folks eventually bought her a trampoline, so she moved the show there."

God, he remembered his bright and cheerful sister, how she used to do cartwheels in the kitchen to greet him in the morning. She always had a smile on her face. And when Ava was there, her sunny disposition ramped up tenfold.

"They were quite the pair. If they could be outside, that was where they were."

"Was Ava into gymnastics?"

"Yeah, but I think it had more to do with Tabby being into it. Ava was good but not quite as graceful. Turn here," Magnus instructed. "It's the back way into the camp."

Trey followed his instructions onto the dirt road that ran around the outside of his property, winding around until they reached the house.

"Why do I feel like I should be doing something?" Magnus asked, staring at the metal building that housed the Camp K-9 office and kennels. "How do you do this? How do you function?"

"It's not easy," Trey mumbled in response, then sounded surprised when he added, "I'd rather be doing anything else."

"I thought you liked it."

Trey's gaze slid over to him briefly. "You want the truth?"

Magnus nodded.

"I fucking hate it. I hate immersing myself in everyone else's pain while trying to find their loved one. It's killing me slowly."

Magnus was pretty sure that was the most honest thing Trey had ever said to him in all the time they'd known one another.

"I can imagine it's not easy. Hell, we sat down to dinner for fifteen minutes, and I felt like I'd abandoned Ava completely."

"Try sleeping at night when there's an active case," Trey said on a rough breath. "But I can assure you, Brantley's on it. JJ's doing her thing, too. We'll find her."

Because he was at a complete loss as to what to do or where to look, Magnus nodded his head.

"I'm gonna check in with Gia." He glanced over at Trey. "Want a tour?"

Trey was staring at the building, and Magnus wished he could read the man's mind. He could tell there was something he wanted to say, but knowing Trey—what little he truly did know about him—he would keep it bottled up.

"I'd love one," Trey finally said, glancing over as he shut off the truck.

And then there they were, staring at one another, the center console the only thing between them.

Whenever they were together, Magnus usually conceded control to Trey, allowing him to lead. Or at least he gave him the illusion that was what he was doing. He knew Trey needed that for whatever reason. But here and now…

Magnus lifted his hand, reached for Trey. When the man didn't immediately shift out of his grasp, he slid his hand behind his neck, pulled Trey closer as he leaned in. He didn't kiss him immediately. He certainly wanted to, but something told him to tread lightly. Even after all the time they'd spent together, this man was skittish, though Magnus wasn't sure why that was.

Leaning in a little closer, Magnus brushed his lips against Trey's.

"I can't stop thinkin' about you," Trey whispered.

Magnus was surprised by the words but certainly not disappointed.

"I shouldn't be," Trey added.

"Why not?" Magnus lightly kneaded the back of Trey's neck, pressed his forehead to Trey's, and waited.

"One night. That was all it was supposed to be."

"Yeah. We surpassed that a long time ago."

They were both breathing harder than they had been, and Magnus knew it was just a matter of time before they ended up in the same place they did whenever they were together. The only reason he hadn't pursued him was that they had more pressing matters to deal with. Namely, finding Ava. And yet, Magnus still wanted this connection he had with Trey. This man was the only one who could settle him, ease some of the pain that was eating at his guts. Even if it was only for a little while, he welcomed that. Needed that.

"There's no reason to keep fightin' this," Magnus whispered.

Trey didn't respond immediately, and for a brief moment, Magnus thought he was going to give in.

Only disappointment reigned supreme when Trey pulled back suddenly, dislodging Magnus's hand.

"Yes, there is," Trey said, his voice low and dangerous. "This is all I have to give."

Before Magnus could argue, Trey was out of the truck.

Knowing better than to push, Magnus took a deep breath, got out of the truck, and headed into the building, leaving Trey to pace the gravel parking lot.

CHAPTER THIRTEEN

REESE SAT AT ONE OF THE EMPTY desks in the barn, a Google search opened in front of him. He'd spent the past hour doing his best to contribute to the search for Ava. He used the information JJ and Baz passed along but had come up with very little on his own.

Although he could tell they were attempting to make him feel as though he was part of the team again, he still felt like he was on the outside looking in. Brantley occupied most of his time with Evan and Slade, the three men discussing what they'd come up with so far and attempting to hash out a plan. Reese caught bits and pieces. Last he'd heard, Slade had offered to pull an all-night stakeout, keeping an eye on the senator's house. It was a good idea, but Reese didn't contribute to the conversation. Last thing he wanted was to overstep, and it was clear the team had fallen into a new pattern of doing things in his absence.

He'd known returning would be a gamble, and integrating himself back into the fold wouldn't be easy. Now it was a matter of proving to Brantley and the team that he was sorry and that this was where he truly belonged.

By the time night fell, Reese felt his energy flagging. He wanted nothing more than to take a shower and get a solid eight hours of sleep. Preferably *not* on anyone's couch.

Problem was, he didn't want to make any assumptions about where he was going to lay his head tonight. Worst case, he could get a motel room down the road, although he preferred to spend the night on Brantley's couch if he had a say in the matter. Not because he expected anything or because he enjoyed the knots and kinks in his neck and shoulders, but because he didn't want to lose the forward progress they'd made. Knowing Brantley, the second Reese left, he'd revert back to hating him.

Again, he didn't want to overstep, so he was waiting the others out so he could talk to Brantley privately.

JJ was the first to give up.

"Y'all, I could do this all night, but I don't think we're gonna get much further," she said, her tone riddled with disappointment.

"I agree," Brantley said, strolling over to the stairs as she was coming down.

"I'm still game to stake out the senator's house," Slade offered.

"I'm with him," Evan chimed in. "We'll take tonight. Someone else can keep watch tomorrow. If we don't find her before then, of course."

Reese respected Evan's optimism.

Brantley looked at Reese. "Thoughts?"

Reese rolled his neck as he got to his feet. He didn't pass up the opportunity to get back into it. "Until we've got somethin' more concrete, it's a good plan. If he knows where she is, chances are he'll leave to check on her at some point."

Brantley nodded, looked at Slade and Evan. "Let me know if something comes up."

"Will do, boss," they said in unison.

"I'll keep searchin' when we get home," JJ offered. "But only if Baz agrees to feed me."

Baz chuckled. "I'm not sure where she puts all the food."

Brantley laughed, and Reese felt better hearing it. Despite the somber atmosphere related to the case, Brantley's mood had improved since Friday night when Reese showed up on his doorstep. He only hoped it would continue for a little while longer.

Reese waited until the others left, then turned to Brantley. "If it's all right with you, I'd like to help with the case until it's closed."

Brantley stared at him, remained silent.

He decided to bite the bullet and said, "I'll get a room up the road. Come back in the mornin'."

"You can stay with me tonight," Brantley said. "It's the least I can do for your help today."

Reese felt as though he'd been mule-kicked in the gut. He didn't want Brantley's charity, but he also didn't want to give the man too much time to think about what had happened between them.

Feigning indifference, Reese started toward the door. "If there's still a couch upstairs, would you mind if I—" A hard hand on his arm drew him up short, had him turning to look at Brantley.

"I don't regret earlier," Brantley said softly, his tone firm. "Doesn't mean anything, though."

Reese ignored the tightness in his chest, told himself he deserved that. "Understood."

Before he could turn around, the hand returned to his arm. This time Brantley gripped him hard, jerked him toward him. Reese stumbled forward then found himself in Brantley's embrace. Strong arms banded around him, his mouth hovering close to Brantley's smooth, warm lips. He dragged in a deep breath, then fused his mouth to Brantley's.

"Fuck, Reese," Brantley groaned softly. "I hate that you do this to me."

Reese wanted him to elaborate, but he wasn't sure his heart could handle Brantley telling him this was nothing more than sex. He knew it was. Of course it was. But he wanted to pretend otherwise for a little while.

He didn't put up a fight when Brantley manhandled him toward the wall, slamming him up against it. He gripped Brantley's shirt, held on tight as their tongues thrashed. When Brantley pulled back and pressed his forehead to Reese's, Reese ignored the emotion churning in his chest. It was the same feeling he'd had for the past six months whenever he thought about never getting to kiss this man again, to touch him. To love him.

"I never could resist you," Brantley said, not sounding thrilled by the acknowledgment.

They swapped air for a moment, both of them breathing hard. Reese still gripped Brantley's shirt, and Brantley's hand was kneading the back of Reese's neck. As far as Reese was concerned, they could remain just like that for the rest of his life. He would be content.

Unfortunately, the moment ended far too soon.

"You hungry?" Brantley asked, releasing him as he took a step back.

"Yeah."

"I'll order pizza."

Reese chuckled. "Or I could cook."

"I'd let you," Brantley said with a smirk, "but it's been a while since I've gone to the grocery store."

Reese knew because he'd made sandwiches earlier. It was like the man had been living off of bread and cold cuts. The rest that was in Brantley's refrigerator left little to be desired.

"How about the diner?" Reese suggested. "My treat."

Brantley held his stare, and Reese could see his indecision. A second later, Brantley nodded. "The diner works."

Reese exhaled as silently as he could, not wanting Brantley to hear his relief, but it was there all the same.

TWENTY MINUTES LATER, BRANTLEY STROLLED INTO THE crowded diner. It wasn't unusual for a Sunday night. Being that it was the only restaurant in town, those who didn't want to venture into neighboring towns or one of the bigger cities surrounding them tended to congregate here.

On the way in, several people greeted them both like they were family. Then again, several of Brantley's family members did appear to be out and about for dinner tonight.

"What can I get you boys?" Rachel asked when she approached.

"I'll have the chicken fried steak, mashed potatoes, and fried okra," Brantley said. "Hold the salad and add peach cobbler for dessert."

Rachel shot him a grin. "So the usual, huh?"

"Yes, ma'am."

She looked at Reese. "And you'll have your usual?"

Brantley noticed the surprise on Reese's face. He'd been gone for so long, he probably thought everyone in town had forgotten him. What he didn't realize was that these people cared about him. Every time Brantley had ventured into town, someone always asked about Reese. It was one of the reasons he'd become reclusive for a while. He'd had a hard enough time not thinking about Reese on his own. Didn't need the help of nosy neighbors.

Reese's shoulders relaxed. "I'll have what he's having."

Rachel beamed a grin as though that was the greatest request she'd ever received.

She glanced between us. "And two sweet teas?"

"Yes, ma'am," Brantley answered.

When she strolled off, Brantley glanced at Reese. "Changin' up the diet, huh?"

"I still eat salads," he said with a smirk. "But it's good to change it up from time to time."

Brantley wondered what else had changed for Reese in the past six months. "I heard you were workin' out of the Sniper 1 Security office when you were in Dallas. Any assignments?"

Reese fiddled with the paper napkin, his gaze on the table. "Mostly busy work. Z wouldn't let me outta his sight."

Yeah, Brantley had heard that, too. "I take it you're up to speed on the cases we worked?"

"I paid attention, sure." Reese looked up. "Look, Brantley—"

"No," Brantley said firmly. "Not right now. I'm not lookin' for more apologies, Reese. You said your piece. Let's move forward."

Granted, Brantley wasn't sure what forward looked like for the two of them yet, but he wanted to take this opportunity to see where things might go.

"At least let me tell you what happened that night," Reese insisted.

Brantley leaned back, regarded him coolly. "I already know."

"Then listen to my side of it, please."

"I said I already know, Reese. JJ hacked into the restaurant's camera feed. I saw exactly what happened."

He'd witnessed Reese and Madison share a hug, sit down to dinner, and then gaze into one another's eyes. They never made it to the meal part because two assholes came in wielding guns, hunting for Maximillian Adorite's sister. That was when Reese had stood between her and a bullet, urging her to safety. A skirmish ensued, Reese got in a few good hits, but then he'd taken a bullet point-blank to the chest.

"It doesn't make up for it, I know," Reese prompted, "but I was confused."

Brantley leaned in, planted his elbows on the table, and pointed a finger in Reese's direction. "I said I—"

Reese reached for his hand, cupping it between both of his. He held firmly, pulling his hand down. "I'm not confused anymore, Brantley. I know exactly what I want."

He couldn't help it; he stared at where his hand was embraced by Reese's. The man had never touched him in public before. Not like this. And certainly not when there were so many people around.

Reese's eyes were serious when he said, "If you want me to stand up and pledge my love for you right now, I'll be happy to." His voice remained steady as he continued. "I love you. That's all there is to it. And my life was so much better with you in it. I'm not in denial any longer."

Brantley continued to stare at their hands as Reese's thumb brushed back and forth along his wrist.

"I know I hurt you, Brantley. I know I fucked up."

Rachel stepped up to the table with their teas, but Reese didn't release his hand—didn't so much as flinch—and Brantley didn't pull away. She didn't say a word, setting down the glasses and disappearing.

"I'm sorry," Reese finally stated, releasing Brantley's hand. "I don't mean to—"

"I'm not complainin'," he interjected. "Let's leave it at that and enjoy our dinner."

Their meal arrived fifteen minutes later, and they made it through with talk about the case. Brantley filled Reese in on the experience he'd had with Magnus over the past six months, keeping everything professional.

"Him and Trey?" Reese pushed his plate away. "Are they a thing?"

"Based on what Trey told me … there's some stuff between them, yeah."

"I don't mean that to be gossipy," Reese said with a chuckle. "Although it sounded like it."

Brantley smiled. He found Reese's slight embarrassment endearing. Then again, he found most everything about him endearing.

"And the team? How are they working out?"

On to safer ground, Brantley answered with, "It was tough in the beginning, but they've found their way. Evan and Slade tend to gravitate toward one another as partners."

"And you? Who're you partnering with?"

Brantley knew Reese was fishing, so he purposely kept his answer vague. "If I need someone, I take whoever's available."

Reese nodded, his gaze shifting back to the table.

"I want you back on the task force," Brantley told him. "As far as the team's concerned, you were just on sabbatical. We've expected you to come back."

Now, that was only mostly true. While the team had anticipated Reese to return, Brantley hadn't expected it. With every week that'd passed, he'd lost more and more hope of anything returning to normal. With Reese here, he wasn't even sure what their new normal would look like.

"Is this a private party? Or can anyone join?" a deep voice bellowed.

Brantley's gaze darted to the end of the table where his cousin Ethan and Ethan's husband, Beau, were standing.

"He's kidding," Ethan said. "We're not here to crash. Just wanted to welcome you back to town since we didn't get to last night."

"Don't y'all have dinner with your folks on Sundays?" Brantley prompted, draping an arm over the back of the booth and regarding his cousin.

"We did." Ethan motioned to the kitchen. "It was Sawyer's night for dessert, and he said he forgot. We ran up here to get a pie."

"Heard you spent the night on Travis's couch," Beau mentioned. "Woke up to some little heads in your face."

Brantley watched Reese interact with the two men Reese used to work with. They chatted for a couple of minutes before Ethan turned his attention to Brantley.

"Rumor has it Magnus is havin' problems. Let him know if he needs anything, we're here."

"I'll tell him," Brantley promised.

"Well, we'll let y'all get back to it; they'll start bitchin' if we're not back soon." Beau winked. "But I ain't leavin' until I force my husband to request extra whipped cream for later."

Brantley chuckled, turning his attention to Reese when the pair sauntered off.

Rachel arrived to deliver their dessert and the check. Brantley used what was left of their time to enjoy Reese's company. It was difficult not to. Despite the anger he harbored and the pain he felt from Reese's betrayal, he knew deep down that this was what he wanted. He just wasn't sure he was ready for it yet.

CHAPTER FOURTEEN

BAZ STARED AT JJ, WHERE SHE SAT cross-legged on the kitchen island, her laptop sitting in front of her. She was leaned over, her fingers flying over the keyboard, lost in thought.

He could've watched her all day, every day. The woman mesmerized him.

"I really wanna know what happened to that girl," JJ mumbled to herself. "You can't hide her forever."

He loved the way she talked to herself or her computer when she worked. It was fascinating to see how her brain processed everything she was dealing with. What was even more adorable was the fact she didn't seem to care who else was around, who might overhear. During their time together, he'd heard a number of things come out of her mouth, some that were questionable in polite company.

She must've sensed him watching because her fingers stopped, her eyes darting up. "What?" She sat up straight. "Did you tell me dinner's ready, and I didn't hear you?"

He laughed softly, turned back to the stove. "Not ready yet."

JJ exhaled heavily. "I know this girl exists, but for the life of me, I can't find her. I've even got her name on the marriage license, so I know she's real."

Baz stirred in the teriyaki sauce with the chicken and vegetables he'd combined. "We're not talkin' about Ava March, are we?"

"No. Her name's Shayla Andrews. She's the underage girl Rivers was with back in the day."

"Maybe she changed her name after they called off the wedding."

"Possible," JJ grumbled. "But you'd think I'd still find her."

"And why are you looking?" he asked, turning off the stove and pulling the sauté pan from the hot burner. He pulled the lid off the five-minute rice JJ favored, checked to ensure it was done.

"I'd like to talk to her. Find out what happened. Thought maybe she could give me an idea of Rivers, what he's capable of."

That was the question they were all seeking an answer to. More specifically, Baz wondered whether or not Harrison Rivers was capable of murder. If so, there was a good chance this search for Ava March would result in a recovery, not a rescue.

After he dished the food on the plates, he motioned for JJ to join him at the dining room table. She hopped down with enthusiasm, singing his praises. Baz got the feeling JJ was happier with the fact that he cooked for her rather than what it was he made. He knew if he left it to her, she would eat packaged donuts or canned soup before making an effort on something with more nutrients.

"Take a breather," he insisted. "Want some wine?"

"Not tonight, but thanks. I need to keep a clear head."

"Water? Or tea?"

"Water's fine."

While she sat, he got two glasses, filled them with ice, added water. When he returned to the table, he found she was waiting for him. He loved that she didn't dig in, preferring to share a meal with him.

It was the little things, he realized. And there were so many little things he'd learned about JJ over the past six months. Ever since the truth had come out about Molly and the baby not being his, things between him and JJ had progressed. So much so he was already thinking about the next steps for them. Of course, he kept those thoughts to himself because he knew better than to push her. The last time he did, back when he'd invited her to Thanksgiving dinner with his folks, he'd caused the implosion of their relationship. He wasn't willing to risk that again.

"What's on your mind, Detective?" she asked, her eyes dancing with amusement. "You said to take a breather."

He liked the fact she now used the detective moniker as a nickname rather than a way for her to keep him at arm's length.

"I am." He picked up his fork. "Swear it."

"Well, if you don't have anything pressing, I might have some news," she said smoothly.

"News?" he prompted when it was clear she wanted him to. She nodded.

"Does this have anything to do with you and Bristol conspiring last night?"

Her grin widened. "Maybe."

"What're you two cookin' up?"

JJ took a bite, chewed. "Bristol might've mentioned she's gonna put her house on the market."

Baz set down his fork, picked up his water. "And what's that mean for you?"

Her cheeks turned a fascinating shade of rose, her smile disappearing. "I might've mentioned I'd be in the market for a house in the near future."

Suddenly the few bites he'd managed sat heavily in his gut.

JJ was watching him intently. "Maybe I should amend that." Her grin returned, slow and wicked. "I told her that *we'd* be in the market for a house in the near future."

"We?" He refrained from feeling hope. With JJ, he'd long ago learned to take things slow.

"Yep. You know, me and a certain sexy detective."

"We're in the market for a house?" he asked, keeping his tone cool.

"We are."

He couldn't hold back the smile any longer. "And she has one?"

"It's the house she grew up in. When she moved in with Kaden and Keegan, they kept the house. She's been sitting on it for a little while but told me she'd be willing to part with it if she found the right buyers." JJ held her fork up, wiggled it. "It needs work."

"You saw it?"

"No. She told me. I wanted to wait to see if you'd even be interested."

Baz was back to holding his breath.

JJ's eyes narrowed. "Are you not interested?"

"Oh, I'm interested," he relayed gruffly. "You know me. I'm just takin' baby steps here."

JJ laughed, the sound something he'd gotten used to hearing lately.

"Well, this is not a baby step. It's a major leap into a vast ocean." She pinned him with a million-megawatt grin. "You interested in takin' a dip with me, Detective?"

"JJ," he growled roughly.

"Hmm?"

"Are you sayin' what I think you're sayin?"

"That I want to move in with you?" She giggled. "I think we're past that point, don't you?"

"That you wanna buy a house with me?" he clarified.

"Oh, good. I thought for a second you weren't processin'——"

He cut her off when he launched to his feet. Baz grabbed her up, spun her around, and crushed his mouth to hers as he guided her toward his bedroom. She giggled as she walked backward, her arms wreathing his neck.

JJ's laughter echoed around them, cut off abruptly when he tossed her onto the bed, followed her down.

"The house is gonna need some work," she mumbled against his mouth.

"I'm not scared of work." He yanked her T-shirt over her head, tossed it to the floor.

JJ unhooked her bra, pulled it off. "Lots of work. Like a total gut job."

"I don't mind gettin' my hands dirty." He yanked on the button of her jeans, dragged down the zipper.

JJ lifted her hips, letting him strip her pants down her legs.

"It would mean no more days off for a while," she continued, tugging at his shirt when he shifted over her beautiful naked body.

"I'm sure I can suffer through," he said, nuzzling her neck when she dipped her hands into the waistband of his shorts. He groaned softly when she cupped his ass, pulled him closer.

"Gonna have to get those shorts off," she rasped.

Baz ground his hips to hers, let her feel the hard ridge of his cock against her delicate flesh.

"Now, Baz," she snapped.

With her help, his shorts disappeared, and a short breath or two later, he was sinking into her silky, wet heat. Baz growled low in his throat as her pussy enveloped him, the smooth walls stroking along his shaft. He shuddered from the exquisite sensation.

"God, you're tight," he moaned against her mouth. "So fucking tight."

He groaned again when she tightened those inner muscles, clamping down on his throbbing cock.

When he pressed in deep, rocking his hips to hers, she reciprocated with a guttural mewl that went right to his head.

"Fuck me, Baz," she demanded, her nails clawing at his back as she fought for control beneath him.

He retreated slowly, smiled down at her, then rammed in deep.

JJ cried out, her head tipping back, her beautiful breasts thrusting upward as she begged and pleaded, unashamed to voice exactly what she wanted from him.

He fucked her then. Hard and deep, giving her everything she begged for and more. She was wild beneath him, rolling her body, meeting him thrust for thrust. And when he lifted up, they both watched as his cock sank deep inside her again and again.

"More," she demanded.

Baz gave her more, sliding his arms under her knees and bending her in half, drilling down into her with the force of every emotion building inside him. He loved this woman with a passion that defied rationality. He'd been captivated since the first day he met her and found himself so far gone that he knew he would never survive this life without her.

"Tell me you love me," she urged, cupping his face as he stared down at her.

"I love you," he ground out, reaching the pinnacle and holding on as he fucked her harder, faster, deeper.

"Baz!" JJ's inner muscles locked down on him. "Oh, God ... I'm... Please..."

"Tell me," he insisted, holding back just enough to keep her from tipping headlong into ecstasy.

"I love you!" she shouted.

He drilled into her once, twice...

"Tell me again, JJ."

Before she could get the words out, he drove in deep, sending her careening along with him.

"I. Love. You!" she screamed, her back arching as she came.

Baz's release slammed into him at the same time those precious words did.

AFTER THAT INTENSE BOUT OF LOVEMAKING, JJ opted for a quick shower. When she was finished, she joined Baz in the living room. He had transferred the chicken stir-fry to bowls, reheated it in the microwave, and joined her on the sofa.

While she continued her search on the computer, he fed them both.

"Tell me about this house."

She glanced over at him. She could see the interest in his gaze, and her heart felt lighter. She hadn't been sure whether now was the right time to bring it up, but she was glad she had.

"I told Bristol we'd be interested," she admitted.

"Did you?" His intense blue eyes glittered with amusement. "Without talking to me?"

"I kinda thought I knew what your answer would be. Is that okay?"

"It's more than okay."

JJ exhaled her relief. Although she was all in when it came to Baz, more than willing to take things to the next level now that she'd been given a second chance with him, it wasn't easy for her. All too often, she wanted to fall back on old habits, putting up walls to protect herself from the hurt and pain she knew came with relationships. Each time she did, she reminded herself that they'd been through so much already, and somehow they'd toughed it out. Moving forward seemed the best option for them. And while she was still battling her own demons, JJ was making an effort to put Baz first. It only seemed fair considering he'd been putting her first all along.

"She said it's a two-bedroom, one-bath."

"Small."

"Yes, but…" She held his gaze. "She said the lot's big enough we could add on some square footage. I figured maybe enough to make it a three-bedroom, two-bath."

"Sounds reasonable."

"I've got the money," she blurted. "I mean, I got the settlement for my house, and I can sell the lot. It's not worth much, but—"

"Money's no object, JJ. You know that."

Oh, she did. JJ knew that Baz came from money. His mother and father were both sitting high on the hog, and based on this apartment alone, JJ knew Baz wasn't hurting either. He didn't make much working for the task force, nor had he when he was with APD. Certainly not enough to afford these digs. However, JJ wanted them to do this on their own. She didn't want to rely on handouts from anyone. She'd spent her entire life taking care of herself, and she wasn't about to let anyone start now.

"When can we look at it?" he prompted.

"She said to get the keys anytime."

He seemed to consider that. "Maybe we can stop by and check it out tomorrow."

"I'll text Bristol in the morning." Since Brantley lived next door to Kaden and Keegan's ranch, it would be the work of a minute to drive over and grab the keys.

"JJ?"

She met his gaze again. "Hmm?"

"I love you."

Every time he said the words, she felt them deep in her soul. More importantly, she found she wanted to say them back because she loved the way his eyes lit up when she did.

"I love you, too, Detective."

CHAPTER FIFTEEN

REESE FIGURED HE COULD CONSIDER TONIGHT A success.

Dinner, at least.

They'd made it through without a knock-down, drag-out, so that was a good thing.

Granted, he'd been hoping for a chance to talk to Brantley about what happened, to tell him exactly what went down between him and Madison, and his reasons for doing so. It didn't surprise him that Brantley wasn't eager to engage in a conversation that might involve emotions or the chance to pick at recently gaping wounds. Didn't mean they shouldn't do it. Reese knew they couldn't move forward until they did.

Of course, the option of moving forward might be little more than a pipe dream. Brantley had told him that what transpired between them earlier didn't mean anything. Before he'd come along, Reese knew that Brantley saw sex as little more than a means to an end. That had never been the case for Reese, but he was shoving that down, reminding himself he'd created this mess all on his own.

"Would you mind if I shower?" Reese prompted when they walked into Brantley's house. "I can use the guest bath."

"You can use mine," Brantley told him, not bothering to look his way as he headed for the fridge, snagging a beer.

"Thanks."

Figuring it was better to let sleeping dogs lie for a bit, he went to Brantley's room, headed for the closet. Brantley hadn't put Reese's clothes back on hangers, but he hadn't packed them up either. Reese grabbed a T-shirt from the pile, pulled a pair of shorts out of the dresser, then headed for the bathroom.

A million memories returned when he stepped inside, turned on the light. They'd indulged so many times right here in this very space. Reese recalled every single moment, every breath he took, every moan that had escaped during those passionate encounters. He ignored the knot in his stomach that he got every time he thought about what he'd lost because of his own insecurities.

He should be grateful Brantley hadn't kicked his ass to the curb already. Perhaps he was gearing up to do that in the near future, but for now, Reese had a chance to redeem himself.

Well, not right now. He would save his confessions and apologies for tomorrow after they'd had a chance to sleep.

Reese got through the shower in record time, only a little disappointed that Brantley hadn't joined him. He finished up by brushing his teeth with his toothbrush, which was still in the holder on the counter. He stared at it for a moment, wondering why Brantley had kept it. He wasn't sure he could've done the same if their roles had been reversed.

When he came out of the bathroom, Brantley was standing at the back door, staring out into the night. The door was partially opened, Tesha sniffing around the yard.

Before Reese could say anything, Brantley spoke. "I hate you for what you did."

You know that painful moment when you take the plunge into icy water and it steals your breath and makes your body hurt? Or that moment when a bullet pierces your chest and the fires of hell sear every nerve ending? This was so much worse than that.

"I know." Reese exhaled heavily. "Not as much as I hate myself for it."

Brantley continued to stare out the door. "I thought nothing could be worse than the day that building came down on top of me. I knew that my career was over, my life irrevocably changed." He glanced back at Reese, his eyes spitting fire. "It didn't hold a candle to the pain I felt when you went to her that night."

Reese swallowed past the lump in his throat. "I didn't—" He stopped himself. "I know."

Brantley spun around then. "You *don't* know, Reese! You don't fucking know." His eyes glittered with what looked like unshed tears. "It fucking gutted me when I found out you were with her. I trusted you. I trusted you to fucking talk to me."

Reese inhaled, and it felt like shards of glass were rattling around in his lungs, nicking him at every turn.

"I fucking loved you!" Brantley exclaimed.

Ah, hell. Those shards turned into sharp, jagged blades slicing him open from the inside. Hearing that word in the past tense shredded him.

Brantley dragged in a ragged breath, then shoved out an exhale. "I'll see you in the morning."

Reese stared as Brantley stormed past him, through the living room, and down the hall.

He didn't dare go after him. The last thing he wanted was to push Brantley past his breaking point. It was clear he was hovering on the brink, so it was best to keep his distance.

With his heart shattered in pieces and a physical ache gnawing through his insides, Reese closed the sliding door, ensured the dog door was open so Tesha could come back in when she was ready, then headed upstairs. He went to the office they'd designed for him shortly before things fell apart. Like the toothbrush, he was surprised to see everything was the same, right down to the notepad sitting on the desktop, covered—like everything else—in a fine layer of dust. He walked over, glanced at the writing. It was his own. Notes about the case they'd been working on right before they left for the training session in Dallas.

Right before Reese had single-handedly brought it all down.

He dropped into the chair, leaned back, and closed his eyes.

His chest was tight, but not from the bullet wound that had pained him for so long. No, this was emotion clogging his insides. The same emotion he'd been battling for months. He should've come back as soon as they'd let him out of the hospital. He should've explained himself to Brantley, admitted he was at fault, begged for forgiveness. He probably would've received it.

Instead, he'd opted to work on himself, to piece himself back together. While his body had been on the mend, his heart slowly broke down, torn apart by his own actions.

He opened his eyes, stared out the door to the open door across the way.

Getting to his feet, he headed over to Brantley's office. The desk lamp was on, the laptop no longer sitting on the top, another layer of dust coating the top of everything. It looked as though Brantley hadn't used this space in a while. Probably spent most of his time in the barn with the rest of the team.

He peered down at the black leather sofa, remembered the time Brantley had fucked him right there. Hell, there weren't many places in this house that he could look that wouldn't offer a reminder of an intimate moment they'd shared.

The grief of losing the best thing he'd ever known resurfaced, had his knees going weak. He sat down on the couch, yanked his shirt off, tossed it to the floor, and then stretched out his legs. For some strange reason, he felt closer to Brantley here in this room.

With those memories filling his mind, he closed his eyes and drifted off.

Brantley couldn't sleep.

He tossed and turned, his mind running a million miles a second.

He should've been thinking about the case, about finding the missing woman, but the only thing he could focus on was the fact that Reese was in the house with him. It took effort not to go searching for him, to take the solace he knew Reese was willing to give. Brantley craved it, needed it more than the air he breathed.

But as much as he wanted Reese, as desperate as he was to find his way back to him, Brantley wasn't sure he could commit. And fucking for the sake of fucking wasn't something he was willing to indulge in with Reese. For some fucked up reason, Brantley didn't want to hurt him that way. He didn't want to lead him on or pretend that everything was all right. What'd happened earlier never should've happened. Brantley had taken advantage, and for that, he was disappointed in himself.

So he remained where he was, staring up at the dark ceiling, listening to the silence of the house. He heard the flap of the dog door. A minute later, he felt a soft shift on the bed, knew Tesha had hopped up there to join him. She curled into a ball at the end of the bed, exactly as she'd done every night since Reese left.

When she started to snore softly, Brantley let the sound lull him to sleep.

A sharp bark sounded, dragging Brantley from his dreams. He opened his eyes, stared around, realized he'd already reached for his gun but hadn't grabbed it.

With his hand hovering over the grip, he listened for noise to signal something was wrong, heard nothing.

Tesha huffed a bark, her attention on the open bedroom door.

"What is it, girl?"

She answered with a soft whimper.

Brantley forced his feet to the floor, stood upright. He left the gun on the nightstand and sauntered to the hallway. The lights in the living room and kitchen had been turned off—Reese, no doubt—so he moved in the dark.

"Let me out!" The shout came from upstairs.

Without hesitation, Brantley bounded up the stairs, taking them three at a time. His body was primed for a fight, adrenaline flooding his bloodstream.

Once at the top, he heard rough breathing, followed by a garbled moan.

"Let me out!"

Brantley found Reese thrashing on the couch in his office, his arms flailing as though he was fighting his way out of something.

"Reese," Brantley said firmly, refraining from rushing to his side. He knew the effects of those night terrors all too well, and he had no desire to put himself in striking distance.

Reese punched and kicked as though fighting someone off.

"Reese," he barked harshly. "Wake up, Reese. You're safe."

Reese went stone still, his eyes still closed, his chest heaving.

"Reese?"

Those eyes opened slowly, head swiveling on the arm of the couch as he scanned the room. There was still terror in the golden orbs, but it faded away almost instantly when their gazes met.

"You're safe," Brantley repeated, unable to resist moving toward him now that he was awake.

He stared down at Reese for a moment, considered his next move, then said fuck it. He perched on the edge of the cushion near Reese's hip, laid his hand on Reese's chest. His skin was clammy, his heart pounding.

Brantley's gaze snagged on the scar on his chest and he sucked in air. He remembered the first time he watched the video that had captured Reese being shot. Nothing in his life had ever caused such a painful, gut-wrenching feeling. Seeing that bullet pierce Reese's chest … the thought that he could've lost him that very instant … it was still too difficult to think about.

Reese stared at him, his eyes hard, his breaths still coming fast and shallow.

"Where were you?" Brantley dared to ask, curious as to what nightmare he'd just relived.

"In that shithole," Reese rasped, not moving a muscle. "Locked in that fucking shithole."

Brantley knew what Reese was referring to, even if he didn't know the specifics. Over the past six months, he'd done his homework and learned a few tidbits about Reese that the man had never shared.

"You want to talk about it?"

Reese didn't move, didn't blink. "Not really, no."

Brantley understood all too well the ghosts that haunted a man. He knew because he had his own, had been battling the night terrors brought on from the night his world had come crumbling down on top of him.

Tesha appeared, creeping into the room slowly as though assessing whether the danger was real. Brantley reached for her, patting her head, assuring her she was also safe. She moved closer, pressed her nose to Reese's arm.

"It's all right, girl," Reese whispered.

Seemingly content, Tesha turned and strolled out of the room. Brantley heard her huff when she flopped down on the floor just outside the door.

Brantley began to pull his hand away from Reese's chest but stopped when Reese placed a firm hand over his.

"Please don't go."

"This couch ain't big enough for both of us."

Reese's hand moved off his as though Brantley had rejected him outright. He should have, he knew. It would've been the smart thing to do. Then again, Brantley'd never been smart when it came to Reese. He'd been all in from the jump, common sense be damned.

"Brantley...?"

He held that familiar stare, felt his heart kick into high gear. Every emotion he'd battled these past months hit him with a vengeance. Pain, anger ... but most importantly, longing. He'd missed Reese fiercely, and wondering where he was, who he was with had gutted him on more than one occasion. He no longer had to wonder because Reese was here. Right here.

Reese sat up.

Brantley didn't move.

Reese touched his face, his fingers sliding along his jaw.

Brantley held his breath.

"If we do this..." Brantley wasn't even sure what warning he wanted to relay or who exactly he was speaking to.

Reese's hand slid to the back of his neck, a firm weight that soothed something deep in his soul.

"Jesus fuck," Brantley rasped roughly, leaning in and pressing his mouth to Reese's.

For a few seconds, they remained like that, trading air, chests heaving as those emotions began warring once more. Their lips brushed once, twice, then Brantley bit Reese's bottom lip gently.

"I need you," Reese whispered.

"I don't want you to *need* me, Reese," he countered.

"I *love* you," Reese clarified, his voice sandpaper rough.

Ah, hell. He was so fucking screwed.

Brantley slammed his mouth over Reese's, shifted so that he could move over him, forcing him back roughly. He took Reese down to the couch, settled his weight over him, and soaked up the sensation of those calloused hands as they roamed over his naked back while he fucked Reese's mouth with his tongue and swallowed the deep groans that came from Reese's chest.

He'd ached for this, for Reese's hands on him, his mouth. He'd woken up too many times to count, expecting Reese to be at his side so he could slide into him, seek comfort in his arms. He hadn't been there. And night after night, his hope for Reese to come back had dwindled until it had been replaced with a deep-seated fury.

With Reese here, Brantley couldn't control himself, grinding his aching cock against Reese's, dry-humping the man like a goddamn teenager. He'd missed this so fucking much. His breaths sawed in and out of his lungs as he sought the friction that would provide only a fraction of relief. It would be enough, he told himself. It had to be.

"Fuck … Brantley … it's been too long."

Brantley lifted his head, stared down at Reese. He held that tormented stare even when he shoved his hand between them, snaked beneath the cotton of Reese's shorts, and found the hot, hard length of Reese's cock. Reese did the same, shoving Brantley's shorts down his hips, gripping his steely erection. Their fists bumped as they jerked each other, a jarring attempt to slake the lust. Desperate for skin-to-skin contact, Brantley batted Reese's hand away, gripped both their cocks, and stroked, never looking away from Reese.

"When's the last time you came?"

"When you made me," Reese drawled roughly.

Brantley knew his eyes were wide with shock. If that admission had come from any other man, he wouldn't have believed it. But Reese was exactly the type of person who would've punished himself by practicing abstinence in the most punishable form because the last time they'd had sex had been before the trip to Dallas.

"Fuck…" Reese hissed. "Brantley … oh, fuck … oh, fuck…"

Brantley jerked their cocks roughly, determined to make Reese come if it was the last goddamn thing he did.

Reese's hips began to buck, his cock thrusting into Brantley's fist, gliding against his own dick.

"I can't stop," Reese groaned. "Oh, fuck … Brantley!"

Reese's cock jerked in his fist as cum shot onto their naked chests. Brantley couldn't hold back, growling roughly as he followed him right over.

CHAPTER SIXTEEN

TREY SAT ON THE EDGE OF MAGNUS'S living room sofa, elbows on his knees, head in his hands.

He'd spent the better part of the last two hours with Magnus, helping him with the dogs while Gia and her husband, Randy, went home to get some rest. Magnus had called in a couple of people to keep watch on the dogs tonight, telling Trey he wanted to be available in the event they found Ava. The man was convinced they would.

Trey wished he could be as optimistic. He'd spent the past year and a half of his life working these cases, hating it more and more with every passing minute. It wasn't that he felt he wasn't making a contribution, because he was. He did have the highest close rate of the team when it came to the cold cases they were working. What they didn't realize when they were patting him on the back and offering high fives to celebrate another accomplishment was that Trey was slowly dying inside.

He hated the task force.

Hated it with a ferocity that bordered on crazy.

Trey had no idea how people could do this. How they could be expected to live a relatively normal life when there was someone else's life that could precariously hang in the balance while Trey was having dinner or taking a shower or, heaven forbid, having a beer at the bar. His brain told him he needed to be focused and working at all times, that someone needed him while his body begged and pleaded for him to take a breather.

If he didn't work for his brother, if he didn't worry Brantley would think he was a pussy, Trey would've quit a long time ago. Instead, he found himself in the same predicament once again, feeling guilty because he was sitting down while someone else might need his vigilance.

"Why don't you sleep in my bed? I'll take the couch," Magnus said, his voice little more than a hoarse, withering growl. It was obvious exhaustion was settling in.

Trey lifted his head, stared at Magnus. "I can't do that."

He didn't want to ogle the man's bare chest or admire his abdomen's lean muscles, that deep V that dipped into the waistband of the shorts he'd changed into. Unfortunately, want had gone out the window a long fucking time ago.

They remained like that for too many heartbeats to count, Magnus standing there looking sinfully delicious, Trey keeping himself in check by ensuring his ass remained planted on the cushion.

"Trey."

He forced his gaze upward, met Magnus's eyes. The stare captivated, distracted him enough he didn't realize Magnus had just shoved his shorts down his hips, letting them pool at his feet. The moment it registered, he looked down, drew in a shuddering breath when he saw Magnus's cock bobbing proudly out from his body. His mouth watered; his fingers itched. He wanted to taste and touch in equal measure, wanted to fondle and tease until neither of them knew their own name.

Magnus moved first, closing the small distance between them as he skirted the coffee table, pushing it back with his legs, then stopped directly in front of Trey.

Driven purely by his hunger for this man, Trey reached for him, settling his hands on Magnus's hips as he stared up into those gorgeous hazel eyes. Content Magnus was watching him, Trey lowered his head, pressed his lips to Magnus's stomach. He felt the muscles tense beneath his ministrations. He kneaded Magnus's hips lightly as he dragged his lips and tongue over the smooth expanse of his stomach, following the hard lines of his abs, memorizing every inch of him.

He shifted one hand over Magnus's steely erection, pressing it flat to his stomach, and licked the tip every so often while he continued to kiss.

Magnus's hands curled around Trey's head, his fingers linking into Trey's hair and tugging lightly. His hair had grown out in the past year, and every time he thought to cut it, he recalled how Magnus's fingers felt tugging on it. It bordered on too long now, and his family had started giving him shit, but Trey didn't care.

Trey dragged his tongue over the swollen head of Magnus's dick, teased the crest, then kissed his stomach again. He alternated like that for long minutes, spurred by Magnus's deep, ragged breaths.

"Oh, fuck me," Magnus groaned when Trey sucked the head between his lips. "Oh, fuck, Trey."

Magnus's fingers dragged through Trey's hair, down his back, urging him closer. Trey let him lead, taking Magnus in his mouth, dipping his head down to suck the entire length along the flat of his tongue. He lifted his head, lowered it again, all the while Magnus rocked toward him.

"Oh, God, Trey … it feels … your mouth feels so good."

He worshipped Magnus's cock, content to be right here in this moment, needing it for as long as it would last. He wanted to banish all other thoughts from his head, to forget the reason he was here in the first place.

"Trey … keep it up, I'm gonna come in your mouth," Magnus grunted, his hand fisting in Trey's hair.

Trey took him to the back of his throat, drew on him harder as he lifted his head. He was on a mission, one that involved making this man cry out his name when the pleasure consumed him. Over and over, he worked him until Magnus was thrusting his hips forward, fucking Trey's face in an attempt to reach that razor-sharp edge that would signify he was seconds from that satisfying freefall.

"Trey!" Magnus's shout echoed in the space as his cock pulsed violently in Trey's mouth, splashing his throat as he sucked him dry.

When he pulled back, he stared up at Magnus, saw the gleam in his eyes, the satisfaction, and he knew it was futile to try to resist this man. He'd been doing it for so long it had become second nature, but he was tired of fighting it.

So fucking tired.

WHEN TREY LIFTED HIS HEAD, MET HIS gaze, Magnus held still, praying Trey wasn't about to put distance between them. It was what he did. Every time they made progress, every time they succumbed to the desire that tethered their souls, Trey would always push him away.

"Don't make me sleep alone," Magnus whispered.

Trey didn't look away, those steel-blue eyes glittering when he said, "Take me to your bed."

Magnus didn't hesitate, reaching for Trey's hand, gripping his palm, and urging him to his feet. Trey padded behind him down the hall as Magnus flipped off the lights.

He shoved down the guilt that came from knowing he was about to get fucked while Ava was God only knows where. He should've been focused on her, but there was an ache deep inside him that only this man could ease. An ache brought on by a plethora of emotions that churned. Lust, need, and bone-chilling fear. He couldn't separate them, didn't know which was more prominent, which was the very reason he needed this man to comfort him for a little while, to provide a flicker of light in the never-ending darkness.

When Magnus reached for the light switch in the bedroom, Trey grumbled, "Leave it on."

Magnus lowered his hand then let Trey lead the way to the bed. A moment later, he was on his back while Trey was discarding his clothes. He watched in awe, just like he always did, then welcomed the man with open arms.

Trey crawled over him, sighed when Magnus reached for him, sliding his hands over all that warm, velvet-smooth skin.

"I can't fight this anymore," Trey mumbled against his mouth. "I don't want to."

Hope sparked in his chest when Trey's mouth settled over his in a kiss fueled by something they'd been fighting all this time.

"I need you, Magnus," Trey moaned softly, pressing his hips down, his cock thick and hard between them.

"You've got me," he answered, palming the back of Trey's head, letting their tongues do the communicating for the next few minutes.

They were both panting when they came up for air.

Trey lifted his head, stared down at him, and Magnus saw it. That beautiful spark he'd been desperate to see signifying Trey's surrender.

"Love me, Trey," he rasped, never breaking eye contact.

Something flashed hot then winked out almost instantly, as though a curtain had been drawn.

Magnus spread his legs wider, urging Trey to take what he was willing to give.

"Right here," Magnus told him. "Right now."

Trey sat back on his haunches, and Magnus saw the indecision as it flitted across his ridiculously handsome face. As usual, he was overthinking.

"Love. Me," Magnus demanded.

Trey hissed, then jerked as though he'd been yanked from a glorious dream. He turned, reached toward the nightstand.

Magnus's breaths became heavier as he watched the muscles in Trey's body shift and bunch. He twisted back, the bottle of lube in his hand. Magnus had set it out because he'd been praying they would end up here.

His lungs worked overtime as his body prepared for the sensual assault. He watched as Trey slicked his cock, every muscle standing out in stark relief as he stroked it, lubricating it in preparation for what was to come.

When Trey turned again, Magnus reached out, halted him with a hand on his arm, stopping him from reaching the condom.

"We don't need it."

Trey's eyes flashed again.

"I haven't been with anyone but you," Magnus told him. "And I'm clean. Got the results to prove it if you want them."

Trey's nostrils flared, his eyes darkening.

"I trust you, Trey. You can trust me, too." He tugged Trey's arm, urging him closer. "No more barriers."

Trey huffed a harsh breath, then slammed his mouth on Magnus's. He swallowed Trey's ragged groan as he shifted his hips, providing the angle Trey needed to push deep inside him.

"Ah, fuck, yes," Magnus moaned, his head falling back as Trey's cock sank to the hilt inside him.

Trey pumped his hips once, twice, then paused. He sat up, grabbed a pillow, and shoved it under Magnus's hips. The entire time, Magnus watched, not wanting to miss a second of this. Trey was surrendering; of that, he had no doubt. And it was a glorious thing.

The next thing he knew, Magnus's legs were draped over Trey's shoulders as Trey bent him in half and drove down into him.

Magnus gritted his teeth as pleasure consumed him. Every cell in his body sparked as Trey fucked him hard, ramming his hips forward, pulling them back. Again and again, he impaled Magnus, their eyes locked. There were no words, but the conversation that took place was life-altering.

Trey grunted with every thrust, driving them both to that elusive pinnacle.

Magnus gripped Trey's biceps, held himself still, and gladly accepted the sensual assault.

"Magnus…"

He fucking loved when Trey said his name during sex. Fucking loved it.

"Jesus, Magnus." He breathed harshly, fucking him harder, deeper.

"Come inside me," Magnus pleaded. "Come for me, Trey."

Trey shouted his name, his hips driving forward brutally hard. He stilled inside him, then Magnus felt that wicked pulse of his cock as he came. His own cock spurted despite being drained from their earlier encounter.

Half an hour later, Magnus was draped over Trey's naked body. They had cleaned up then returned to the bed. If they were lucky, they'd get a few hours of sleep before dawn broke and the new day started.

"Do you think I should get a haircut?" Trey asked, his voice whisper soft.

Magnus turned his head, peered up at Trey in the darkness. He chuckled softly. "No. I happen to be fond of it."

"Okay."

With that, they drifted off, holding one another.

CHAPTER SEVENTEEN

Monday, March 14, 2022

REESE STRETCHED HIS LEGS AS FAR OUT as he could, shifted to get more comfortable.

They'd been sitting in Brantley's truck for the better part of two hours now and still had endless more to go. When Brantley had volunteered to stake out the senator's house tonight, Reese had invited himself to come along.

"Move the seat back," Brantley grumbled, a pair of binoculars pressed to his eyes as he stalked the senator from their spot a few houses down.

"Already did." Sometimes it didn't pay to be so fucking tall.

He forced himself to relax, glancing down the dark street. This was an up-and-coming neighborhood with cookie-cutter houses that had benefited from the last economic boom, taking a middle-class neighborhood and converting it into a prime spot for wealthy Austinites.

To be fair, Reese had expected something a bit more glamorous for a senator, but JJ had kindly informed him that government officials don't make all that much money. What Harrison Rivers did have came more from the family coffers than from his biweekly paycheck, and it didn't appear the family was all that keen on bankrolling him.

They sat for a few more minutes in silence. Brantley kept an eye on the house as though he was getting paid for every second he peered through the binoculars. Reese figured it was an avoidance technique, something to make him look busy so Reese didn't bring up the uncomfortable subject he'd attempted to broach at dinner last night.

"Brantley, we need to talk about this," Reese finally said.

"About what?"

"About ... what happened that night."

Brantley lowered the field glasses, set them on the dashboard, and fell back in his seat with a huff. Reese was almost certain he'd seen one of Brantley's nieces do the very same thing when they were told to go to a time-out. Had they learned it from Brantley? Or vice versa?

"Can you at least listen?" Reese prompted, staring at the back of Brantley's head because he refused to look his way.

"If it'll get you to shut up about it," Brantley grumbled.

Reese took a deep breath, blew it out slowly. "It doesn't make it any better, but I want you to know I didn't reach out to Madison first. She texted me."

He noticed Brantley's shoulders stiffen.

"It was right after we started working for Sniper 1, and since her brother's married to a Kogan, she caught wind of it. I've got the text thread if you want to see it."

No response.

"It's mundane bullshit. I didn't always respond." Reese turned his attention to the front windshield so he could center himself. "I did, however, agree to meet up with her. I told myself it was because she needed closure or because I did, but that was a lie. I needed ... something. Validation, I guess. Things between you and me ... they were good. Too good. I thought for sure something was going to go wrong."

"So you sabotaged us?"

He peered over, saw Brantley was still looking the other way.

"Not purposely, no, although it would seem that way." He exhaled heavily. "I was trying to make sense of it all. My feelings for you, how they came on so fast. I couldn't rationalize how I'd gone from never having considered a man attractive to falling in love with you. I still don't look at men like that. There is only one."

"But you find women attractive?"

"To a degree, sure," he admitted. "But it's not the same. Not anymore. No one has captured my attention the way you do." He ensured he maintained present tense, wanting Brantley to know he still saw a future for them. "When Madison texted me, I thought if I talked to her, it might make sense. I might be able to figure out how I'd gone from proposing to her years ago to wanting to spend the rest of my life with you."

Brantley's head rolled along the back of the seat as he turned toward Reese. "Did it help?"

Reese looked away. "That night, when I pulled into the parking lot, I knew it was wrong. The only place I wanted to be was with you, but I didn't want to stand her up. I decided I was going to tell her the truth. I figured admitting it aloud might help."

"From what I saw on the recording, she didn't look all that surprised. I take it you didn't tell her."

Reese swallowed the hard lump in his throat. "I didn't get a chance. When she mentioned our past, I realized she'd altered it to fit the present. She'd rewritten history because it was easier. I don't know why; I don't know what's going on in her life that made her feel the need to seek the comforts of the past. I corrected her, and I think the blinders fell away. She assumed I'd met a woman. I didn't get a chance to tell her you were the one who turned my world upside down and set me on a new path. I wanted to." He peered at Brantley. "But I was terrified."

Brantley continued to stare at him, so Reese forged ahead. "About that time, the two guys came in. My only thought was to get her out of there."

"She got," Brantley muttered harshly. "Left you for dead."

Reese understood the frustration because he'd dealt with it, too. "If she'd come back, they would've taken her, Brantley. And I would've still been shot. Or worse, dead because I would never let that happen."

The silence in the truck was so loud Reese battled the urge to get out.

"I haven't talked to her since. I blocked her number, so I don't even know if she's attempted." Reese tried to relax, couldn't. "I told RT to get a message to her. To let her know I was fine but that I'd moved on with my life."

"So that's what you did for the past six months? You moved on?"

"Not from what matters, no. I focused on healing and getting my shit together. You deserve more than what I was giving you, Brantley. You had my whole heart, but I was still terrified of what that meant."

"A lot of self-reflection?"

Reese looked at him, met his stare. "I went to counseling while I was up there. Z insisted. I worked through the trauma of getting shot, and I finally admitted that I was not the same man I was before I met you."

"You didn't deal with the other trauma."

It wasn't a question, but Reese responded anyway. "I can deal with only so much at a time, so I didn't bring it up, no." He ensured Brantley was looking at him when he added, "But I'm willing to tell you if you want to hear it."

Neither of them spoke for a few heartbeats.

"You would, wouldn't you?" Brantley frowned. "Tell me, I mean."

Reese nodded. "I love you. I've never been confused about that, but now I'm comfortable with it."

Brantley looked away again. "Then why were you comin' to pack your shit?"

"Because I thought that's what you wanted. I fucked this up; I know I did. I should've come back a long time ago. Probably would have the day Z told me you left. I'd been confined to that hospital bed, but I'd done my damnedest to get out of it." He sighed. "I'm no match for Z, by the way. Especially not when I'd been sliced open the day before. They told me that's why I ended up back in ICU."

Brantley's head snapped over, and he frowned. "What?"

"I was back in the ICU for several days after that. They said I went from stable to critical. I don't remember much of anything."

"I had no idea," Brantley muttered under his breath. "No one told me."

Reese figured that had been the case. Or rather, he had hoped, because the thought of Brantley not coming when Reese had been back at death's door had been too difficult for him to process.

"I would've been there," Brantley insisted.

"I know."

More silence ensued, but before Reese could bring up where they would go from there, the senator's garage door opened. A moment later, his car was backing out, and their night was taking a very different turn.

"LET'S SEE WHERE THIS MOTHERFUCKER IS GOING," Brantley grunted, starting the truck.

He waited for Harrison Rivers to get a couple of houses down before he pulled away from the curb, another couple before he turned on his headlights and began following at a discreet distance.

It was possible the bastard was making a trip to the liquor store to pick up a bottle of Jack to drown his sorrows, but Brantley doubted it. Based on the conversation he'd had with the man earlier, he didn't get the impression the senator did much on his own. He had employees who took care of the menial tasks, leaving him plenty of time to … well, to do whatever the fuck a shithead like him did.

Without the radio on, Brantley could practically hear Reese breathing, although he knew his own heartbeat was louder. Hell, for a minute there, when Reese had been telling his version of events, Brantley'd thought his damn heart was going to beat right out of his chest. It had taken tremendous effort to remain calm so he could feign an emotional detachment he certainly hadn't felt.

Brantley kept his focus on the road while he processed all the information Reese had given him. Admittedly, he'd known some of it. Reese had been acting suspiciously long before the night he went out with Madison, but Brantley had refused to call him on it. Instead, he'd all but shoved his head in the dirt and pretended everything was fine. It had been easier that way.

Right up until it wasn't.

Which meant Reese wasn't the only one at fault. Brantley had to carry some of the weight.

With his hands gripping the steering wheel, his eyes locked on the asphalt laid out before him, Brantley took a deep breath and said, "I want you to come back home. If you want to, I mean."

"More than anything," Reese mumbled softly from the passenger seat.

Relief filled him, so potent he swore his fingers tingled a little.

"Looks like he's gonna take the toll road," Reese stated.

Brantley changed lanes, using his turn signal when he did. If Harrison was paranoid, he didn't want to give the guy any reason to think they weren't some law-abiding couple out for a school-night date.

The thought made him smile. This wasn't a date, but it very well could've been. This was the exact thing they both enjoyed doing, and the day of the week didn't matter.

A short time later, the senator's car exited the toll road, turned right onto Highway 79, which would take them right to Coyote Ridge, although his destination was likely a good distance past it. He had two guesses as to what the man was doing. Either he was going to confront Magnus because he honestly didn't know where his wife was, or he was headed to wherever he knew Ava to be. Brantley would bet his life it was the latter.

Forty minutes later, they were in the small town of Embers Ridge, not too far from Camp K-9, pulling down a narrow dirt path with the headlights off. The senator had gone this way, and Brantley'd stayed back until he felt it safe to follow.

"He's up ahead, parked off on the right," Reese told him, using the binoculars to see farther down the road.

"What the fuck is he doin' out here?" Brantley mused aloud.

There wasn't a house for miles. This land was pasture based on the wooden fence posts stringed with barbed wire.

He looked past Reese out the passenger-side window, saw another barbed-wire fence—this one in better condition—several yards back from the road.

"What's that sign say?" he asked, noticing a small metal square attached to one of the posts.

Reese glanced his way, then turned the opposite to look out the window. "Dead Heat Ranch. Private property."

"Well, I'll be damned," he muttered as he grabbed his phone, turned on the camera, and zoomed in.

He snapped pictures of the senator's car by the side of the road. He figured evidence of him being here would go a long way toward getting a confession if there was one to be had. Unfortunately, the senator was on the side not belonging to DHR. Otherwise, Brantley could've asked his cousin Jared if they could take a look at the game cameras they likely had posted throughout the property.

Several minutes passed as they sat in silence, Reese continuing to keep an eye on things.

"Looks like he's comin' back," Reese noted.

Brantley turned on his phone again, watched the camera screen as it brought Harrison Rivers into view. He snapped a few more pictures to prove the senator was here.

"He looks pissed," Brantley said.

"At least he's not carryin' a body."

Brantley exhaled a mirthless laugh. That was definitely a good thing.

"He's gonna know we're followin' him," Reese said when the senator's car did a K-turn on the narrow path, turning back toward them.

"Oh, he's gonna know, all right," Brantley stated, flipping on the headlights and starting the engine. He pulled forward, effectively blocking the senator's exit.

Once he was close enough, he put the truck in park, opened the door, and stepped out. He grabbed his flashlight, flipped it on, then popped the snap on his holster and put his hand on the butt of the gun as he approached.

"Out for an evenin' stroll, Senator?" he shouted to be heard through the closed window of the car.

The window slowly lowered, and the senator glared up at him, blinded by the beam of light Brantley shined into the car.

"You come to visit someone?"

The senator's eyes were wide, his mouth open. He looked distraught. Or, more accurately, guilty.

"Where is she, Senator?" Brantley demanded. "Where's your wife?"

The senator's head snapped to the other side of the car when Reese's flashlight beamed into the vehicle's backseat.

"I don't know," Harrison said roughly, his voice trembling. "I ... I just came out here to think."

Brantley barked a laugh. "Like hell." He lifted his gaze to the dark field. "Is her body out there? Is that where you dumped her when you killed her?"

"No!" he insisted, blocking the light from his eyes. "This is Magnus's land. I just ... I thought I'd look for her."

Brantley glanced at Reese, shot the flashlight beam toward his face to see his reaction. When he shook his head, Brantley glanced back at the senator.

"That's not Camp K-9 property."

"What?" Harrison's head snapped up. "Yes, it is."

"Naw, you're a couple miles shy of the trainin' camp." Brantley gazed down the road as though seeking it out. "Was that your intention? Dump her body on Magnus's property so you could blame it on him?"

The senator's hands returned to the steering wheel, his death grip turning his knuckles white. Brantley knew he was about to bolt, and he didn't try to stop him. The guy already knew they were on to him, so where the hell was he going to go?

The car's engine revved, and Brantley saw Reese step back out of the way to avoid being run over. A second later, the senator punched the gas, the car lurching backward.

Brantley moved to stand in front of his truck, watching as the senator did another three-point turn, aiming in the opposite direction. He figured there was no way out at the other end, or the guy would've gone that way in the first place. That, or he'd miscalculated where he was since he believed this to be Magnus's property.

"Give me a minute," Brantley told Reese. "If I get shot for trespassin', just haul my ass to the hospital, would ya?"

With that parting shot, he carefully slipped between the barbed wire to the other side of the fence. With flashlight in hand, he did a quick skim of the terrain. In the distance, he heard a donkey braying, figured it was doing its job, attempting to warn off a predator. He kept his attention on the ground, followed the crushed and broken grass where the senator had likely trampled. It looked like something had been dragged through there, but the damage wasn't recent. He went as far as he figured the senator had before turning back.

"Find anything?" Reese called to him when he made his way back to the road.

"Besides a few stray beer bottles and evidence someone's been tramplin' through, no."

Reese carefully gripped the top wire of the fence, then put his foot on the middle and separated them to give Brantley room to ease back through.

"Could be kids," Reese said. "Popular hangout for the local teenagers, maybe?"

"Could be." Brantley pulled out his phone.

"Who're you callin'?"

"Magnus." Brantley looked up at Reese. "Figured we could get his dogs out here to search."

Reese turned, his gaze swinging along the darkened pasture. "I think you should wait till dawn. Get a full search team, and we can go door to door."

"You don't think she's here?"

Reese glanced back. "I think the senator came here for a reason, sure. I think it's possible she *was* here at some point. But based on his reaction, he didn't find what he was lookin' for, so no, I don't think she's out here."

Brantley nodded. Reese made a good point.

"We can get the Lamberts to call the sheriff," Reese continued as they moved back toward Brantley's truck. "Get him out here at first light."

The Lamberts owned Dead Heat Ranch, Brantley knew.

With that decision made, they returned to the senator's house to keep an eye on things.

CHAPTER EIGHTEEN

Tuesday, March 15, 2022

"I'M GONNA TAKE TESHA FOR A RUN," Brantley said when they returned with the sun on the horizon and the new day nearly underway.

Reese wanted nothing more than to grab a few hours of sleep, but he knew that wasn't an option. He'd managed to sleep for roughly an hour in the truck while they'd kept watch over Harrison Rivers's place, but it hadn't been nearly enough.

"I'll grab a shower, put somethin' together for breakfast," Reese told Brantley.

"You're welcome to go with us," Brantley said, hands on his hips as he stared back at Reese.

As much as he wanted to, he wasn't sure he was up for it. Ten miles had been easy for him before getting shot. These days, five was more his style, but he didn't want to admit that to Brantley.

"Next time," he told him, meeting that steel-blue gaze.

Brantley nodded then whistled for Tesha, who'd slipped out into the backyard when they returned.

She came bounding through the door, tail wagging furiously, tongue lolling out of her mouth. Just seeing her made Reese's heart swell. He'd missed her so damn much.

After Brantley changed clothes and harnessed Tesha, they took off out the front door, leaving Reese alone with his thoughts. He figured he had a little time before they returned, so he dropped onto the couch, stared at the blank TV for a minute. In the dark screen, he could see the reflection of the kitchen behind him, and he found himself relaxing a bit.

He was home again.

He wouldn't deny being relieved when Brantley had told him he wanted him to come back. As for what that meant for their relationship, Reese didn't know yet; however, he considered it a good first step. He had a lot to atone for, and he had every intention of making it right with Brantley. He wanted nothing more than for them to get back to a good place again, back to where they'd been before Reese had let his insecurities get the best of him.

His thoughts drifted to one of the last sessions he'd had with his therapist.

"The last time we talked, you mentioned Brantley had tipped your world on its axis," Dr. Regina Sanders said, her gaze skimming the notepad in her lap. *"I'd like to know what you meant by that."*

Reese took a deep breath. "I don't know," he said honestly.

"Are you saying he makes you feel different?"

Reese frowned. "Different?" He snorted. "More like an entirely different person."

"In a good way? Or bad?"

"I don't know."

Dr. Sanders was silent, as was her way. She tended to keep quiet when she expected Reese to talk.

That was the reason he was here, though. To talk through his problems. Had Sniper 1 not forced him to go to counseling after getting shot, Reese wasn't sure he would've volunteered. From time to time, he would recall what Evan had told him—how therapy had helped him process after his wife's murder—but Reese still had difficulty buying into all the hype. Did he feel better now that he'd shared his private thoughts? Not really, no. However, he knew he wanted to make a life with Brantley, and in order to do so, he had to put in the effort. If it meant coughing up some of his secrets, so be it.

"Tell me about the night you met him," Dr. Sanders prompted.

"I was out with friends. We were at the bar, having a couple of beers. Someone suggested we go to IHOP," Reese recalled.

"Is that usual?"

"For me to go along with them?"

"The events. Do you usually hang out with your friends, grab an early breakfast?"

"Hang out, yes. I don't usually make it much past the beers, though."

"But that night was different? Why?"

Reese shrugged.

"Were you hungry?"

"No." Reese knew what the doc was angling for, so he gave in. "I wasn't hungry. I was … curious."

"About?"

"Brantley."

"Something about the introduction intrigued you?"

Reese considered telling her he'd been intrigued by the idea that Brantley was a Navy SEAL, but he knew that was just the excuse he'd told himself at the time.

"I felt something," Reese admitted, holding the doc's stare. "A connection, I think."

"A connection?" The doctor seemed to mull that over. "You've got a military background. Was it a kinship of some sort?"

"No. It was intrinsic," he admitted. "As though our introduction was meant to happen."

"Interesting. Go on."

"I was attracted to him." Even as the words came out, Reese felt his face heat. He'd never admitted that to anyone.

"Based on what you've told me about him, it sounds as though he's got a magnetic personality. Just because you're attracted doesn't mean anything more than that."

"I'm not talkin' a fondness for his presence, Doc," he blurted. "I. Was. Attracted."

Her gaze remained on his face, encouraging him to continue.

Reese didn't know how to make it much clearer than that except to tell her he'd wanted to know what it would feel like to have Brantley's hands on him. While they were both naked.

He decided to keep that to himself.

"Was there a physiological response?" she inquired.

Reese hated this part of it, the weird dance that took place to get him to put a voice to his thoughts. Because he knew they could go round and round for another session or two, and he had no intention of being here much longer, he decided to confess.

"If you mean did he make my dick hard, yeah, he did."

She didn't look away, didn't seem at all bothered by his harsh statement. "And he's the first man you've had that reaction to?"

"The only man," Reese clarified. "There were none before him and none since."

"Have you not felt an attraction to women since you met him?"

Reese recalled meeting Jessica James that night. He remembered thinking she was a beautiful woman, but he hadn't been stirred by her the way he'd been by Brantley. Of course, he'd done his best to pretend, because it made a hell of a lot more sense than his reaction to Brantley.

"I tried to be," he admitted. "I met JJ that night, too."

The doctor glanced down at her notepad. "She works with you. She's Brantley's best friend."

"Yes."

"And what happened after you met her?"

"I asked her out."

"Because you were attracted to her?"

Reese shook his head. "Because I didn't want Brantley to know I was attracted to him."

Staring at the television screen now, Reese remembered how he'd felt when he admitted that openly. It had been the truth. From the day he'd met Brantley, he'd felt as though he'd been sucked into the vortex of another dimension. Everything had changed for him that night. Everything.

It had taken a few more sessions to get to the heart of the matter, but that one had signaled his progression. Since then, Reese had accepted the fact that Brantley Walker was the only person in the world who could make him happy. And with Dr. Sanders's help, he'd learned that his sexual orientation did not have to define him.

He was still the same person he'd been before Brantley came along.

The same but better, he had realized.

Because Brantley Walker made him a better person.

Brantley didn't take the long way for their morning run, choosing the shorter route instead.

He told himself he was tired from a night in the truck, but that wasn't true. He was wide-awake, his blood pumping hot, and it was all thanks to the man who was back at his house.

Figuring he'd given Reese enough time to shower—ultimately removing the temptation—Brantley returned with five and a half miles under his belt. Time-wise, it was quite possibly a personal best for him, which told him he'd amped up his game in order to get back to Reese. He wasn't sure how he felt about that.

"One treat and water," Brantley told Tesha when they walked into the house. "Then I'm gonna hit the shower."

He went to the kitchen, expecting to find Reese at the stove, but he wasn't there. He gave Tesha her bacon treat from the fridge, then refilled her water bowl from the filtered pitcher.

It wasn't until he'd completed his task that he realized the shower was on in his bathroom.

Brantley glanced at Tesha, over at the hallway, back to Tesha.

Maybe he should take her for another few miles. He knew she certainly wouldn't complain.

But his legs didn't lead him to the front door. Nope, he strolled down the hallway to the bedroom, toeing off his shoes before he stepped inside. He stripped off his socks, tossed them aside. The bathroom door was ajar, so he pushed it open, walked in.

Reese was in the shower, head tilted back as water rained down on him, over his broad shoulders, his muscular chest, down the ridges of his abdomen, farther to caress his semi-hard cock, and then down his long, *long* legs.

Brantley didn't hesitate for a second. He continued striding toward him, heading right for the shower. He managed to get his shirt over his head, tossed it to the floor. And then he was walking into the shower, not caring that he still had his shorts on. He was on a mission, one that involved getting close to the naked man in his shower.

Reese's head tilted up, his eyes opening as Brantley approached.

Brantley closed the distance between them, intending to press his body to Reese's, but stopped short, his gaze finding the scar on his chest, the one from the bullet that could've ended his existence. For some reason, seeing it in the bright light of day made what happened to Reese all too real. Since the day RT had called to tell him Reese was in the hospital, Brantley's mind had grazed right past the reason for him being there. He'd been too focused on what went wrong between them and the fact that Reese hadn't come back to fully process the fact that he'd nearly lost the man.

He stared as he reached up and grazed his fingertip over the healed wound that would forever remain as a reminder that someone had nearly taken Reese from Brantley. As pissed as he'd been that Reese hadn't come back, Brantley'd never let himself think what his life would've been like if Reese had been gone forever.

His chest swelled as a foreign emotion filled it. He swallowed the lump in his throat, lifted his gaze to Reese's.

"I'm here, Brantley," Reese said softly, as though knowing exactly what he was thinking.

Brantley nodded, holding his gaze as Reese pressed his hand to Brantley's, securing it over his heart.

"I could've lost you."

"But you didn't. I'm here," he repeated, his voice rougher than before.

Brantley leaned forward, pressed his chest to Reese's, and then pushed him back until he was against the tile wall.

"I've missed this," he admitted, cupping Reese's head as he sealed their lips.

Reese's soft grunt was encouragement, the hard hands that gripped his back were promise.

Brantley had spent months dreaming about this moment, about getting Reese right here again. This shower held some of his best memories with Reese, and whenever he was in here, he'd thought about each and every one of them. It was the reason he'd taken to showering in the guest bath.

But here they were again.

"I've missed *you*," Reese mumbled when Brantley pulled back.

NICOLE EDWARDS

Brantley growled softly, then grabbed Reese roughly, slamming his mouth down. This time he kissed him with every ounce of pent-up passion he'd collected over the past six months. He let Reese feel his need and his fury as he plundered his mouth, groped every inch he could reach. And when his hands made it to Reese's ass, he gripped firmly, pulling his cheeks apart, letting Reese know his intention.

"God, yes," Reese moaned, grinding his hips forward, their cocks bumping in their haste. "Touch me, Brantley, and don't ever stop."

"I'm gonna do more than touch," he rasped against Reese's mouth.

"Please…"

Before he could process what he was doing, Brantley spun Reese around, pinned him to the shower wall with his chest to his back. He didn't speak, wasn't even sure he could. The only thing he managed was to shove his shorts down to his ankles and kick them out of the way as he guided his cock between the tight, firm globes of Reese's ass. His brain wasn't functioning, or he would've reached for the lube sitting on the ledge. Instead, he pushed the head of his cock past the tight ring.

"Oh, fuck," Brantley hissed, overwhelmed by the pleasure he'd been missing all these months.

Reese was breathing heavily, thrusting his hips back, attempting to take more of Brantley. The water and his pre-cum provided enough lubricant for Brantley to sink in deep, his hips cradled against Reese's ass. He remained like that for several heartbeats as he mentally pulled himself back from the edge. He was dangerously close to coming, and he hadn't even moved yet.

"Don't stop," Reese pleaded, his hand gripping Brantley's thigh. "Please, don't stop."

Brantley pulled his hips back, thrust them forward.

A strangled groan escaped, but he wasn't sure who it belonged to. Him. Reese. Both.

It didn't matter because the tight clasp of Reese's body was the only thing he could focus on. He drove into him repeatedly, his skin tingling as pleasure consumed him. He reached around, cupped Reese's throat, and pulled his head back, forcing him to arch his back so Brantley could continue to pound inside him. He fucked him hard, deep, every thrust jarring Reese's body.

"You hurt me, Reese," he bit out, fucking him harder.

"I know."

"You won't fucking do it again."

"Never."

Brantley's chest heaved, and he realized it wasn't from exertion; it was from the emotion bubbling to the surface.

This man was all he wanted, all he needed.

His hips slowed, his violent thrusts becoming unhurried, gentler, although just as intense. He kept his hand on Reese's throat and pressed his face to the side of Reese's neck as the emotion burst free. The water masked the tears that came, but Brantley wasn't trying to hide them. The dam had burst, and this was the release he needed to move forward.

"Love me," Reese begged, his voice hoarse from the angle of his throat. "Love me, Brantley."

"Always," he moaned.

When the wave subsided, Brantley released Reese's neck and gripped his hips. He angled their bodies for maximum penetration, then pounded him again and again until they were both grunting and groaning, the sound echoing in the room.

And when Reese growled his name, his ass squeezing Brantley's cock, he let himself go, his body shuddering violently as he came with Reese's name tumbling from his lips.

CHAPTER NINETEEN

After that overwhelming encounter in the shower, Reese managed to get dressed. He went to the kitchen, started a pot of coffee.

"You're gonna have to go to the store," Brantley informed him when he joined him a short time later.

"One step ahead of you," Reese told him. "I placed an order for delivery yesterday. Slade stuck around to put it away."

Brantley was staring at him like he was from another planet.

"What? You never thought to have groceries delivered?"

Brantley's dark eyebrows rose slowly. "Actually, no." He went to the refrigerator, opened it. "Holy shit."

Yeah, Reese might've gone overboard with the order but at least now they wouldn't starve to death.

"I was gonna make bacon and eggs. Unless you'd prefer something else?"

Brantley closed the refrigerator. "Perfect. You've got just enough time to make it. The team's on the way over."

Reese glanced back, noticed Brantley was typing something on his phone. There was a definite shift in the air, one that made him feel lighter than before. He knew if he attempted to bring up what had happened, he would be shut down because that was how Brantley operated. Brantley's theory was to let bygones be bygones, and he was quite possibly the only person Reese knew who didn't hold a grudge, who didn't bring up the past. It was a trait Reese admired, even though he didn't understand it.

He appreciated it now, though, because he did not intend to dwell on the past any longer. He was ready to move forward, and to do that, he had to accept Brantley's forgiveness and learn to forgive himself in the process.

Reese got to work preparing breakfast like he'd done a hundred times. It wasn't much, but it would get them through the morning.

Coffee went a long way to clearing the fog from his sleep-deprived brain. He was on his third cup when JJ and Baz arrived. They brought kolaches and a handful of orange juice cartons, dumping their loot on the island.

"I've seen his refrigerator," JJ explained.

"You haven't seen it lately," Brantley quipped.

JJ's gaze darted to him and Reese smiled.

"So, what's the plan?" Baz asked.

"We'll wait until Magnus gets here," Brantley told them.

Ten minutes later, the rest of the team had arrived. Trey, Charlie, Holly, Elana, Deck, Evan, Slade, Darius, and Jay. Luca was the only person missing, but Holly told them her brother was heading in and would be reachable by phone if they needed him. Magnus had brought Gia, introducing her to them as the woman who managed things better than he could, as well as Gia's husband, Randy. With them, they'd brought three of their best tracking dogs, which gave them four with Tesha.

With everyone standing around the kitchen, Brantley explained what they'd encountered last night. He pulled up a map of the area, showed them the general vicinity he wanted to look in.

"We think he believed that land belonged to you," Brantley told Magnus.

"He's a couple of miles off," Magnus noted.

"Yeah." Brantley pointed to the vast area on the opposite side of the dirt road they'd been on. "This belongs to Dead Heat Ranch. I talked to Mercy Lambert this mornin'. She agreed to call the sheriff and fill him in on what's goin' on."

"We should head out there," Magnus stated, his tone ripe with urgency.

Reese could see the fear he was trying to mask.

"I'm ready," Reese told him when Magnus shot a look his way.

"What're we waitin' for then?" he demanded, his gaze darting to Brantley.

Brantley didn't appear bothered by Magnus's impatience, instead taking a minute to outline how things would work.

"Evan, Deck, and Slade, I want you to start door-to-door in this area. Show them the photo of Ava, ask if they've seen her. If not, ask if they've seen anything suspicious in the area," he instructed, pointing to a section on the map. "There's a lot of land out in these parts, so you'll have fewer houses to visit. Cover as many as you can.

"Charlie, Jay, and Darius, I want you to focus in town. It's early, and it's Tuesday, so you might not find many people out, but talk to anyone you can," he said, pointing to a section on the map. "And Charlie, some of my cousins are gonna meet you in town. Divvy it up however you think it'll work best and let them help. Baz, take JJ and head over to DHR. Mercy's expecting you." Brantley looked at Holly. "I want you and Elana to stay here, man things from HQ."

Both women nodded.

Brantley turned to Magnus. "The ball's in your court. I've got a dozen more who're willin' to help in the search. They'll meet us where we found the senator last night. Reese and I'll take Tesha; you just tell us where you need us."

Reese ignored the look JJ shot him, but he knew she was trying to determine whether that was an undying admission on Brantley's part. While she glared holes through him, Reese watched Magnus shift from worried friend to experienced tracker. Being that he led the S and R team for the county, he already had a plan.

It took him only a few minutes to hash it out, give orders, then everyone was on their way. Reese followed Brantley, opened the door for Tesha, then climbed in the front seat.

"You wanna drive?" Brantley offered.

Reese cut his eyes over. "Seriously?"

"Of course not." He laughed, started the truck, then whipped around and followed Magnus and Trey down the driveway.

Admittedly, he was glad some things hadn't changed. Even if it meant he had to ride shotgun with a man whose only setting was ASAP.

JJ MANAGED TO REFRAIN FROM MAKING AN outburst until she was in the truck with Baz, and he was pulling down Brantley's long dirt drive.

"They're back together," she told him with a wide grin. "They made up."

Baz's teal-blue eyes slid to her, shifted back to the road. "You sound convinced."

"I *am*."

She knew those two couldn't stay apart for long. For the past six months, she'd been watching Brantley unravel. He was a bear to deal with on a good day, but he'd been more of a terror since Reese got shot. It was nice to see a smile on his face again.

"Do you know anything about this Dead Heat Ranch we're goin' to?" Baz asked.

JJ rolled her eyes. She should've known he wasn't going to indulge her need to gossip. When it came to Brantley and Reese, Baz tended to keep his nose out of their business. Not always easy since JJ had been working herself up these past months, desperate to find a way to get the two of them back together.

"I do not," she admitted. "But give me a minute or two, and I'll get you all you need to know."

While Baz drove, JJ pulled out her laptop, did a search for Dead Heat Ranch.

"Wow. It's an actual dude ranch," she said aloud. "People come from far and wide to spend time on the ranch and..."

She narrowed her eyes on one of the pictures. It showed a happy couple shoveling what appeared to be cow manure.

She barked a laugh. "Why would anyone in their right mind want to shovel cow shit on vacation?"

"To each his own," Baz commented. "But I was thinkin' more along the lines of who owns the place."

"Right." She pulled up the information. "Looks like the Lamberts own it. It sits on a good majority of the land in Embers Ridge." She skimmed more details. "Jerry Lambert and his five daughters, Hope, Grace, Trinity, Faith, and Mercy, keep it running. Hope's married to Jared, one of Brantley's ten million cousins."

Baz chuckled.

"Should we throw them a party?" JJ asked.

Baz's gaze slammed into her. "What? Why would we throw the Lamberts a party?"

"Not the Lamberts." She huffed. "Brantley and Reese."

He shook his head adamantly. "Absolutely not."

"Why? It'll be fun."

"No."

"But—"

"JJ, I know you mean well, but please don't interfere. They've had a hard enough time as it is. Just let it be."

She turned her attention out the window with a heavy sigh. He was right, of course. If she threw them a party, Reese would just be embarrassed, and Brantley would end up pissed.

"Fine," she muttered, then slowly looked back at Baz. "However, when they get married, you can bet your ass I'm gonna make it the event of the year."

Baz snorted. "Yeah? And who says they're gonna get married?"

She narrowed her eyes, stared out the front window. "I do. Mark my words."

Half an hour later, Baz was parking the truck in the front lot at the ranch's main office.

Rather than go in through the guest entrance, JJ wandered around to the back, looking for someone who could tell her where to find Mercy Lambert.

She spied a woman walking her way. She was decked out in cowboy boots, painted-on jeans, and a T-shirt with the sleeves rolled up like they'd done back in the day. Despite the somewhat masculine attire, she was a beautiful woman. Long blond hair pulled back into a ponytail that swished back and forth when she walked.

"You must be JJ," the woman shouted as she approached.

"And you must be Mercy."

"One and only." Mercy thrust out a hand when she neared. "Nice to meet you."

JJ shook it, then glanced at Baz. "This is Sebastian Buchanan."

"You can call me Baz," he insisted, shaking Mercy's hand.

"Sorry you had to come this way under the circumstances," she said politely, motioning for them to follow her. "The sheriff's inside talkin' to my dad. Y'all wanna head that way?"

JJ was about to tell her that she had no desire to talk to the sheriff, but Baz spoke up first.

"Why don't I take care of that? Maybe you could give JJ a tour." Baz gifted them one of those wicked smiles. "She mentioned somethin' about wantin' to learn how to shovel—"

"Shut it!" JJ shouted over him. "Ignore him. He's the funny one in this relationship."

Mercy laughed, then pointed toward the house. "Go right on in there. They're at the dinin' room table."

"Be good," Baz said softly, then squeezed her hand before moving past her toward the porch.

"I didn't even know this place was out here," JJ admitted once she was alone with Mercy.

"Yeah, well, I didn't know there was a dog kennel just a couple miles down the road, and I've lived on this patch of dirt my whole life."

JJ laughed. "It's a canine camp," she clarified. "Magnus Storme, he owns the place. Does training and boarding, also runs the search and rescue team."

Mercy stopped, stared at JJ. "Magnus Storme? He owns that place?"

"He does," JJ confirmed. "You know him?"

"Not personally, but I've heard the story about what happened to his family. Sucks."

Yeah, JJ would agree. It broke her heart to think that Magnus had lost his entire family in a fire. She never would've known the man had suffered such a tragic loss in his life. He was one of those people who was quick to smile and faster to flirt. She liked him tremendously, so it pained her to know he'd had to endure so much so young.

"Well, why don't I give you the dime tour of the stables," Mercy offered. "I promise, you won't have to shovel anything while you're here."

JJ laughed. "Thanks. I appreciate that."

BRANTLEY SPENT THE MAJORITY OF THE MORNING tracking through the open field they'd caught the senator in last night. With help from Ethan, Beau, Kaden, Keegan, Sawyer, Braydon, Brendon, and Kaleb, they walked a grid pattern up and down, starting at the southernmost end of the field and working their way north. Another team that included Trey, Magnus, Gia, Randy, Rex Sharpe, his husband, Jack, his brother, Rafe, and Brantley's father, Frank, and his uncle Curtis, started at the northernmost end and began working south.

So far, the dogs hadn't scented on anything, but he had to admit, Tesha was doing a damn fine job. She'd come a long way in the past six months, and he could tell even Reese was impressed.

As they went, Brantley filled Reese in on the training Tesha had undergone since he left. He made sure there was no accusation in his tone because he genuinely believed that once you decided to move past something, you did just that. And the only way to do that was to put the past in the past. Brantley sensed Reese was expecting a snide comment from time to time, but Brantley ensured they didn't come. It would take some time before the memories would fade, but he vowed he was moving on. Hell, he loved Reese. Had never stopped loving the man, and the truth was, he'd held out hope for a future for them despite the shit they'd gone through.

"Hey, Brantley," Trey's voice sounded over the two-way radios they were carrying. "I think Adira's alerted on something."

"Roger that," he answered. "We'll head your way."

"And what way would that be?" Reese asked.

Brantley grinned. "Hell if I know. Can't be too far away; they were movin' toward us."

Based on the expression on Reese's face, they could've been a couple of miles away.

Brantley lifted a hand, pointed toward the northwest from where they were standing. "They've worked away from the road."

It took ten minutes at a brisk jog for them to get to where Trey, Magnus, Gia, and Randy were currently standing.

"What'd she find?" Brantley asked, coming to a stop near them.

Trey pointed, and Brantley felt his heart drop. "Is it a body?" he demanded to know because the suspense was going to take him out at the knees.

"We don't know. We didn't … move anything," Gia answered for the group. "There's a rug, and there's blood."

"Call the sheriff out here," Brantley instructed Reese before he started toward the direction they were pointing.

As he walked, he was careful where he stepped, pulling a pair of latex gloves out of his pocket. He knew he should probably wait for the sheriff, but if he did that, there was a good chance Magnus was going to implode. He figured the least he could do was check to see whether or not Ava was wrapped up in the rug. As he moved closer, he sent up a silent prayer.

Carefully, he tugged one corner of the rug, pulled until it unrolled.

"No body!" he called out. "She's not here."

However, he suspected she had been.

On a high note, the rug looked antique and probably cost a pretty penny. If someone could tie it back to the senator, then there was proof of foul play.

He pulled his phone from his pocket, dialed JJ's number. "Hey. We found what looks to be the dump site. I need you to get my coordinates and pass them on to the team going door to door. Tell them where to focus their efforts. They need to talk to anyone who lives within a mile of here first."

"On it, boss," she said before disconnecting the call.

He approached the others and focused his attention on Magnus.

"There's blood, but it's not a significant amount."

"Meaning?" Gia asked, her voice a bit too high.

"Meaning if that is her blood, she could've survived."

"Could've?" Magnus's face turned a shocking shade of green.

"She's not here," he repeated, stepping closer and lowering his voice. "Last night, when the senator was out here, he didn't find what he was lookin' for. Which we're gonna take as a good sign."

Magnus nodded, but Brantley could tell he wasn't listening.

"So what now?" Trey inquired.

"We keep lookin'. There's a chance she walked away from here, so we need to keep trackin'. She could be out there somewhere."

"I need to get the dogs some water," Gia noted. "Might be a good idea to trade them out. Bring Sarge and Aurora."

Magnus nodded, his gaze still on where the rug had been found.

"I'll go with her," Randy stated. "You want us to take Tesha with us?"

Brantley looked to Reese for a decision. He saw the man's surprise, but he waited for a response.

"Yeah. I think she could use a break."

Brantley stepped over to Magnus, blocked his view of the rug. "Look, man. This isn't easy, but it's not over. She's not here, which means she's somewhere. We keep lookin' until we find her."

He nodded. "Yeah."

Brantley pulled a bottle of water from one of the many pockets on his tactical pants. He passed it over. "Drink this, and let's keep movin'."

Perhaps he sounded harsh, but he knew how easy it would be to get lost in your own head in a situation like this. Magnus was terrified for his friend, but now they had a glimmer of hope. If she had been dumped, she either walked away or someone found her and took her somewhere. Now it was a matter of finding her. And he was crossing his fingers that she was still alive.

CHAPTER TWENTY

DAY TURNED TO NIGHT, AND MAGNUS'S HOPE dwindled.

Admittedly, he'd nearly lost his lunch when he'd come across that rug in the middle of that damn field. The field he now knew like the back of his hand, thanks to hours of trekking over the terrain looking for signs that Ava was alive. He would've still been out there if it weren't for Brantley calling it quits. Magnus had wanted to punch the man in the face, but he figured the only thing that would do was break his hand on the guy's granite jaw.

He understood the reasoning, sure. The team Brantley had pulled together was tired, having spent hours out in the sun poking through knee-high grass. So he got it. At least, he did after he'd made his way back to his SUV and realized his legs were like noodles, his muscles overtaxed from all the walking.

"Come on," Trey said when they pulled up to the house. "Let's get some food and a shower."

Magnus's gaze swung over to Trey, who was driving since Magnus's mind wasn't in any shape for something so complex. "You're stayin'?"

There wasn't an ounce of hesitation when Trey said, "Yeah."

"I don't have much in the way of food," he admitted, wrangling with the door handle to get out.

It took a minute for him to calm down enough to pull the handle, then he was stepping out. His knees were jelly, but he managed to remain upright.

"I need to check on the dogs," he said, starting toward the kennels.

Trey pulled him up short with a hand on his arm. The next thing Magnus knew, he was being herded toward the back door of the house.

"It's bein' handled," Trey told him. "Gia said Billy's stayin' overnight, and your day crew's well aware of the situation. They've got it covered. Once I get you settled, I'll go see if anyone needs anything."

Magnus stared up at Trey and frowned. "Who are you, and what'd you do with *my* Trey?"

He'd meant it to be funny, but there was a flash of something in Trey's eyes, and quite possibly for the first time since the day they met, it didn't look like panic.

"Come on." Trey nudged him forward. "Shower first. I'll order pizza."

"Shower with me," Magnus insisted, glancing back as he managed to move forward.

"Okay."

Magnus stopped, turned to face Trey fully. "Are you *handling* me, Mr. Walker?"

Another flash in those beautiful blue-gray eyes. "I wouldn't dare."

Magnus soon learned that Trey hadn't actually intended to get in the shower with him, using the excuse he wanted to get the pizza ordered, but he helped urge him that way. He took his time, letting the hot water wash away the dirt from the day. It went a long way to easing some of the tension from his shoulders. Afterward, Magnus scarfed down three slices of pizza, but it wasn't until he'd had three bottles of water that he started to feel more like himself. He figured it had something to do with the fact Trey was still there.

"Billy wasn't over there earlier. I want to introduce myself," Trey told him. "You go ahead and get in bed."

Magnus shook his head. "I'll go." He started toward the door, stopped when he realized Trey was coming along. "You can grab a shower. It'll only take me a minute."

Trey looked determined, reaching around him for the doorknob. "I'd like to know what needs to be done. That way, I can help out if necessary."

It took effort to keep his eyebrows from launching into his hairline, but Magnus managed. He considered asking Trey why he wanted to help out but decided the why of it didn't really matter. The fact that he did told Magnus that they'd finally taken that first step past the booty call phase and into … well, he honestly didn't know where this was headed, but he damn sure hoped to find out.

They walked out to the main building side by side, then Trey opened the door, held it for him. Magnus smiled to himself then schooled his expression when he saw Billy standing behind the counter, the computer keyboard on the top, monitor angled toward him.

"Hey, Billy," Magnus greeted.

The older man smiled, revealing a missing front incisor that had been knocked out in his younger, wilder days. At least that was the story Billy usually told.

"Hey. How's it?" he asked, eyes imploring as though Magnus might have some answers to make the world a better place.

"No news yet, but we'll head back out at first light."

Billy glanced between Magnus and Trey briefly.

"Oh, sorry," Magnus said. "Trey, this is Billy Daniels; he usually takes care of the dogs during the day. Billy, this is Trey Walker, my … uh…"

"Boyfriend," Trey supplied, stepping forward and offering a hand to Billy. "Nice to meet you."

"Nice to meet you, too," Billy said with a satisfied grin.

Magnus wasn't sure he could move or speak. In fact, he wasn't even sure he was breathing anymore.

Had Trey really just…?

What the fuck was going on?

TREY BLAMED THE EVENTS OF THE DAY for his slip, and no sooner was the word out of his mouth than he wished he could've taken it back. At least, that was his initial thought. Unfortunately, it was out now, and he figured recalling it would make him look like an idiot, so he forged ahead.

"Magnus came to check in, see if you needed anything," Trey told Billy when it looked as though Magnus was too stunned to speak.

"Everything's good." Billy glanced toward the back of the building. "I just got Sarge and Aurora settled in. Gave 'em an extra treat for working so hard today."

"Anything we can do to help?" Trey offered, purposely avoiding the stunned expression on Magnus's face.

Billy wasn't doing as well in the avoidance department because he continued to glance at Magnus, and if Trey was right, that was amusement in the man's eyes.

"Naw. I think I've got it handled. Gia said she'd be back in the morning, but I should be good. I'll just sleep in the bunkroom."

Trey nodded. "Well, I need to get him … back in the house." He was grateful he'd recalled what he'd nearly said. He figured telling Billy that he needed to get the man to bed was probably a little TMI for the situation. Not to mention Trey's sanity.

Hell, he deserved a pat on the back for handling things so well this far.

"You ready?" Trey asked Magnus.

That seemed to shake him out of his stupor because he shook his head as though dislodging something, then looked at Billy. "Did they get their meds?"

"Yep." He tilted his head in the direction of the monitor. "I was logging it when you came in."

"What about tomorrow? Who's comin' in to relieve you? Do they—"

"It's handled," Trey and Billy said simultaneously.

Magnus's eyes narrowed as he looked between the two of them.

"Fine."

"If you need anyth—"

"I'll just holler," Billy interrupted with a smirk. "Go on, now. Get some rest. You've got another long day ahead of you tomorrow."

Trey guided Magnus toward the door, then followed. He stopped short when Billy said, "Magnus, I hope you find Ava. If there's anything I can do to help … I'm here."

Magnus's head tipped forward as though it had become too heavy to hold up. "Thanks."

Trey nudged him toward the door, then outside into the cool evening air. They'd had an unseasonably warm day, but according to the weather reports, the temps would be dropping into the freezing range mid-week as another cold front blew through. Trey didn't have to think about what that would mean for Ava if she was out there somewhere, wandering around alone, maybe hurt.

He closed the door behind him. No sooner did he turn than he found himself up against a firm body.

"Boyfriend?" Magnus whispered roughly.

Trey skimmed his face in the dim light from the exterior spotlight. It was cast partially in shadow, making it impossible to read whether Magnus was pissed or relieved that he'd said something so juvenile.

"I didn't—" Trey's words were cut off when Magnus pressed his lips to his.

"Don't take it back," Magnus whispered. "Not tonight, please."

Trey nodded, pulled back.

"Did you mean it?"

"I don't say things I don't mean, Magnus. You should know that by now."

He heard Magnus's sigh and released his own heavy exhale in relief.

"Come on," Trey insisted. "You need sleep. Dawn comes early, and we'll need to be back out there."

CHAPTER TWENTY-ONE

Wednesday, March 16, 2022

AFTER MANAGING TO SLEEP FOR SIX SOLID hours, Reese was up with the rest of the team on Wednesday morning. They headed out at first light to resume their search for Ava March.

While Magnus took his team, as well as a handful of Brantley's cousins, with the dogs back to the area where they'd found the rug, Reese and the rest of the task force, minus Trey, continued going door to door. They had decided to split up to cover more ground. Reese was on his third house of the morning, this one belonging to Gloria Steiner, a sixty-seven-year-old retired ER nurse and grandmother of three.

He walked up onto the wraparound porch, went to the door, and knocked gently on the wooden screen door.

"Who are you?" she demanded in a raspy, two-pack-a-day voice.

"Ma'am, my name's Reese Tavoularis. I'm with Sniper 1 Security." He held his credentials up to the security hole in the door. "I would just like to ask you a couple of questions."

"Does your dog bite?" she shouted back.

"No, ma'am." Reese glanced down at Tesha. "Her name's Tesha."

"How do I know you're who you say you are?"

He understood her reluctance, despite the fact they could've been done by now.

"Ma'am, my team's workin' with Sheriff Starr. If you'd like to call him, I'll be more than happy to wait."

As though that was the trigger, he heard the deadbolt release, then the door slowly opened.

"I've got a shotgun," she said wearily, keeping the door mostly closed.

"I mean you no harm, ma'am." He held up the credentials again so she could see them more clearly, then held up his phone to show her a picture of Ava March. "Have you seen this woman?"

Gloria leaned closer to the screen, squinting. "No. Who is she?"

"Her name's Ava March. She's been missing for a few days. We believe she was in this area."

"And why d'ya think she'd be here?"

"I don't, ma'am. I'm askin' if you've seen her. We believe someone was tryin' to hurt her, might've left her out near County Road 126."

"Haven't seen her," she stated, her tone a bit cooler than before. "Then again, I don't get out much these days. Haven't even been to town in…" She glanced up as though thinking. "Well, it ain't been for 'bout a month, I guess. Gonna have to get out there, stock up on some food if this cold snap is comin' in."

"Yes, ma'am." He pulled a card from his pocket. "Well, thank you for your time. If you happen to hear anything or see anything, would you mind givin' me a call?"

Reese tucked the card in the edge of the wood so she could get it when he left.

When she didn't say anything more, Reese turned and headed back to his truck. He paused when Tesha nosed around one of the scraggly bushes that had probably been part of a nice landscape design once upon a time.

"Come on, girl," he told her, hoping she wasn't about to do her business while Gloria watched.

Tesha sat, stared up at him expectantly.

Frowning, Reese nodded toward the truck. "Come on. Let's check in with Brantley. See if he's fared better than we have."

That perked her right up, had her bounding toward the truck.

"What d'ya say we stop by one more before we head back to town?" Reese asked, feeling guilty that he'd promised her they'd meet up with Brantley.

Tesha's response was a single bark, her tongue lolling out of her mouth as she stared over at him.

Reese chuckled, rubbed her head affectionately. "I missed you, girl."

The next house they came to was owned by Rafael Sanchez. According to the notes he'd been given, Rafael was a father to four grown children and two grandchildren and spent his days farming the fifteen acres of land he'd bought forty-something years ago.

Reese pulled up to the big white farmhouse that reminded him of Curtis and Lorrie's spread in Coyote Ridge. It looked as though the house had received a fresh coat of paint in recent years, the shutters on the front painted deep hunter green, the floorboards of the porch were the same dark red as the front door. And the plants in the front had been replaced recently, the flowers beginning to bloom as spring grew near.

He took the steps up to the house, knocked on the door, then moved back.

No one answered, but he could've sworn he saw the curtains move in the big window overlooking the front porch.

"Mr. Sanchez? My name's Reese Tavoularis; I'm with Sniper 1 Security."

Still no answer.

He waited another minute, then tucked his card into the screen. If they were lucky, Mr. Sanchez's curiosity would get the best of him, and he would give them a call to see what was what.

Reese looked down at Tesha. "I guess no one's home, girl. Now you ready to meet up with Brantley?"

Her ears perked up, her tail slashing the air with excitement.

"All right. No more teasin'. Let's go see how he's doin'."

He shot Brantley a text to let him know he was coming his way, then left the Sanchez residence and headed back to town. Fifteen minutes later, he met up with Brantley outside the lone convenience store/gas station.

"Any luck?" Brantley asked, coming to stand near Reese's open window.

"Nothin' so far. No one home at two of the houses, so I've noted them for follow-up. The others didn't know anything." Reese jerked his chin toward the store. "What about here?"

"Nothin' unusual, unless Martha Danbury buyin' three pints of Ben and Jerry's counts." Brantley's eyes glittered with amusement. "Evidently, she's lactose intolerant, but she recently broke up with her boyfriend, so she said fuck it." His head nodded in the direction of the store. "Lee's words, not mine."

Reese chuckled. Gotta love small towns.

Tesha barked from the backseat, so Reese rolled down the window, allowing her to get closer to Brantley.

"What's up, girl? Not enough excitement for ya?" Brantley rubbed her head then moved back to Reese's window. "I've got a few more to talk to. You wanna head back to HQ, outline what we've got? I'll have the team join us when they're done."

Reese nodded, his gaze lingering on Brantley's mouth a little longer than was appropriate.

It earned him a grin.

Next thing he knew, Brantley was leaning in. Reese got the feeling it was a dare, figured Brantley thought he wouldn't follow through. Reese proved him wrong by closing the distance and kissing his mouth. He lingered for a long second, not pushing but ensuring Brantley knew he was no longer concerned about what others might think. Reese was ready to live his life the way he'd always done: without shame.

"Do that again, you might find yourself bent over the tailgate," Brantley growled, his warning seductive enough to have Reese's cock standing at attention.

Reese laughed, and this time his ears warmed. He knew there was a blush on his face, but it definitely wasn't from shame.

"Make it the kitchen island, and you've got a deal," he countered, planting another kiss on Brantley's mouth.

When Brantley pulled back, his eyes flamed with the same desire that coursed through Reese's veins. "I'm gonna hold you to that, Tavoularis."

"I hope you do."

Brantley's grin warmed Reese from the inside out.

"HOW'RE WE DOIN'?" BRANTLEY ASKED THE TEAM when he joined them in the barn several hours later.

JJ, Baz, Evan, Slade, and Reese were standing around, staring at the electronic screen where they'd compiled the information they had gathered over the past few days.

"We've covered a lot of ground," JJ noted.

"Anyone hear from Charlie?" Brantley asked.

"She's followin' up at the two Reese listed as no one home," JJ answered. "Once she's done, she's headin' back this way. Darius and Jay are headin' over to the senator's house to relieve Luca and Deck." She glanced up at the second floor. "Becs and Elana are double-checkin' the map, makin' sure we've covered everyone. Anything from Magnus or Trey?"

"They headed over to Dead Heat Ranch," he told the team. "Jared called, said he got the recordings from a couple of the game cameras. They were gonna review them."

"You hear anything from the sheriff?" Evan asked.

"They secured the scene where we found the rug. They've got a forensic team runnin' blood samples to see if it matches Ava. No news yet."

"What do you want us to do next, boss?" Slade prompted, clearly eager to keep looking.

Brantley was, too, although they'd pushed themselves hard throughout the day. With every passing second, he felt as though they were getting farther from answers than when they began.

"Why don't I make burgers," Reese offered. "We can take a breather, regroup after."

"I won't turn down food," Baz said with a grin, his gaze sliding to JJ as though they shared an inside joke.

Brantley was glad to see things were still going well for them.

"Come on, then," Brantley said. "Let's move this to the house for a little while."

A short time later, after they'd rehydrated and scarfed down burgers and fries—which Reese had picked up at the grocery store on his way back from Embers Ridge because his online order hadn't had enough food for a full army—Brantley was sitting at the kitchen island looking at JJ's laptop screen.

He knew he should've been paying attention to what she was showing him, but his mind kept wandering to Reese. Namely, to an image of Reese bent over this very island. He couldn't deny he'd been shocked to shit when Reese had kissed him by the truck. It had taken every ounce of willpower he possessed not to launch himself through the window and take the man right then and there.

It had been the first time Brantley had kissed anyone in a public place. Not that he'd been ashamed to do so, but he'd never been much for public displays of affection. When he'd been in the teams, he'd kept his sex life on the DL for proprieties sake. Then again, he'd never been with a man he'd cared to take out in public, much less kiss in front of others.

Meaning Reese had been his first.

"Hey, B? Please tell me you're not thinkin' about gettin' Reese naked right here in this kitchen."

His head slowly turned, his gaze pinning JJ in place. "What?"

She motioned with her hand, drawing a ring around his head. "This right here." She laughed.

Brantley rolled his eyes. He knew that was her subtle attempt to get him to open up about the status of his relationship with Reese. She'd been dropping hints the past couple of days, her curiosity like a lighthouse beam, drifting over him every time he came into the room. She was nosy, that one.

JJ leaned in closer to him, lowered her voice. "Just tell me one thing."

He cocked an eyebrow.

"Is it good now?"

Brantley's gaze shot to Reese, who was sitting on the couch talking to Evan and Luca. "Yeah. It's good."

She squealed. "Sorry. I'm happy for you."

"Yeah, well, you should be focused on the case, not my love life."

Her smile made her eyes bright. "I'm rather good at multitasking, thank you very much."

"So you say."

Headlights through the front windows washed over the living room, drawing all conversation to a halt. A minute later, Trey and Magnus strolled in, Adira on their heels.

Brantley got to his feet to ensure Tesha's water bowl was filled, but Reese beat him to the punch.

"Any news?" Baz asked the two men, coming to stand behind JJ.

"No," Trey answered, his tone ripe with disappointment. "She's not out there."

At least not where they'd been looking, Brantley thought to himself. There was far too much ground for them to cover, even if they had a dozen teams. Dead Heat Ranch was three thousand acres, the surrounding ranches significantly smaller but still vast. It would take them a month to cover it all.

He was willing, of course, but he knew the team was beginning to feel the effects of days of searching. They needed to rest and regroup, although not a single one of them would admit it.

"The sheriff closed down the county road," Magnus informed them. "He posted deputies out there to stop anyone who attempts to go that way and to keep an eye out in case Ava is out there."

"Anything on the cameras?"

"Nothing useful," Trey told him, his eyebrows lowering as he glanced at Magnus then back to Brantley. "Mountain lion sighting."

Brantley knew all too well that there were mountain lions, bobcats, and coyotes running rampant through these parts. Most were scavenging for food. Rarely were they a threat to humans. He didn't know what that would mean for a wounded woman wandering around, but he told himself she wasn't out there; otherwise, those animals wouldn't need to hunt for a little while, so their presence was a positive sign.

"It's gettin' late," Baz said, clearly sensing the tension building over the revelation. "I think it's best to turn in for the night and start early again."

"I agree," Brantley said, standing. "I'll call the sheriff, see if I can get an update, and find out what his plan is. Tomorrow, Charlie and Jay can relieve Deck and Slade, keep an eye on the senator. The rest of you need to be here early."

There were a couple of relieved sighs, as though they hadn't been able to shut down until they'd been given the go-ahead.

Brantley understood that feeling all too well. The desire to keep going even when exhaustion took over was something he'd been plagued with all his life.

CHAPTER TWENTY-TWO

"WHAT'RE YOU DOIN' UP?"

Reese looked up from the computer screen, saw Brantley padding toward him, scraping a hand down his face.

"Couldn't sleep," he admitted. "Thought maybe if I looked at this again, I might see somethin'."

Brantley walked around behind him, warm hands settling on his shoulders. "Any luck?"

"No. I just have this feelin' she's out there."

"Out there? Meaning where we've been lookin'?"

"Yeah."

"That feelin' tell you whether she's safe or not?"

Reese sighed when Brantley pressed his lips to the back of his neck. "Unfortunately, no."

"Hmm."

Reese reached back, cupping Brantley's head as he nuzzled his neck. Goose bumps formed over his skin and his blood heated.

"Question is, do you wanna keep lookin', or do you want me to take your mind off it for a little while?"

He knew there was no right or wrong answer. If he chose to keep looking, Brantley would put on a pot of coffee and settle in for the long haul. If he chose the latter, there was a good chance he might get a couple hours of sleep after Brantley had wrung every last drop of energy from his body and mind.

Brantley sucked on his neck, making his cock swell.

"Don't stop doin' that," Reese rasped, tilting his head and welcoming those smooth, warm lips.

Brantley's mouth fused to his skin, sucking roughly, drawing a ragged moan from Reese's chest. His strong arms banded around Reese's middle, his hands sliding over his thighs then venturing inward and finding his aching cock.

"As much as I want to bend you over this counter," Brantley whispered in his ear, "I think I need to have you beneath me this time."

Reese inhaled sharply when Brantley stroked his cock through his shorts. The exhale that followed was harsher when Brantley released him.

"This way," Brantley said, taking his hand and pulling him to his feet.

Reese followed him to the bedroom, wasted no time discarding his shorts while Brantley did the same. And then all thought fled because he found himself beneath Brantley's hot, hard body.

"Right where I want you," Brantley mumbled, taking Reese's hands and lifting them over his head as he pinned him to the mattress.

Heat brewed beneath his skin and traveled like warm honey throughout his entire body, making his skin prickle with awareness. Brantley's touch, all that smooth skin against his own, brought his nerve endings to life, causing his breaths to deepen. He was aware of the crisp hairs on Brantley's legs rubbing his own, the bristle of his day-old stubble abrading his chin. It was heaven and hell at the same time, so fucking amazing but not nearly enough.

They breathed together for long seconds, their lips grazing lightly as Brantley stared down at him. Despite all the times they'd made love, nothing felt as intimate as this.

Brantley's hips dropped, pressing to his, and Reese hooked his leg behind Brantley's knee, pulling him closer, eager to feel every inch of him.

When Brantley lifted his head and held his stare, Reese said the three words he hadn't said nearly enough. "I love you."

"I love you, too," Brantley rumbled softly.

It felt like a band snapped in his chest, freeing him from the tension that had burdened him for so long. The pain and anguish he'd suffered because of his own actions. He'd hated himself and too many times during his self-loathing phase, he'd decided he didn't deserve Brantley. He still wasn't sure he did, but he'd learned he didn't know how to exist without him. Didn't even *want* to.

Reese didn't try to pull out of Brantley's firm grip on his wrists, but he lifted his head, finding that delectable mouth with his own. He kissed him, willed Brantley to feel all that it contained. Love, need, desire. Want, hope, promise.

"I missed how you taste," Brantley moaned against his lips. "Missed the heat of you beneath me."

Reese used his leg to nudge him closer, silently requesting more.

"You want me inside you, Reese?"

"So fucking much," he admitted roughly.

A soft growl escaped Brantley, and then the heat of him disappeared as he sat up, reached for the nightstand.

Reese didn't move except to use his hands to caress Brantley's thighs while he watched the man lube his cock. Reese's ass clenched, a desperate ache consuming him. The only one who could sate him was this man, the man he loved, the man he wanted to spend eternity with.

"Pull your knees back," Brantley instructed.

Reese did, baring himself to Brantley's hungry gaze.

He hissed when cool liquid dripped onto his balls, lower, dribbling down toward his anus. He moaned when the head of Brantley's cock painted the lubricant along his taint, lower. When Brantley's cockhead pushed against his hole, Reese relaxed, pulling his legs closer to his chest, urging Brantley to fill him completely.

Reese kept his eyes locked on Brantley's face, watched every expression, how his mouth tightened when he slipped the head in, stretching him. And how his eyes narrowed as he watched where their bodies would soon be joined. He loved that face, loved every single nuance about it.

Brantley's eyes darted up, catching Reese as he ogled him.

"You ready for me?"

"Always."

The steel blue of his eyes darkened as he shifted his hips forward, pushing his cock in slowly. Reese breathed deep, expecting pain but only receiving pleasure. Even though there was discomfort, it felt insanely good because this was Brantley. Reese's body had acclimated to this intimacy, made him crave what only Brantley had ever given him.

Brantley teased him with shallow penetration, pulling out, pushing in an inch.

"You want more?" Brantley asked.

"I want everything."

Although the heat flashed in his gaze, Brantley didn't thrust into him the way Reese expected. He sank in slow, a never-ending slide that grazed every part of him. Brantley shifted forward until he was balls deep, then leaned forward until Reese's calves rested on his shoulders.

"Put your hands over your head," Brantley instructed. "Grip the headboard."

He did, holding himself still as his body stretched to accommodate Brantley's thick cock.

Brantley met his gaze and held him captive as he began to retreat before slowly sinking into him. Over and over, he repeated the incredible slide and retreat. Reese let the pleasure rush over him, tilting his hips to take more each time Brantley filled him. It was heaven.

"Can you come like this?" Brantley taunted.

"Most definitely."

Brantley smirked. "Then let's see how long you can last."

Minutes felt like centuries as Brantley tormented him with slow, deep thrusts. Reese endured because he never wanted it to end. When the electric spark in his spine would tingle in warning, Brantley would pull back, as though he knew how close Reese was. Their bodies remained joined as Brantley fucked him with exquisite torture.

"Next time you're close, I'm not gonna stop," Brantley warned.

Reese gripped the headboard to keep from reaching for Brantley, wanting the man to do whatever he wanted to him. His cock wept as the friction pushed him higher and higher. He wanted more … needed more, but he wasn't going to say it. He was completely at Brantley's mercy.

"Squeeze my cock," Brantley growled.

Reese's ass clamped down on the thick shaft invading him.

"Oh, fuck, yes." Brantley held his stare. "So tight. So fucking hot. I'm gonna make you come; then I'm gonna fuck you. Hard."

Reese cried out as his balls drew up tight. The words alone were going to send him into the stratosphere, and he was helpless to stop it.

Brantley's hips bumped his ass when he pushed in deep. He maintained the brutally slow pace, but he somehow fucked him more insistently.

"Come for me, Reese. Come so I can drill this tight fucking hole and spill myself inside you."

"Oh, fuck." Reese tilted his head back, felt the cords in his neck stretch tight as his body coiled, sensation blooming into a fireball.

"Just like that," Brantley whispered as he continued to torment him. "I want you to come."

Reese gritted his teeth, sought the release that was just out of reach.

Brantley shifted his hips forward, sank in on a deep, bellowing growl, and that was enough to send him over. Reese shouted his name as he came, his cock jerking and spurting without so much as a graze.

"Fuck … that's what I wanted," Brantley snarled, pulling his hips back and driving in hard. "Oh, fuck, Reese. I'm gonna come."

Reese groaned, loving how verbal Brantley was. "Come inside me, Brantley."

"Aw, hell." Brantley's hips bucked as he drilled down into him again and again. "Fuck … Reese!"

Reese's ass tightened around the cock lodged deep, milking Brantley as best he could. He released the headboard, shifted his legs down from Brantley's shoulders, and welcomed Brantley's weight as he fell over him. He held him, loving the feel of Brantley's heart beating against him, the heavy gasps fanning his neck.

He felt tears form at the corners of his eyes, but he fought them back. He didn't want Brantley to see him cry, but the emotional turmoil was proving to be too much. The relief was omnipotent, dragging a sob from his chest. Reese banded his arms around Brantley, held him tight so he wouldn't see the way he was unraveling even as he felt as though he was being stitched back together.

"I've got you," Brantley whispered against his ear. "No matter what, Reese, I've always got you."

This time the sob tore free of its own volition, and Reese was powerless against it.

BRANTLEY WAITED UNTIL REESE HAD STILLED BEFORE he forced himself out of bed. He washed up in the bathroom, returned to find Reese lying there with his arm draped over his eyes. As he stared down at the man, he realized he'd never truly known what love was until he came along. Never understood the depth it could reach inside him. The way Reese had come undone had sealed Brantley's fate. He'd felt his remorse, understood the pain he'd suffered. Brantley hadn't been the only one in pain these last few months.

And something about that moment had settled everything inside him. He felt whole again despite the fact he hadn't been the one to cry. Not this time, anyway. And yes, his earlier breakdown in the shower hadn't been the only one he'd experienced in the past six months. He'd blamed the tears on fury and rage, but he knew better.

"I'm gonna grab some water," he told Reese. "Need anything?"

Reese's arm fell away, and he smiled. "I'm good. Thanks."

Brantley pulled on his shorts, then went to the kitchen, grabbed a bottle of water. He glanced at the computer Reese had been looking at before he'd dragged him back to the bedroom. As he cracked the lid on the water, he walked around the island, tapped the mouse to bring the screen to life.

He realized he was looking at Reese's notes, things he'd jotted down about the people he'd visited. He knew most of it already, but he figured another pass might help.

He was still skimming the data when he heard footsteps.

"You find something?" Reese asked, coming over and taking the water bottle from his hand.

"Not y— Wait a minute." Brantley pulled the barstool out, dropped onto it. "This here." He pointed to the screen. "Did Gloria Steiner actually *say* that?"

Reese glanced over his shoulder. "That she hadn't been out of the house in a month? Yeah. She offered it up. I didn't ask."

Brantley cut his gaze to Reese. "The guy at the gas station … he said Gloria came in a few days ago and cleaned out all the milk, eggs, and bread he had. Said it wasn't unusual since they were expecting a freeze."

"That's odd." Reese stood tall. "Maybe she forgot?"

Brantley cocked an eyebrow. "Who forgets somethin' like that? Or more importantly, who claims the opposite without bein' asked?"

"Oh, shit."

Brantley's gaze snapped over to him. "What?"

"Tesha. I didn't realize … I think she alerted on the house." He exhaled roughly. "She was curious about the bushes out front, then her butt instantly went to the ground. I … You think…?"

Brantley pushed back the stool, stood. "Oh, I definitely think. Come on. Get dressed. We've got some recon to do."

"She did mention she had a shotgun," Reese offered.

"Then I guess if we don't wanna get shot, we probably shouldn't get caught."

Brantley left Tesha at the house, not wanting to risk exposing them if she got anxious and barked.

With Reese in tow, they parked just down the street from Gloria Steiner's house and moved closer on foot. He probably should've waited until morning, but Brantley was almost positive they were on to something here. If he were lucky, a nosy neighbor would simply call 911 if they saw him or Reese lurking and not take matters into their own hands. He figured he could talk himself out of any situation if someone called the sheriff, but he'd have little leeway with a bullet.

An hour later, they were back in the truck. Their reconnaissance mission had netted them nothing. Brantley had checked out every square inch of the outside of the house, including the small gardening shed. There was nothing that would make him believe Ava was there, but he still couldn't shake the feeling that she was.

"You wanna call the sheriff?" Reese asked as Brantley drove back to Coyote Ridge.

"No. If Ava's there, I don't think Gloria intends to harm her."

"Protecting her."

"That's my thought. Why else would she raid the convenience store? Probably taking care of her, maybe hiding her."

"She's a retired ER nurse," Reese told him.

"Then she's somewhat equipped. Hopefully. If Rivers did dump Ava in that rug, no telling what he did to her first. It's possible she needs medical attention."

"Then I go and walk up on her porch," Reese mused. "She probably thought I was there to do Ava harm."

Brantley went to thrust his hand through his hair but came up short when he remembered he didn't have much anymore.

"Should we call Magnus?" Reese asked.

Brantley shook his head. "We'll call them in the morning after we call the sheriff. I don't want Gloria to get in trouble if she's just bein' a good Samaritan, but I don't want to get an ass full of buckshot either. In the meantime, we'll grab some shut-eye. And at first light, we'll bring Ava March home."

He exhaled heavily, praying like hell he was right.

CHAPTER TWENTY-THREE

Thursday, March 17, 2022

TREY'S PHONE BUZZED, DRAGGING HIM OUT OF a deep sleep.

He woke, rubbing his eyes with his fingers while reaching for his phone with the other hand.

"Yeah," he answered, his voice rough with sleep.

"I think we've got somethin', Trey," Brantley said, his no-nonsense tone in place. "Reese and I are about five minutes out."

"Did you find Ava?" he asked, nudging Magnus with his arm.

"We don't have eyes on her, no. However, we do think she's alive and safe."

"What?" Trey shot up. "What do you mean safe? Where is she?"

"Four minutes out," Brantley stated. "Get up. Get dressed. Meet us outside."

"Fuck." Trey dropped his feet to the floor, ignored the creak in his bones. He felt like he'd gone ten rounds with a heavyweight champion thanks to all the walking he'd done the past few days.

He glanced at the clock, frowned. It was 5:43 a.m., which meant they'd slept for at least five hours. That acknowledgment brought his brain online.

"What's the matter?" Magnus groaned, rolling over and placing a palm against Trey's back.

He hated to part with that touch, but he didn't have much choice, so he pushed to his feet and said, "Brantley and Reese are on the way. They've got somethin'."

"What do you mean they've—"

Trey shut the bathroom door, effectively cutting Magnus off. He wasn't intentionally being rude, but he needed to piss, and he needed a quick shower before his brother showed up. Four minutes wasn't a long time.

It took him roughly five to take care of business. He left Magnus behind to get dressed while he went outside to meet Brantley and Reese. They were climbing out of Brantley's truck when Trey stepped out onto the front porch.

"Where's the rest of the team?" he asked his brother.

"Charlie and Jay are on their way. I asked Deck and Slade to sit tight at the senator's house until Evan can relieve them."

"What about the rest of them?"

"I haven't called 'em yet."

"Then what are we doin'?"

Brantley remained calm, asked, "Where's Magnus?"

Irritated that his brother wasn't telling him anything, Trey motioned toward the door behind him. "Gettin' dressed. Now tell—"

"You want coffee?" Reese offered, carrying a to-go tray with two paper cups. "Added a couple of Splenda."

"Fuck, you're a lifesaver." Trey took one of the cups, popped off the lid to let it cool before taking a hefty swallow.

The door opened behind him, and Magnus came out, shrugging into his shirt before tucking his cell phone into his pocket. "What's goin' on?"

Trey listened while Brantley and Reese carried on something about a woman having bought eggs and milk or some shit. He was barely able to keep up with all the details, but it didn't take long to realize the details didn't matter.

"We believe Gloria Steiner might have Ava at her house."

"Who's Gloria Steiner?" Magnus asked, his expression stony as he glanced between the three of them.

"She's a retired ER nurse," Reese explained. "Her house backs up to the field where the rug was found. We think Ava might've wandered in that direction, possibly caught Gloria's attention."

"What the fuck?" Magnus snapped.

"Our theory is she found Ava, and now she's protecting her," Brantley explained. "We checked out her house last night, but it was closed up tight. We didn't get eyes inside, but it's possible Tesha alerted on the house when she and Reese were there yesterday."

"I didn't realize that was what she was doing," Reese said, his tone apologetic. "I missed it."

Magnus's face sobered instantly, the anger fading away. It made sense to Trey.

"We've called the sheriff," Brantley continued, "asked him to meet us over there. We'll let him do the talkin'. If we're right and Gloria's got Ava, we don't want to bring her any trouble."

"Why're we still standin' here, then?" Trey demanded.

"Waitin' on y'all," Brantley said with a smirk. "Come on."

Trey pulled his keys from his pocket and headed for his truck. He didn't have to tell Magnus to move his ass. The man was in the passenger seat before Trey managed to get his damn door open.

"I hope to fuck they're right," Magnus grumbled. "I don't know if my heart can handle much more of this."

Not for the first time, Trey wondered whether there was more between Magnus and Ava than the man was letting on. He believed Magnus when he said they hadn't fooled around, but he knew there was more to caring for someone than the mere physical aspect. And based on the fear he'd seen in Magnus these past few days, he got the feeling Magnus cared for Ava. Not necessarily in a platonic manner, either.

A few minutes later, Trey pulled up behind Brantley's truck, parking on the grass edge of the street in front of Gloria Steiner's house. There was no option of pulling into the driveway because three patrol cars and an ambulance were blocking their way.

"Oh, Jesus," Magnus rasped, yanking on the door handle.

Before he got the engine shut off, Magnus was out of the truck and racing to the front porch. Trey got out, heard Brantley call after him. He could've told his brother not to bother. Magnus wasn't hearing anything. He had a one-track mind, and right now, the only thing he cared about was finding out whether Ava was in the house. Trey knew because he'd spent every waking hour with Magnus for the past few days. And the sleeping ones, too.

Trey fell into step with Brantley, approaching the house slowly.

"Is she in there?" Brantley asked the deputy.

The man didn't respond immediately.

"I'm the one who called," Brantley clarified, pulling out his credentials. "We're with Sniper 1 Security. We're the ones who've been searchin' for her."

Magnus was pacing back and forth, his gaze darting to the deputy then to the door, likely trying to determine the odds of getting past him.

"She's in there," the deputy finally said. "But she's in bad shape. The paramedics are with her now."

"Oh, fuck," Magnus said, his relief potent.

Trey felt it, too. That sense of calm that descends when the chaos suddenly stops churning because you've found the person you've been looking for … found them alive. His chest expanded as though he was taking his first full breath in days.

"Can I see her?" Magnus asked, although there wasn't much question in his tone.

The deputy's eyes danced between Brantley and Magnus, back and forth until, finally, he gave Magnus the go-ahead.

"Would you mind if we speak to Gloria?" Reese prompted, joining them with Tesha at his side.

Trey tried to care what the old lady had to say, but he didn't. Right now, the only thing he wanted was to go to Magnus. At the same time, he wasn't keen on the idea of watching the reunion between Ava and Magnus. Sure, he was grateful she was alive, but he hadn't considered what it might mean when they found her.

"Would you ask Gloria if she'd mind talkin' to us?" Brantley requested. "We just have a few questions."

The man's dark eyebrows drew down in a harsh V as though he hadn't realized the severity of the situation.

"Go on in." He stepped back out of the way. "She's in the livin' room. Keep in mind, she's not happy we're here."

Trey wasn't sure he was ready for what was on the other side of that door, but when Reese moved forward, so did he.

BRANTLEY WATCHED HIS BROTHER GO INSIDE. HE could see the tense line of his broad shoulders and knew he was hanging by a precarious thread, which was why he'd made the request. *And* why he'd decided they would post someone at Ava's side at least until her bastard of a husband was taken into custody.

Reese repeated his request to speak to Gloria, and this time the deputy granted them permission, although he warned she was not in trouble at this time.

"We only want to thank her," Reese explained. "And try to understand what happened."

"The sheriff's already talked to her," the deputy countered as they passed.

"We know. Oh, and we've got a couple more comin'," Brantley informed him. "Charlotte Miller and Jay Hernandez. I've asked Charlie to accompany Ava to the hospital. You mind lettin' her in when she gets here?"

The deputy nodded, turned back to his post guarding the door.

Once inside, Brantley glanced around to get his bearings. All the curtains had been drawn, making the place feel dreary and cold. The good news was, the house was clean and smelled like lemon, not the sickly scent of death he'd imagined it would have.

"Ms. Steiner?" Reese said softly, moving slowly. "My name's Reese Tavoularis. I was here yesterday. Would you mind if I sit and speak with you a moment?"

Gloria Steiner was sitting on the edge of a couch cushion, her elbow resting on the arm, her hand over her mouth. She was trembling, her gaze swinging to the back of the house as though she was going to bolt at any moment.

"Ma'am?" Reese repeated.

Finally, Gloria nodded, a somewhat nervous action that made her head bob even as her gaze darted to the back of the house again.

"We're with Sniper 1 Security, and we're friends of Magnus Storme. He's a friend of Ava's," Reese explained as though talking down a wounded animal.

Her gaze slammed into him then bounced to Brantley. "How do I know y'all aren't the ones who hurt that poor girl?"

"Because we're givin' you our word," Reese said, his tone ripe with sincerity. "We'd like to understand how Ava ended up here. We know somethin' bad happened to her, and we're tryin' to ensure the person responsible is held accountable for their actions."

"How do I know you boys aren't the ones who did this?" she repeated, her gaze bouncing wildly once again.

Brantley could feel her tension. Throughout his military career, he'd encountered people from all walks of life, those who'd experienced trauma a thousand times, those who'd been on the periphery of it their entire lives. From his experience, they were dealing with a woman who'd once been through something similar to what Ava was going through now. It made so much more sense now. Why Ava was here. Why Gloria was hiding her.

He stood back, let Reese maintain control of the situation.

"We've been searchin' for Ava for several days now," Reese explained. "We were led to this area by suspicious actions. I'm the one who came to your door, remember?"

"Yeah, I remember," she grumbled.

"We were tipped off that Ava might be out this way because we were keepin' tabs on her husband."

Gloria stared up at Reese, narrowed her eyes. "He's the one who did this," she declared.

"Did you see him?"

She shook her head. "She told me. Begged me not to let him find her."

That explained why Gloria had lied when Reese had come to the door.

Reese forged ahead, joining her in the living room, easing down on the edge of the couch cushion at the opposite end from where she was. "During our search, we came across a rug in one of the fields not far behind your house. Can you tell us if that's where you found Ava?"

Gloria shook her head again. "I saw her walking," she said, her voice husky. "I think she was lookin' for a place to go." Some of the tension in her body eased as she angled toward Reese. "Is that where he dumped her?"

"We believe so," Reese confirmed. "We followed him this way, found him searchin' the field. Figured he might've come back for her. Can you tell us how bad her injuries are?"

Gloria nodded, and this time when she looked at them, Brantley noticed tears in her eyes. "It's bad. It's real bad. I told her she needed a hospital, but she begged me not to make her go. Said he'd find her."

Brantley's gut tightened. He wanted to wrap his fucking hands around Harrison Rivers's neck and choke the life out of him. He wanted to watch that smug expression turn to fear for his own life. Any bastard who laid hands on a woman deserved to suffer the way their victims suffered.

His attention shifted to voices coming from the front porch. He walked over, invited Charlie and Jay into the house.

They walked in silently, and Brantley took a moment to introduce them to Gloria. "Charlie works for me. She's gonna stay with Ava," he explained. "She's armed, and she won't let him anywhere near her." He turned back to Charlie. "They're in the back. I need you to go back there, introduce yourself to Ava, then send anyone else out who's not critical. The last thing she needs is to be surrounded by a bunch of men."

"Of course." Her eyes swam with understanding.

Without asking for details, Charlie ventured in the direction Brantley pointed.

He glanced back at Reese and Gloria, still chatting quietly. Hoping Gloria might open up a little more if she didn't feel Brantley looming over her, he headed toward the kitchen with Jay. Sheriff Paul Starr was standing at the island, his hands planted firmly on the butcher-block countertop, head hanging down.

"How is she?" Brantley asked, glancing in the direction of the soft hum of voices.

When he looked up, Brantley got all the answers he would ever need, and what the sheriff relayed with just a look was enough to chill his bones.

"He did a number on her," the man answered gruffly. His brown eyes blazed with fury when he said, "Guy oughta be put down for this."

"She's alive, Sheriff. Her wounds'll heal, and she's got people who care about her. They'll keep her safe." He glanced back at where Reese and Gloria were talking. "And we'll keep Ms. Steiner apprised of what's goin' on. She went above and beyond."

"She went through the same sorta thing," the sheriff noted. "Her bastard of a husband's six feet under 'cause of it."

That meant Brantley's theory was true. Gloria Steiner had come to Ava's rescue, kept her here to protect her. He couldn't imagine how difficult that had been for her. Probably dredged up a lot of bad memories.

"I take it she needs medical attention?"

"Yeah. Gloria admitted as much. I suspect she was gettin' ready to call us."

"You think you've got enough for an arrest? He's gonna be a slippery one."

"Aren't they all?"

"We'll need a solid case," Brantley told the sheriff. "It's imperative this guy not get the chance to do somethin' like this again."

The sheriff's smile was laced with menace and promise. "We'll make sure that doesn't happen."

The sound of footsteps drew Brantley's attention to the hallway. An EMT led the way while another pushed the portable gurney Ava was on. Brantley's gaze went to her face and his rage built to a crescendo. She was so battered and bruised, he hardly recognized her from the picture they had. Didn't help that someone—he assumed the husband—had shaved her head.

He watched as they passed, Trey and Magnus pulling up the rear.

"Did he...?" Brantley couldn't get the words out because *Jesus fuck*.

"Strangle her with a fuckin' rope?" the sheriff growled, a violent rumbling sound. "Yeah."

He'd tried damn hard, too, based on the rope burns on her neck.

"I figure he thought she was dead, dumped her in that rug," Sheriff Starr explained as Ava was taken out of the house. "She's got rope burns on her wrists and ankles, too. Probably had her hog-tied. Gloria said the ankle's definitely broken. How that girl got up and walked off is beyond me."

"We'll have someone watching her twenty-four seven," Brantley assured him. "Now it's your job to nail this fucker."

And while the sheriff took care of things from a legal perspective, Brantley had to figure out a way to get Ava March's mother out of danger, too.

If it wasn't already too late.

Magnus sat silently in the passenger seat of Trey's truck while they followed the ambulance to the hospital. The EMTs hadn't allowed him to go with Ava, but Charlie had assured him she would not leave Ava's side. He'd argued, of course. Although he liked Charlie, even figured she was better equipped to protect Ava since she was armed, it had pained him to let her out of his sight.

"There'll be protocols in place," Trey said, his voice a soothing hum. "That's why Brantley sent Charlie with her. Ava's safe now."

An image of Ava's battered face flashed in Magnus's head. He hadn't recognized her at first. Between the bruises and contusions marring her beautiful face and the fact that the dickhead had shaved her head. But the rope burn around her delicate throat had been more than he could bear. Magnus dragged in a ragged breath. He wanted to kill that fucker.

A warm hand curled over his, squeezed. "We'll take care of her," Trey said softly.

Magnus stared at Trey's profile as he drove. "We?"

Trey's eyes snapped over to his briefly. "I'm in this with you, Magnus. Whatever it takes."

A shudder racked his body as the relief of knowing that engulfed him. He wasn't sure Trey was making the promise that Magnus was hoping for, but he got the sense Trey understood that this was going to get complicated. Magnus couldn't deny that he'd fallen in love with Trey. The problem was, this thing with Ava, the realization that she could've been taken out of his life indefinitely … it had brought his feelings for her to light. And after seeing her again, finding her alive … well, Magnus knew Trey wasn't the only person he was in love with.

Which meant complicated might very well be an understatement.

Trey pulled up to the main entrance of the small hospital, stopping at the curb.

"Are you comin' in?" Magnus asked.

Trey looked over. "No, but I'll be back."

Magnus frowned. "Where are you goin'?"

Trey squeezed his hand. "I thought I'd head back to your place, check on Gia, see if she needs help. That way you can stay here and not worry about anything but Ava."

"Trey, you don't have to do that."

"I know. I want to. I'll be back, I promise."

Magnus glanced at the hospital doors. He knew Ava wasn't just coming in for a checkup. She would be here for a while. According to the EMTs, her injuries weren't necessarily life-threatening—likely thanks to Gloria's help—but it would take some time for Ava to recover.

"I'll come with—"

Trey shut him up by leaning over and kissing him square on the mouth. "You'll stay here. I'll be back." Trey pulled back. "Call me if you need me."

Magnus figured it wouldn't do well to tell him he needed him now, so he kept that to himself, forced himself out of the truck. He took a deep breath and headed inside to see what, if anything, he could find out.

CHAPTER TWENTY-FOUR

"Thank God you found her alive."

Reese smiled up at the fourth person in as many minutes to stop by their table to offer their congratulations on a job well done. Like Brantley, who was sitting across from him attempting to enjoy his dinner, Reese wasn't sure what to say to something like that. He was merely grateful that Ava March was safe and secure for the time being. It only pissed him off that Senator Harrison Rivers was still walking free. At the very least, he should've been dragged down in cuffs the way Magnus had been.

When they were left alone again, Reese picked up his fork, dug back into the chef salad he'd ordered while Brantley was two-fisting a double bacon cheeseburger with a smile.

"You think we should swing by the hospital? See how she's doin'?" Brantley asked, wiping his mouth and reaching for his sweet tea.

"I thought about it, but I think we should give her some time. Charlie said she's not goin' anywhere soon."

According to the update Charlie provided after the doctors had had time to assess Ava's condition, she wouldn't be going home for at minimum a week—wherever home might be. They'd already set her fractured wrist, stabilized her fractured collarbone, and she was scheduled for surgery in the morning to repair her broken ankle. Even as he thought about it, Reese's ankle throbbed at the thought of Ava walking as far as she had on a fractured leg. He imagined it would've been excruciating.

On a positive note, her other injuries were minor, and thanks to Gloria's medical training, Ava was going to be just fine. Physically, at least. It would just take time and rest for her body to heal from the rest of the damage that bastard had inflicted.

"I called RT, asked him to send me a couple of female agents who can remain on Ava's door until Rivers is arrested," Brantley said. "They'll be here tomorrow."

"If we're lucky, they'll arrest his ass soon," Reese grumbled, hating that the man still walked free. Hating even more that Ava's mother was still at the senator's house. They had intended to escort her off the property personally, but RT had intervened, instructing them to stay away from the senator. Evidently, there were some hotheads who weren't keen on the fact Sniper 1 Security had been involved in this high-profile case.

Thankfully, RT had followed that demand with a promise that they'd already submitted paperwork to the courts to have her moved to a mental health facility for the time being. Seeing as the senator was now under investigation for attempted murder, it was just a matter of time.

"Not soon enough," Brantley said as he sipped his tea. "I told the team to take tomorrow off."

"It's been a rough week," Reese noted. He still couldn't believe he'd already been back a week as of tomorrow. It felt like hours since he'd walked into Brantley's house, prepared to pack up his things if Brantley had enforced it.

As though agreeing, Tesha stretched her long body beneath the table where she'd been since they came in an hour ago. Reese had convinced Brantley to keep her with them since she'd worked so hard this week. Although Brantley assured him she enjoyed her time alone at the house, Reese preferred her company, and he suspected Brantley knew that.

A shadow fell over the table as another person stepped up.

Reese turned his attention to the newcomer, saw Travis standing there, his dark gaze skimming over them.

"I hear you found the girl."

Brantley leaned back, put his arm out along the back of the booth, and regarded his cousin. "She's in the hospital, but they say she'll make a full recovery."

"Good to hear. If she needs anything ... or if Magnus needs anything…"

"There's a lot of that goin' around," Brantley told him. "I'll pass it along."

Travis nodded, looked between them once more. "You two figure your shit out yet?"

Reese couldn't contain his smile. He should've known Travis had an ulterior motive for stopping by, and it hadn't been to check on Ava's status. Not entirely, anyway.

"It's all figured," Brantley responded with a smirk.

"Good. Why don't y'all stop by my folks' house for dinner on Sunday? They'd like to catch up."

"We can do that," Brantley answered before Reese had a chance to comment.

Travis nodded, his mood somber, as had been the case for some time now. He looked at Reese, over at Brantley, then tapped two fingers on the tabletop before sauntering off.

An hour and a half later, they were back at the house. Reese got Tesha's dinner served, refilled her water, and then joined Brantley on the back porch, where he sat drinking a beer and staring up at the stars. Reese pulled up a chair, dropped down into it.

"Somethin' on your mind?"

Brantley glanced over. "For the first time in a while, no."

Reese took that as a good sign.

As he settled back in the chair, letting the comforts of home quiet his nerves, he thought about their first date. The one that had started at a fancy steakhouse and ended up takeout right here on this very deck. It hadn't ended well that night because Reese had been overwhelmed by the fact he'd gone on a date with a man. At the time, he hadn't imagined his life could take such a drastic turn. Now here he was, more comfortable than he'd been in his entire life.

The dog door slapped, and he glanced over to see Tesha joining them. She looked their way as though assessing the situation before sauntering down into the yard. Reese couldn't help but smile. Her life had changed drastically in the past year and a half, too. She'd gone from being chained up in someone's backyard to leading the charge on the task force. She was no longer skinny and afraid of her own shadow, and Reese took pride in knowing he'd played some part in that.

"You know that thing you mentioned the other day?"

Reese swung his head toward Brantley. "I remember."

"Were you serious?"

He didn't respond immediately, but he smiled to himself. His hand went to his pocket, patting the ring he'd been carrying around with him for the past couple of months.

"If you weren't, that's all right, too," Brantley said after a minute or two.

Reese looked up at the stars, back to the table where they'd had that first date, then over to Brantley.

For months, he'd fantasized about this moment, sometimes wondering whether or not he'd ever get the opportunity. Like everything else, he'd obsessed over how he would do it, what he would say, but he'd never come up with the ideal scenario. Now, as he listened to Brantley breathing, to Tesha sniffing at the bottom of the steps, he figured he wouldn't get a more perfect moment than this one right here.

Reese pushed to his feet, sliding his hand in his pocket as he turned to face Brantley directly. He stepped closer, then eased down to one knee directly in front of him. He stared at Brantley's ridiculously handsome face, let his gaze drag over the hard line of his jaw, the firm set of his mouth, then up to the blue-gray eyes he'd spent months dreaming about.

"My life hasn't turned out quite like I'd envisioned," he said softly, holding Brantley's gaze. "In more ways than one. I never imagined I would find someone who would captivate me simply by breathing, someone who would hold my heart in the palm of their hand. I never took it for granted, Brantley; I promise you that. However, I did fuck it up by not being straight with you. You've been nothing but patient with me since the beginning, letting me lead, although it went against your nature to do so."

Reese swallowed, his chest churning, his stomach flipping. He took a deep breath, continued. "I thought I knew what love was at one point, but then you came along and pulled the blinders off, made me see exactly what I'd been missing. It took me screwing up to see exactly what I have."

Brantley remained stone still, his gaze boring into him, hands gripping the arms of the chair as though he was holding himself back.

"I love you. I love you with every breath I take, with every beat of my heart." Reese inched closer, still on one knee, leaning toward Brantley as he lifted the ring and reached for Brantley's hand. Part of him expected Brantley to pull away, but he didn't, and Reese felt a tidal wave of relief that propelled him forward. "I don't want to spend another day without you. If you'll have me, that is."

Still, Brantley didn't say a word.

"I want to spend the rest of my life with you." Reese drew in a deep breath, released it slowly, and smiled at the man he loved more than life itself. "Brantley Walker, will you do me the honor of marrying me?"

Even in the dim light from the house, Reese saw the glitter in Brantley's eyes as he sat up, leaned forward, and said the single most wonderful word in the history of words:

"Yes."

BRANTLEY WASN'T THE SORT OF MAN WHO had ever fantasized about proposals or marriage, but he could honestly say, if ever there were a perfect one, Reese had just nailed it.

"I wasn't sure if I was supposed to do this with a ring," Reese rambled. "So I decided I would since it felt right. It's nothin' fancy, but it symbolizes my commitment to you."

Brantley choked back the emotion clogging his airway while Reese slid the ring on his finger. He hadn't expected it, but he knew he would wear that damn thing with pride for the rest of his life.

Once it was settled on his finger, he palmed the side of Reese's face and drew him closer. Leaning forward, he kissed him softly, smiling as he did.

"I hope you haven't given much thought to a wedding," he whispered against Reese's mouth.

Reese pulled back, looked up at him. "Maybe a little. Why?"

"Because we're gonna have little say in the matter."

"Why's that?"

He chuckled. "Between JJ and my mother…"

Brantley could already see it now. His mother and JJ joined at the hip as they prepped and planned for the big day. It was going to be a nightmare, but as he stared back at the man in front of him, Brantley knew he would weather any storm for this man. Even Tropical Storm Iris and Hurricane JJ.

"Enough said." Reese laughed. "Just as long as there's a wedding."

"Oh, there will definitely be a wedding." The likes of which this town had never seen if Brantley knew JJ.

Brantley thumbed the ring on his finger, and the significance of this moment settled over him, heating the blood in his veins and coiling every muscle in his body. He reached for Reese's hand as he surged to his feet, pulling Reese with him.

"Come on before I fuck you right there on that table."

Reese laughed, the sound following him as Brantley dragged him into the house. He gave Reese enough time to slide the back door closed as he considered which direction to go. Did he bend Reese over the counter and fuck him in the kitchen? Or maybe he could turn him over the couch and take him there. Hell, there was enough adrenaline in his veins, he could fuck Reese up against the wall and never tire.

Although he liked the idea of all those options, he tightened his grip on Reese's hand and pulled him toward the bedroom. They'd christen those rooms soon enough. Right now, he wanted to take this man to their bed and make love to him the right way.

No sooner did he cross the threshold into the bedroom than Brantley found himself on the receiving end of Reese's kiss. No man had ever ripped the control away from him so completely, so thoroughly. Then again, there'd never been a man Brantley wanted to relinquish that control to.

No one but Reese.

"My turn," Reese grumbled as he yanked Brantley's shirt up.

"Your turn," Brantley agreed, helping him to discard the shirt, followed by the rest of their clothes, which landed in a heap on the floor at their feet.

As soon as they were naked, Reese manhandled him down to the bed, and while Brantley put up some resistance—it was in his nature—he finally gave in, falling onto the mattress with Reese coming over him. He welcomed the weight of him as Reese's naked body settled over his, their lips melded, the kiss one for the record books.

Just when he thought they were going to get down to business, Reese threw a wrench in his plans, forcing him to turn over onto his stomach before straddling his thighs. Hard hands gripped his shoulders, kneading him into submission. Brantley moaned, his full attention on Reese's hot skin pressed to his back, his heavy cock settling against his ass.

"If you're gonna take me," Brantley taunted, "you better do it hard and fast."

Reese chuckled, his lips dragging over Brantley's shoulder, inching lower. "You're not in charge here, navy boy."

Brantley laughed, but it was extinguished on a rough growl when Reese's lips trailed down his spine. He kissed his way lower, making Brantley's skin prickle with awareness. When Reese bit his ass cheek, he groaned. And when Reese's tongue glided along the crack of his ass, teasing him, Brantley's breath lodged in his throat as pleasure assaulted him.

"Oh, fuck," he whimpered when Reese's tongue rimmed his most sensitive flesh. Brantley pulled his knees beneath him, assuming the position, urging Reese to continue.

He relaxed, Reese's sensual assault making his muscles go lax even as his cock throbbed painfully, a desperate need to be fucked consuming him. He choked down the commands that were as natural as breathing and let Reese maintain control. His hands pressed roughly to Brantley's ass cheeks, spreading him wide as he tongued his hole, making his cock weep with excitement.

When two lubed fingers replaced Reese's tongue, Brantley realized he was panting, a sense of urgency claiming him. He wanted Reese inside him. He wanted to feel the man deep in his soul.

There were no questions, no comments, just the riot of Brantley's erratic heartbeat pounding in his ear as Reese settled over him a minute later, his cock pushing insistently against him.

Goose bumps broke out on his skin when Reese sank in deep, a rough, bellowing groan coming from the man's chest.

"Fuck," Reese hissed. "You feel too damn good."

Brantley pressed his chest to the mattress, held himself still as Reese sank in to the hilt, stretching him wide. An erotic bite of pain morphed almost instantly into pleasure as Reese began to move. He didn't go slow, but he didn't rush. He fucked him thoroughly, his fingers curling over Brantley's shoulders, keeping him in place, forcing him to take every delicious impalement.

Reaching back, Brantley gripped behind Reese's knees, slamming his hips back to take him deeper. Reese groaned. His hips pistoned on short, shallow thrusts as he drove them both higher. Brantley never wanted it to end, but he was close. So fucking close. Every muscle in his body tightened, forcing him to release Reese so he could reach for his cock. He gripped it tightly, staving off his release for as long as possible, but it didn't matter. He was overwhelmed with pleasure, the sensual assault on his body too much for him to fight.

"Oh, fuck, Reese!" he bellowed, slamming his hips back, jerking his cock roughly.

"Brantley…"

He heard the warning in Reese's tone, knew he was right there with him.

And when Reese came deep inside him, it triggered his release, and Brantley was sure every molecule in his body exploded, shattering before fusing back together. It left him feeling replete in a way he'd never experienced before.

CHAPTER TWENTY-FIVE

Friday, March 18, 2022

JJ WOKE UP TO AN EMPTY BED.

She stretched as her brain came fully online, processing the fact that there was light streaming in through the bedroom window. She glanced at the clock, noticed it was after eight. She'd slept later than usual, smiling at the realization. She was still tired, but not so much that she wanted to stay in bed all day. Well, not if Baz wasn't with her. If he'd been here, there was a good chance she would've been sitting astride him by now, slaking the lust that consistently hummed under her skin from his proximity.

"Mornin', sleepyhead."

The dark thunder of Baz's voice had her looking over at the door. He was leaning against the doorjamb, naked from the waist up. She took the opportunity to admire the smooth, hard plane of his chest, the rippling washboard of his abdomen, letting her gaze rake over every delicious inch. The longer she stared, the louder that hum got.

"You hungry?"

She listened for a response from her body, shook her head when her stomach did that little twisty thing it'd been doing for the past month or so. "I don't think I'm awake enough for food," she told him. "Maybe a shower first."

"You do that, and I'll make some coffee. Then when you're ready, we can go check out Bristol's house."

JJ felt a flutter in her chest, a giddiness she was getting used to.

When he left, she sat up slowly, dropped her feet to the floor. Her stomach lurched, so she sat still, breathing in deeply through her nose, out through her mouth until the unsettled feeling dissipated. Once she was steady, she got to her feet and headed for the bathroom.

She stared at her reflection in the mirror, wondering if she was imagining the glow on her face. It was happiness, she figured, another thing she was getting used to, thanks to Baz. She thought about the house they were going to look at, felt the giddiness return as she turned to grab a towel from the closet. She opened the door, reached in, and stopped short, something niggling at her brain when she noticed the box of tampons stashed inside.

Her analytical brain instantly kicked into gear, calculating the days since the last time she used them. It wasn't something she generally thought about, but something told her it was important to do the math.

"Oh, shit," she muttered, closing the door then leaning back against it.

She swallowed hard. How long had it been? She held up a hand, used her fingers to count, although she wasn't sure what exactly she was counting.

Her hand went to her stomach, and she took a deep breath. "Oh. Shit."

"JJ?"

Her gaze slammed into the closed door. "Yeah?"

"You all right?"

"Uh…" Was she?

His voice sounded concerned when he called her name again. A second later, the door opened, and then there he was, filling the doorway, larger than life, his teal-blue eyes pinned on her, worry etched into the lines near his eyes.

"What's wrong?"

Her eyebrows lowered as she tried to think back to the last time she would've had to refrain from having sex with him due to the inconvenience of her period. She was on birth control, but admittedly, there were times she forgot to take it. Not too often, but a slip every now and again. There were also the times she skipped the sugar pills and moved right into the next month just to avoid the blasted period.

"JJ? Baby, talk to me."

"I was just … uh…"

Baz walked into the room, came to stand directly in front of her, his gaze lowering to where her hand was still on her stomach, then meeting her gaze once more. "You okay?"

Not wanting him to worry, she said, "I'm good. Sorry. I was just…" *Just what?* What was she supposed to tell him? She shook off the weirdness and forced a smile. "I think I'm just hungry."

Even as she said it, her stomach churned in disagreement.

"Any special requests?"

"Toast," she blurted. "And coffee."

Another churn.

Maybe she would skip the coffee.

JJ pushed away from the door, stepping around him.

He flipped the end of her hair, then headed back to the door. "Comin' right up. It'll be ready for you when you're done."

"Baz, wait," she called after him.

He looked back over his shoulder.

JJ bolstered her courage, reminding herself that they were in this together, and she was no longer that timid woman who was scared of her future. It wasn't always easy to remember, but she was making a conscious effort these days.

She swallowed past the lump in her throat, met his gaze. "I … uh … think you might need to go to the drugstore."

He turned to face her fully. "You need somethin' for your stomach?"

Realizing her hand was still on her belly, she dropped it. "No, but I do think I need…"

Baz's dark eyebrows rose, his eyes glittering with the endless reserve of patience he seemed to have.

"I need a pregnancy test," she blurted.

His eyes went wide, his mouth opening. His gaze dropped to her stomach, back to her face. It would've been comical if JJ wasn't secretly still panicking.

She waited for him to say something, to see what his initial response would be. She probably should've gotten a test without him knowing, taken it first before springing something like that on him. She would've, she figured, if she'd been smart enough even to notice that she hadn't had a period in … if her calculations were correct, she'd missed two.

To her shock, Baz moved toward her, his stunned expression morphing into what looked a hell of a lot like hope.

"Are you serious?"

"As a heart attack," she said in a strangled whisper.

Baz's hand flattened on her belly, and she instantly soaked up his warmth. "You think…?"

She shook her head no at the same time she said, "Yes?"

His smile blinded her, and JJ felt that giddiness tightening her insides. He leaned down, pressed his lips gently to hers.

"I'm gonna run to the store right quick," he mumbled against her mouth.

She nodded. "Okay."

When he left her alone, JJ turned on the shower water, realizing she was … smiling.

BAZ DROVE TO THE DRUGSTORE IN A haze. He wasn't sure he could even feel his fingers as they wrapped tightly around the steering wheel. He knew for sure his knees were weak when he climbed out, strolled into the store. He skimmed the aisles, looking for the pregnancy tests. He felt utterly helpless as he stared at the wide variety they offered.

"Can I help you find something, sir?"

Baz didn't bother to look up when he responded to the polite young woman who was just doing her job. "I … uh … don't know which one I need."

She stepped forward. "They're all pretty much the same. Some have clearer readouts than others."

He glanced over, his gaze dropping to her name tag. Karen Burke, pharmacist, it read.

"I guess we want the one that'll tell us the truth," he muttered, shifting his attention back to the variety of rectangle boxes in several different colors.

"Then I think this one's exactly what you need." She chuckled, reached forward, and grabbed a box. She tucked it in his hand and then turned him toward the front.

Half an hour later, after sneaking back and grabbing two more different ones to go with the pharmacist's suggestion—one could never be too prepared—Baz was standing beside JJ at the bathroom counter, staring down at the little stick she'd peed on.

He had bought three different ones, not sure why. JJ had picked the digital one the pharmacist recommended, and he was grateful for that because it dumbed it down for him. The little countdown window was one bar away from complete, and his breath was already wedged in his lungs as he waited for the screen readout.

"What does it say?" JJ asked.

He glanced over, noticed she was covering her eyes with her hands.

"Nothin' yet," he told her, glancing back down.

He waited an eternity, which was probably more like ten seconds, before a word started to appear.

He stared.

One single word. Not two.

Baz gasped.

"Damn it, Baz," JJ grumbled. "What does it say?"

He snatched the stick, put it behind his back, and turned to face her.

He waited her out until she lowered her hands. Her gaze shot to the countertop, then up to his face. Her glare was adorable.

"What do you want it to say, JJ?" he asked.

Her light green eyes glittered as they skimmed over his face as though she could read his mind. "What do *you* want it to say?"

"Answer my question first," he insisted.

The words that came out of her mouth next hit him square in the chest, stealing his breath.

"I want it to say that we're gonna have a baby," she said in the softest, sweetest whisper.

He brought the stick around and showed her the small readout screen.

"Pregnant," she read, her eyes darting to his face as tears formed on her lower lashes.

Baz smiled, but it wasn't just on his face. The feeling consumed his entire being.

"We're havin' a baby, Baz."

He tossed the stick in the sink and reached for her, bringing his mouth to hers in a kiss he hoped expressed how fucking happy this woman made him.

Two hours after they'd learned they were going to be parents, Baz was walking through Bristol's childhood home, listening as JJ talked to herself, outlining what was what. He heard her voice but barely processed the words because he couldn't stop thinking about the fact that she was pregnant.

He honestly thought he couldn't be happier than he was right then. If he didn't know better, he would've sworn he was walking on clouds, his head dangerously close to a rainbow as he moved from one room to another. He expected a unicorn to peek out from somewhere and smile.

"Baz?"

"Hmm?" His gaze skimmed the room, but he didn't process much of what he saw.

"Did you hear anything I just said?"

He turned to face her. "We're havin' a baby."

JJ laughed. "I know. You've only mentioned it at least two dozen times since we left the apartment."

His smile split his face, and he repeated it.

"So I take it this would make a good baby room?"

"You're serious?"

She nodded. "I agree with Bristol, it needs work, but I think it's perfect."

He stepped up to her, put his hand on her hip. "I think *you're* perfect."

She laughed again, that sexy husky sound that went right through him. "Detective, I don't think you're payin' attention."

Baz wasn't sure he'd ever be able to pay attention again. He was going to be useless for the foreseeable future because nothing in this world could make a dent in the euphoria he felt.

"So we should make an offer," JJ said.

"We should."

"How long do you think it'll take to renovate this place?"

He shrugged. "How long do we have?"

She giggled. "We won't know until we go to the doctor next week."

"We?" His heart swelled with hope.

JJ's eyebrow arched. "I ain't doin' this by myself, Detective."

He smiled, and he realized he was wrong. He was already happier than he'd been two minutes ago.

Looked as though it was possible after all.

CHAPTER TWENTY-SIX

RENEE MARCH SAT SILENTLY IN THE CHAIR, her attention divided between the television screen, the front door, and the man stomping through the house. The TV was of little interest to her, but she was hoping the front door would open and Ava would come strolling in. She'd been gone too long now, and Renee was starting to worry.

Well, that and she was growing increasingly more uncomfortable being left alone with Harrison. She didn't like the man. At first, he'd snowed her with his promises to take care of Ava, to treat her like the princess that she was. But he'd evidently forgotten he'd made that promise if his actions were anything to go by. He'd long since started treating Ava like she was a child and not his wife.

The one and only time Renee had intervened, Harrison had threatened to have her put away in an asylum. He told her in no uncertain terms that she would never see her precious daughter again if she didn't learn how to toe the line.

So she had.

Since then, she'd done her best to back his requests when prompted and to ignore him any time she could.

It was hard to ignore him now. For some reason, Harrison had been on a rampage the past few days, cursing a blue streak as he hissed and growled at anyone and everyone who dared cross his path.

Renee knew better than to speak directly to him when he was in one of these moods. Instead, she sat quietly, pretending to be doped up on whatever meds he fed her on a daily basis. She'd stopped taking them two weeks ago, shortly after she'd gotten the feeling something was wrong with Ava. Her daughter had been spending a lot of time crying these past few months, and the arguments between her and Harrison had begun to escalate daily. Renee hated that she couldn't console her daughter, hated that the darkness had such a firm grip on her, which was why she'd stopped taking the meds, searching for that glimmer of lucidity she'd had prior to them.

"That fucking bitch," Harrison belted out as he stormed through the room, snatching the remote.

He flipped through the channels, stopping on the nightly news. He loomed over the television blocking her view. Renee watched him, noticing the tight grip of his fists, the tenseness of his shoulders. He was definitely angry, but she didn't know what had triggered him this time. Since he'd told her that Ava was off on a spa retreat, Renee figured he couldn't be pissed at her. Probably one of the maids who hadn't done something to his exact specifications. He was always going off about the worthless help, firing them left and right, never happy with anything anyone did. She often wondered why he didn't just do it himself if he wanted it done right.

Her attention was back on him, which was why she noticed as he stumbled back two steps, a heavy gasp escaping him.

He moved just enough that she could see the television screen. A picture of Ava appeared beneath a heading that read: missing woman found battered and left for dead.

Renee's eyes widened, but she didn't make a sound as she listened to the news anchor, a dark-haired man with a pleasing face and weird cupid's bow lips, explain how Ava March had been discovered early on Thursday morning by a local sheriff in the small town of Embers Ridge.

"Fuck," Harrison thundered, his hands gripping his hair tightly.

She didn't dare speak because it would only result in him taking out his anger on her. Then again, she didn't need to ask questions because she already knew. She'd known all along the danger her daughter was in. Somewhere deep in her drug-induced haze, Renee had known this man was a monster. She'd known, but the drugs had made it impossible to care or to help.

This was her fault, she knew. Her fault that Ava had suffered the wrath of this bastard all these years. Ava had done it for Renee. She'd endured because Harrison had told her that if she didn't, he'd have Renee committed, locked away in a padded room for the rest of her life. Well, that was on a good day. During the height of his tirades, she'd heard him threaten to kill her a time or two, but again, Renee hadn't had enough energy to care. Sometimes she welcomed the idea of death. Now, for instance. It would be so much easier for everyone if she were dead.

Harrison gripped his hair, yanked as he stared up at the ceiling. "I cannot fucking believe this!"

"Where's Ava?" Renee asked.

Harrison lowered his head, glared at her. "Not where she should be, that fucking bitch." He dropped his hands to his sides, took a deep breath, then another personality seemed to slide neatly in place.

"But I can still fix this," Harrison declared. "I can still make it right."

Renee watched him as he began to pace the room.

"She just can't talk to the police," he muttered, stopped abruptly. "I'll need to pay her a visit. Fix it once and for all."

Renee didn't bother to remind him that Ava had probably already talked to the police. If she was found yesterday morning, she'd had nearly two days to reveal the horrors that Harrison had put her through. She prayed she had.

"Did you mean to hurt her?" she asked, keeping her tone bored so as not to rile him more.

"Did I mean to *hurt her*? Fuck no." His eyes burned with menace. "I meant to *kill her!*" he confessed. "That bitch should be dead, not laid up in the hospital, making my life a living fucking hell."

Renee swallowed the bile that rose in her throat. The thought of Ava dead because of her … it renewed her self-loathing, the hatred she had for her mere existence.

Harrison stood tall, his mask falling back into place. The one he used when he was shaking hands and kissing asses, the politician in full force. Renee hated this persona the most because it was the fakest of all.

"Tomorrow morning," he said confidently, glancing over at Renee. "Tomorrow, I'll visit my poor, battered wife in the hospital, play the dutiful, terrified husband, explain how I've been worried sick because she's mentally ill like her mother."

I'm not the only one in this house who's mentally ill, she thought.

Renee didn't move, watching as his vicious smile pulled at the corners of his mouth.

Several hours later, in the dark of night, Renee got out of bed. She retrieved the gun she'd stashed under her pillow. It was the one she'd found in Harrison's desk drawer, the one with the spinning barrel that held the bullets, the kind that was easy to load. A revolver, she believed it was called. There were only three bullets, although it held six. She knew because she'd hidden three of them. A backup plan in case he found the gun and emptied it.

Renee turned the gun this way and that, staring at it as her plan firmed in her mind. She was familiar with the weight of it in her hand because she'd picked it up and held it a few dozen times over the course of the past few years. Each time she was driven by the dark thoughts, the ones that told her to use it because it would end all the suffering, she had gone back to find it.

She'd never had the guts to pull the trigger.

Until now.

CHAPTER TWENTY-SEVEN

Saturday, March 19, 2022

"I'm surprised that thing still works," Brantley said when he came out of the bedroom, dressed after his shower.

Reese had woken early and joined Brantley and Tesha for a run despite his reluctance to commit to ten miles. Fortunately for him, Brantley'd gone easy on him today, cutting the time in half as long as Reese promised to make it up to him when they returned to the house.

Reese had gladly made it up to him, and his knees were still sore from where he'd knelt on the shower floor while Brantley had fucked his face and rasped vulgar words until he came. Then Reese had endured while Brantley jacked him off under the guise of getting him clean.

Needless to say, he was willing to get back to the morning runs, especially if he had that to look forward to each day.

"I had to clean two layers of dust off it, but it turned on," Reese said with a grin, shifting his attention to the television.

"What're you watchin'?"

"I was hopin' to catch the Formula 1 qualifying, but it's not on yet."

Brantley glanced at the TV. "So you're watchin' the news?"

Reese shrugged. "Nothin' else on."

"Well, I can certainly think of somethin' else that'll keep you busy, if you're—" Brantley's words cut off, and his eyes widened, still locked on the television.

Reese turned back to see a picture of Harrison Rivers along with a live feed of a reporter standing outside the familiar house they'd staked out the other night.

"Did they arrest him?" Brantley asked at the same time Reese was turning up the volume.

"We're standing outside the home of Senator Harrison Rivers. As you can see behind me"—the reporter motioned with her hand—"it's a hub of activity this morning. Police were called out shortly after eight when they received a 911 call from a distressed employee of Mr. Rivers. The barricade tape has been erected, and we're being told that it's the scene of a murder/suicide. We don't have all the details, but we will be bringing you more on this breaking news as we have it."

"Murder/suicide?" Brantley asked, his eyebrows lowered. "Where's Ava?"

"Still in the hospital," Reese told him, already on his feet and heading for his cell phone on the kitchen counter. "We got an update from Charlie half an hour ago. Yesterday's surgery went well, and Ava's awake and alert this morning."

"So, what?" Brantley chirped. "He killed Ava's mother and turned the gun on himself?"

The screen flashed back to the reporter outside the house, and Reese paused before placing the call to listen.

"We've just been told that police believe the senator's mother-in-law shot him while he was asleep, then turned the gun on herself." Her expression sobered. "It's a sad, sad day for all involved, Tom."

"Holy shit," Brantley muttered.

"Do they believe this has something to do with the senator's wife, who was found beaten and left for dead just two days ago?" the news anchor questioned, the man's voice far too pleasant to be discussing something so morose.

"How would they think that?" Brantley grumbled. "Are they fuckin' mind readers?"

Reese dialed Charlie's number, greeted with a clipped "Hey" when she answered.

"Everything's good here," she said with a smile in her voice.

With the phone on speaker, he turned to face Brantley as he spoke. "Charlie, don't let Ava turn on the news. And don't let anyone in to talk to her."

"Why? What's wrong?"

He gave her the high level of what they'd just seen on the news, most importantly the fact that her mother was dead.

"Oh, shit. Do you want me to tell Magnus? He's been with her the entire time."

Across the room, Brantley was shaking his head.

"No," Reese told her. "We'll head up there, fill him in so he can tell her."

"Okay. I'll keep everyone else out until you get here."

Reese disconnected the call, tucked his phone in his pocket.

By the time they got to the hospital forty-five minutes later, there were already swarms of news vans parked outside. Reese figured the vultures were looking to land a firsthand account from Ava. Hopefully, Charlie had managed to keep everyone out.

They were able to sneak into the building without any questions lobbed their direction. They made it up to the floor Ava was on, saw that Charlie was stationed down the hall, keeping anyone from making it as far as Ava's room.

"Trey's outside her door," Charlie stated. "We've already had three people try to get up here."

Didn't surprise him. Reese knew the news outlets were greedy for a story. Their only goal was to get the information to the public first. Didn't matter that a woman was lying in a hospital bed after her husband tried to kill her or that that woman was about to learn of her mother's death, as well as her husband's. Just because Harrison Rivers was a monster didn't mean Ava didn't care what happened to him.

"Does Trey know?" Brantley asked.

"I had to tell him," she said, her tone reluctant. "But I don't think he told Magnus yet."

Reese nodded. "Understandable. We'll talk to him first, see how he wants to proceed."

She turned back to her post when Reese and Brantley started down the hall.

Trey's gaze slammed into them as they were approaching, his expression shifting to one of relief.

"You have a chance to talk to Magnus yet?" Brantley asked as he stopped in front of his brother.

He shook his head. "I didn't want to pull him away from her until I had to."

"I think it'd be best if we told him first, let him decide how he wants to relay the information to Ava."

"It won't go over well, regardless," Trey mumbled. "Bad news never does."

"You wanna grab him?" Brantley prompted, nodding toward the door.

Trey slipped inside, returning a moment later with Magnus beside him. Based on the grimace on his face, Magnus wasn't too keen on the idea of being pulled out of the room.

"We'll make this quick," Reese told him. "But we figured you needed to know before someone leaked the information."

"What information?" Magnus glanced between the three of them. "Did they arrest that bastard?"

Reese waited, let Brantley take the lead.

"Harrison Rivers is dead, Magnus."

His dark eyebrows slashed downward over tired eyes. "Dead? How?"

Reese's gaze dropped to the floor, unable to look at Magnus when Brantley delivered the other news.

"Ava's mother shot and killed him."

Magnus's eyes widened.

Brantley plowed forward. "Then she took her own life."

Magnus staggered back, but Trey was right there, putting his arm around his shoulders. Reese stepped back out of the way, giving them a moment.

"She's gonna be devastated," Magnus whispered, turning into Trey's arms. "She's been through enough."

"She has," Brantley agreed, his tone somber. "I hate to be the bearer of bad news, but if it makes it easier for you, I can be the one to tell her."

Magnus shook his head, pulled himself together, and extricated himself from Trey's arms. "No. I'll do it. She needs to hear it from me."

Brantley nodded. "As of right now, you've officially contracted the services of Sniper 1 Security. I'm gonna talk to the hospital, let them know that we'll be stationing agents in the building to ensure no one gets up here. Give the media some time to die down."

Magnus nodded. "I can't afford it, but I'll do whatever it takes."

Brantley smiled, although there wasn't any humor in it. "We're doin' this free of charge, man."

"You don't have—"

"You're family," Brantley said firmly. "There's no other way *to* do it."

It was because of those things right there, Brantley's generosity and his compassion, that Reese had fallen in love with this man. And why he was now going to spend the rest of his life with him.

Brantley put a hand on Magnus's shoulder, squeezed. "We'll get goin', but if you need anything at all, just holler."

Before he could drop his hand, Trey grabbed it. "What's this?" he asked, tapping the ring on Brantley's finger.

Reese felt a smile pull at his mouth when he noticed the bashful way Brantley pulled his hand away.

Trey looked at Reese. "Did you...?" His gaze shot to Brantley. "Are y'all...?"

"He did, and we are," Brantley said firmly. "And that's all we're gonna say about it." Brantley narrowed his gaze on his brother. "And don't you dare tell Mom and Dad."

This time, Reese couldn't hold back the laugh.

It was nice not to be the one turning crimson for a change.

"WHAT'RE YOU LAUGHING AT?" BRANTLEY ASKED REESE as they walked toward the exit after talking to the head of security regarding the stationing of his agents at the hospital.

"Just thinkin' about your reaction to Trey." Reese's tone turned mocking when he added, "Don't you dare tell Mom and Dad."

Brantley scowled. "You found that amusing, did ya?"

"I did, yeah."

Brantley grunted. "Just for that, I'm gonna make you tell my family the story of how it all went down."

He looked at Reese, expecting a grimace, but instead, he found the man smiling.

"It couldn't be any harder than when I got your father's permission," Reese said, deadpan.

Brantley came to a grinding halt right there in the busy hallway. "You did not?"

Reese barked a laugh. "Of course *not*. Hell, I never would've been able to stand in front of Frank and ask for your hand." He laughed again. "I should've, though. It would serve you right. Your brothers and sisters would've given you shit for the rest of your days."

They would've, that was for sure.

"Speakin' of." Brantley continued walking now that the shock had worn off. "You know we've gotta tell JJ. If she hears it from Trey, she'll have my head."

"You wanna tell her before your folks?"

That was a good question. "What about your mom and Z?"

"Already told 'em," he answered with a smile. "Via text message. That's how the kids do it now."

Brantley barked a laugh, drawing the attention of a couple walking into the hospital.

"Well, I can't text JJ. She'll kick my ass, but maybe I tell her, then we'll swing by my parents' later, give them the good news."

"What're we waitin' for? Call JJ. See if they're home. We can stop by before we head back."

"I've already beat you to it," he told Reese. "This ol' boy knows how to text, too. JJ sent me back this cryptic message, said something about big news. I figure she wants to tell us they're buyin' Bristol's house."

"And you'll rain on her parade and tell her we're gettin' married. Smart."

Brantley laughed. "I already know how to make it up to her."

"How's that?"

"They're gonna need all the help they can get to fix that house up, so I figured I'd start by volunteering our handyman services."

"*Our?*"

"Yep." Brantley shot him a winning grin. "You're my partner, remember?"

"Oh, brother," Reese grumbled.

Because he liked to keep JJ on her toes, Brantley didn't bother to call to announce they were coming over. He figured the more surprises, the better.

"Are you expectin' someone?" he heard Baz say from inside the apartment.

"Have I ever invited anyone over here?" she retorted as Baz opened the door.

"Hey," Baz greeted, his eyebrows dipping low. "Somethin' wrong?"

"Why's anything hafta be wrong?" he said with a grin. "Can't a guy just come over to hang out?"

"He can, but he doesn't," Baz answered, stepping back and opening the door. "Come in. We were just about to figure out what to get for lunch. Y'all hungry?"

"I never say no to food," Brantley told him. "As long as it's not lettuce or fruit, I'm game." He peered over at JJ, who was standing at the kitchen island, her laptop open in front of her. "You workin'?"

"Nope. I'm researchin' real estate."

"Yeah?" He pretended to be surprised. "You movin'?"

Her eyes lifted to meet his, and he saw something he hadn't seen in a long time. True happiness.

"Well, I was gonna let it be a surprise, but since you're a know-it-all," she said, turning her computer around so that Brantley could see the screen.

Expecting to see an image of the house, he was surprised to see a note. "You're gonna be an uncle," he read.

When he peered back at her, he saw she was giving him that look that said she had plenty of patience to wait for it to sink in.

He frowned, glanced at Baz, then back to her. "I'm already an uncle."

Reese laughed, then turned to Baz. "Are you serious?"

Baz nodded, his eyes shining bright.

"Congratulations," Reese offered, clasping Baz's hand and pulling him in for a hug.

"Congratulations? For what? What the fuck?" Brantley asked, glancing between them. He knew whatever the riddle was had to be simple, but he wasn't getting it.

"I'm pregnant, you goober," JJ said with a grin.

Brantley went stone still, stared at her.

"It's a good thing, B," she whispered, as though knowing his head was filling with a million questions. "A really good thing."

Brantley's confusion faded, elation taking over. He reached for JJ, pulled her in for a hug. Then did the same to Baz.

"I have to say, her news certainly trumps ours," Reese said when the love wasn't flowing anymore.

JJ squealed, eyes wide as they slammed into Reese. "You didn't!"

Reese smiled. "I did."

"I told you!" she shouted to Baz. "I told you they were gonna get hitched."

Brantley smiled, and for the first time in a really long time, he felt it throughout his entire being.

LATER THAT NIGHT, REESE FOUND HIMSELF ON the receiving end of congratulations from Brantley's family.

He hadn't lucked out and only had to share the news with Frank and Iris. Nope. Brantley had gone and invited his brothers, sisters, nieces, and nephews over so he could knock it out in one fell swoop. Everyone, with the exception of Trey, who was still at the hospital with Ava and Magnus, had come to hear the big news.

"Have you set a date?" Bryn asked, beaming up at Brantley.

"What do you think?"

"I think that's the first step." She canted her head, studied her brother critically. "I'm not sure you'd make a good June bride, but a fall wedding might be nice."

"Fall in Texas is just an extension of summer," Killian noted, coming to join them. "Don't really see much of a difference."

"Have you told your mama?" Iris asked Reese.

"Yes, ma'am."

"He texted her. Can you believe that?" Brantley joked.

Iris's eyes widened as though he'd committed a cardinal sin. "I called her, too," he said quickly. "This afternoon. So yes, she knows."

"Maybe I could get her number," Iris said, her eyes dancing with amusement. "See what her thoughts are."

Before Reese could respond, Brantley was right there. "Of course you can. Then the two of you can get with JJ and nail down all the specifics. Y'all just tell us when to be there and what to wear."

"You sure you wanna give them that much power?" Tori teased, coming to stand next to her husband. She glanced up at Killian. "Remember our wedding?"

He smiled, winked. "Some of it, but mostly the after."

She smacked his chest. "Not in polite company."

"Ain't no one polite here," Frank added with a wide grin.

"Well, we'll get it figured out." Iris looked at Reese. "Can I proceed on the assumption y'all will be tyin' the knot this year?"

"Yes, ma'am." If he was being honest, he didn't care if they got married tomorrow. He just wanted to marry Brantley. The rest was semantics.

It was dark by the time they got back to the house. Reese made quick work of filling Tesha's bowl, getting her settled for the evening. Once that was done, he went and changed into shorts, returned to the kitchen to find Brantley standing at the calendar on the wall.

"September seventeenth," Brantley noted.

"What about it?"

"That's the day we're gettin' married."

Reese stopped. "Is there somethin' special about that day?"

Brantley dropped the calendar pages, turned to look at him. "That's the day after you kissed me for the first time." He bobbed his head to the side. "I would've done it on the sixteenth, but that's a Friday."

Reese's jaw was unhinged, his disbelief evident. Of all the things he knew about Brantley, he didn't realize the man was sentimental. Not to this degree, anyway.

Brantley stepped forward, pressed a finger to his chin. "Unless you want me to fill that mouth with somethin', you might wanna close it."

"You remember the day you first kissed me?" he asked.

"I remember the day we met, the first time we kissed, the first time you let me make you come." His voice dropped an octave. "I remember the first time you fucked me, and yes, I remember the first time I sank my cock into that hot, tight ass of yours."

Heat grazed every inch of his skin as he stared into those blue-gray eyes.

"And I'm about to add another first to that list."

Reese liked firsts. "What's that?"

Brantley took his hand, pulled him toward the kitchen. Reese went willingly, his body pliant as Brantley turned him to face the island. He felt the heat of Brantley at his back, then the warmth of his breath as it fanned his ear.

"And I remember the first time I fucked my fiancé right here on the kitchen counter."

Reese shivered, tingles jolting down his spine, his cock thickening in anticipation.

"You like that."

Since it wasn't a question, Reese didn't feel the need to answer. They both knew the truth.

Brantley's hands slipped beneath his T-shirt, calloused palms gliding up his sides, lifting his shirt. Reese raised his arms, allowed Brantley to strip it from him. He remained where he was as Brantley pulled his shorts down, let them pool at his ankles.

"I sure do love this ass," Brantley rumbled, kneading Reese's ass as he moved behind him.

"You have lube?"

"When have you known me not to be prepared?" Brantley's voice was a seductive rasp against the back of his neck.

Reese spread his feet wide when Brantley's hand trailed down the back of his thigh, then moved inward before sliding upward. He drew in a ragged breath when Brantley reached between his legs, cupped his balls, kneaded them with deft fingers.

"I think I'm gonna make it my mission to fuck you on every surface in this house before we're married," Brantley declared, his hands falling. "And then we'll do it again after."

Reese's breaths were sawing in and out of his lungs as he waited for Brantley's next move. He heard a bottle being squirted.

"Bend over," Brantley commanded.

Reese leaned forward, his ass jutting toward Brantley.

"Now reach back and spread your ass for me."

Chills danced down his spine, the eroticism of the moment making his blood pump.

With his chest pressed to the cold granite, he reached back, did as instructed.

"Now that's nice," Brantley crooned, his hand gripping Reese's hip, the head of his cock sliding along the crack of his ass.

Reese gritted his teeth as the pleasure consumed him, the stretch of his body as it acclimated to Brantley's cock pushing deep inside.

"Oh, fuck me," Brantley grumbled. "You're so fucking tight like this."

From there, Reese let Brantley fuck him until they were mumbling nonsense in their quest for orgasm. He shifted and moved when Brantley instructed, but it wasn't until he had one leg lifted and stretched out on the island top that he knew he wouldn't last much longer. The position allowed Brantley to drive in deep and hard. There was no holding back, every thrust rocking Reese on his steady leg as Brantley plowed into him.

"Don't you come," Brantley growled. "Not yet."

Reese bit his cheek to hold back. The pain recentered him but it was only brief. When Brantley bucked his hips forward and gripped Reese's hip tightly, he felt the pulse of the man's cock inside him.

"Fuck," Brantley growled, lingering briefly while Reese was still holding back.

The next thing he knew, both feet were back on the floor as he was spun around. His ass bumped the cabinet as Brantley went to his knees, sucking Reese deep into his throat. Reese took over, palming Brantley's head and holding him while he fucked his mouth.

He stared down, admiring the way Brantley's mouth stretched wide around him, his eyes glazed with desire. He could get behind the idea of doing this in every room of this house, that was for sure.

"Your mouth…" he rasped. "So … fucking…" Reese grunted when Brantley moaned, the vibrations traveling up his dick and into his balls. He groaned roughly, punching his hips forward and coming with a violent shudder.

Brantley slowly stood, leaned into him, and pressed a kiss to his mouth. "Better?"

"Definitely." Reese hugged him, holding on tight as he came down from that intense rush.

He felt the warmth of Brantley's breath against his ear. "The next time you're cookin', I expect you to remember the way my cock felt inside you."

Reese groaned, then a laugh escaped.

He got the feeling that was exactly what he would be doing for the foreseeable future.

CHAPTER TWENTY-EIGHT

Thursday, April 14, 2022

TREY WALKED INTO MOONSHINERS ON THURSDAY NIGHT, grateful to find the place was nearly empty.

He stopped at the bar, ordered a beer from Rafe Sharpe, then sauntered back to where Brantley and Reese were sitting at a table. He could tell by their expressions that they weren't sure why Trey had asked them here. Sure, he'd been vague about his reasons, but Trey knew it was time to be honest with Brantley. He had an excuse for why he wasn't at work right now—helping with Camp K-9 while Magnus was taking care of Ava—but soon enough, he would have to make a choice. He told himself on the drive over that it was now or never.

"Hey," he greeted, pulling out a chair and easing into it.

"How's Ava?" Reese asked.

"She's doin' all right. Slow goin'."

It had been nearly a month since they'd found Ava at Gloria Steiner's. Four solid weeks of recovery both mentally and physically after her ordeal. They'd been through a lot already, and Trey knew it wasn't over. They had a long way to go before Ava was back to living a full life, but things were steadily progressing.

"And you?" Brantley asked. "You ready to come back to the task force yet?"

Trey took a pull on his beer, held his brother's gaze. He'd taken the last month off from working with the task force, filling in at Camp K-9 to pass the time. He found the work enjoyable, and after a brief conversation with Magnus, he'd come to a decision.

Hence the reason he was here.

"You're not comin' back," Brantley stated, his tone carrying a hint of disappointment.

"I'm not, no."

He expected Brantley to blast him for abandoning the team, but it didn't come. The longer his brother sat there, staring back at him, the more unease he felt.

"Look. I know—"

"This is a good thing," Brantley interrupted. "Even I know that."

Trey frowned, feeling a tad defensive. "What's that supposed to mean?"

"You might not give me much credit, but I'm pretty astute," Brantley said with a smirk. "I'm damn good at readin' a man and I knew you hated it."

"I did," he admitted with defeat. "I fuckin' hated it."

"It's not easy," Reese inserted. "Takes a lot out of you."

Trey nodded.

"So you're workin' with the dogs now?" Brantley inquired, sipping his beer, continuing to stare at Trey as though he was unearthing his deepest, darkest secrets with only his eyes.

"I am."

"It's what you wanna do?"

"It is."

At least for now. Trey had no idea what the future would hold. He was still getting used to everything that was going on. The fact that Ava was staying at Magnus's was the most difficult thing. Magnus had shut down some since finding Ava, and Trey figured that was partly his fault. He'd told Magnus he would give him space, but he would be around if he needed him. And since he'd worked at Camp K-9 for the duration of Ava's stay in the hospital while Magnus had been with her, he'd managed to work himself into the routine. He found he enjoyed it, and he actually looked forward to working each day.

"How's JJ doin'?" Trey asked, referring to her pregnancy.

"Still ornery, still nosy," he said with a smirk. "But she's good. Baby's due October twenty-seventh, so she's got time. You could swing by, you know. The team misses you."

Trey hadn't mustered up the courage yet and he figured that was mostly due to his guilt over wanting to quit. "I still plan to keep in touch."

"Well, I'd hope so. You *are* my brother."

Trey laughed. "You know what I mean."

Brantley took another pull on his beer, set it down. "And you know if you ever wanna come back, we've always got room for you."

"I appreciate it."

"I do have *one* question for you," Brantley said, his expression serious.

"What's that?"

He canted his head. "Any chance we can get a discount on Tesha's trainin'? I mean, you've got an in with the owner, right?"

Trey laughed, and for the first time in a long time, he felt less weight on his shoulders. He'd been dreading this conversation, reluctant to let his brother down even if he knew it was the right move for him.

"He's kidding," Reese said, taking Trey's silence as confusion.

"Hell no, I'm *not*," Brantley countered. "I'm payin' for a wedding. I need all the help I can get."

 Stay Tuned

I hope you enjoyed the seventh installment of the Off the Books Task Force. The team continues to morph and grow, and they'll continue to do so because it's not over for Brantley and Reese, JJ and Baz, and the rest of the task force. And for those eager for Trey and Magnus to have a happily ever after, there will be more for them. Their full story will be told in TREY (The Walkers of Coyote Ridge).

Each book in this series is a full-length novel involving a new case and the continuation of the relationships between them all. And I promise not to keep you waiting long for each installment.

If you enjoyed *Confessions*, please consider leaving a review.

ACKNOWLEDGMENTS

Of course, I have to thank my wonderfully patient husband, who puts up with me every single day. If it weren't for him and his belief that I could (and can) do this, I wouldn't be writing this today. He has been my backbone, my rock, the very reason I continue to believe in myself. I love you for that, babe.

Chancy Powley – As always, you keep me going, and I thank you for that.

Jenna Underwood – I always look forward to the random notes in the mail. They make me smile. As do the phone calls (even if I can't always answer).

I also have to thank my street team – Nicole Nation Street Team – Your unwavering support is something I will never take for granted.

I can't forget my copyeditor, Amy, at Blue Otter Editing. Thank goodness I've got you to catch all my punctuation, grammar, and tense errors.

Nicole Nation 2.0 for the constant support and love. You've been there for me from almost the beginning. This group of ladies has kept me going for so long, I'm not sure I'd know what to do without them.

And, of course, YOU, the reader. Your emails, messages, posts, comments, tweets… they mean more to me than you can imagine. I thrive on hearing from you; knowing that my characters and my stories have touched you in some way keeps me going. I've been known to shed a tear or two when reading an email because you bring so much joy to my life with your support. I thank you for that.

ABOUT NICOLE EDWARDS

New York Times and *USA Today* bestselling author Nicole Edwards lives in the suburbs of Austin, Texas with her husband and their youngest of three children. The two older ones have flown the coop, while the youngest is in high school. When Nicole is not writing about sexy alpha males and sassy, independent women, she can often be found with a book in hand or attempting to keep the dogs happy. You can find her hanging out on social media and interacting with her readers - even when she's supposed to be writing.

CONNECT WITH NICOLE

I hope you're as eager to get the information as I am to give it. Any one of these things is worth signing up for, or feel free to sign up for all. I promise to keep each one unique and interesting.

NIC NEWS: If you haven't signed up for my newsletter and you want to get notifications regarding preorders, new releases, giveaways, sales, etc, then you'll want to sign up. I promise not to spam your email, just get you the most important updates.

NICOLE'S BLOG: My blog is used for writer ramblings, which I am known to do from time to time.

NICOLE NATION: Visit my website to get exclusive content you won't find anywhere else, including sneak peeks, A Day in the Life character stories, exclusive giveaways, cards from Nicole, Join Nicole's review team.

NN ON FACEBOOK: Join my reader group to interact with other readers, ask me questions, play fun weekly games, celebrate during release week, and enter exclusive giveaways!

INSTAGRAM: Basically, Instagram is where I post pictures of my dogs, so if you want to see epic cuteness, you should follow me.

TEXT: Want a simple, fast way to get updates on new releases? Sign up for text messaging. If you are in the U.S. simply text NICOLE to 64600. I promise not to spam your phone. This is just my way of letting you know what's happening because I know you're busy, but if you're anything like me, you always have your phone on you.

NAUGHTY & NICE SHOP: Not only does the shop have signed books, but there's fun merchandise, too. Plenty of naughty and nice options to go around. Find the shop on my website.

Website:	NicoleEdwards.me
Facebook:	/Author.Nicole.Edwards
Instagram:	NicoleEdwardsAuthor
BookBub:	/NicoleEdwardsAuthor

By Nicole Edwards

THE WALKERS

ALLURING INDULGENCE
Kaleb
Zane
Travis
Holidays with The Walker Brothers
Ethan
Braydon
Sawyer
Brendon

THE WALKERS OF COYOTE RIDGE
Curtis
Jared (a crossover novel)
Hard to Hold
Hard to Handle
Beau
Rex
A Coyote Ridge Christmas
Mack
Kaden & Keegan
Alibi (a crossover novel)

BRANTLEY WALKER: OFF THE BOOKS
All In
Without A Trace
Hide & Seek
Deadly Coincidence
Alibi (a crossover novel)
Secrets
Confessions

AUSTIN ARROWS
Rush
Kaufman

CLUB DESTINY
Conviction
Temptation
Addicted
Seduction
Infatuation
Captivated
Devotion
Perception
Entrusted
Adored
Distraction
Forevermore

DEAD HEAT RANCH
Boots Optional
Betting on Grace
Overnight Love
Jared (a crossover novel)

DEVIL'S BEND
Chasing Dreams
Vanishing Dreams

MISPLACED HALOS
Protected in Darkness
Salvation in Darkness
Bound in Darkness

OFFICE INTRIGUE
Office Intrigue
Intrigued Out of The Office
Their Rebellious Submissive
Their Famous Dominant
Their Ruthless Sadist
Their Naughty Student
Their Fairy Princess
Owned

PIER 70
Reckless
Fearless
Speechless
Harmless
Clueless

SNIPER 1 SECURITY
Wait for Morning
Never Say Never
Tomorrow's Too Late

SOUTHERN BOY MAFIA/DEVIL'S PLAYGROUND
Beautifully Brutal
Without Regret
Beautifully Loyal
Without Restraint

STANDALONE NOVELS
Unhinged Trilogy
A Million Tiny Pieces
Inked on Paper
Bad Reputation
Bad Business
Filthy Hot Billionaire

NAUGHTY HOLIDAY EDITIONS
2015
2016
2021

Made in the USA
Columbia, SC
16 November 2022

71354069R00139